TWELVE
HOURS
IN
MANHATTAN

TWELVE HOURS IN MANHATTAN

A Novel

MAAN GABRIEL

SHE WRITES PRESS

Published 2023
Printed in the United States of America
Print ISBN: 978-1-64742-395-7
E-ISBN: 978-1-64742-396-4
Library of Congress Control Number: 2022916961

For information, address:
She Writes Press
1569 Solano Ave #546
Berkeley, CA 94707

Book Design by Stacey Aaronson

She Writes Press is a division of SparkPoint Studio, LLC.

AUTHOR'S NOTE

I am no expert on cultures or races of any kind, but I am a fan of great storytelling. I wrote *Twelve Hours in Manhattan* during the height of my love for Korean drama (well, I never really left; my heart is forever captured, and my idea of self-care is binge-watching them on weekends). But let me say that I am not an expert on Korean culture—whatever I wrote was simply a product of my love for their storytelling approach, and their *Oppa*. Also, there are some themes here that might trigger deep emotions—abortion, drug use and overdose, abandonment, and profanity. What I tried to accomplish here is the feeling of hope and love and self-discovery, and so I hope you'll enjoy this as much as I enjoyed writing it.

To all *Kdrama* fans,

I see you.

I am you.

Oh, the fun we have together . . .

PART 1

Chapter 1

5:55 P.M.

"They fucking hated it."

I grit my teeth together, trying with all my might not to lose it because I'm close. I'm darn close. I drop my head down in defeat, my forehead accidentally hitting the thick wooden bar with a loud thud, causing three empty bottles of beer to topple noisily together, rattling my already exhausted brain. "Geez!" I stutter in frustration, pulling my head back up, rubbing my furrowed forehead aggressively with one hand while the other presses my iPhone firmly to my ear in fury, in fear. I start to tremble lightly.

I'm losing it. God, I'm losing it.

"Fuck it! I mean they didn't even wait a few days, even a few hours, to tell me that my presentation sucks. They spit it out right in the middle of it." I whine vehemently as I say this. I simply do not have the capacity to calm down right this minute because the stakes are too high.

The demand letter from the bank is like a ticking time bomb inside the purse that hangs tauntingly under the bar, proving me powerless. *"We demand that you send us the four months of missed mortgage payments within thirty days or you will need to vacate the property fifteen days after the grace period indicated above."* My heart tightens. I have four hundred and twenty-seven dollars to my name and maxed out credit cards that are all in default. My beat-up car, parked somewhere in Jersey City, looks like my next housing option if I don't get my shit together. Homelessness is real, and it can happen to anyone. I'm on the brink of it.

"What did they say, exactly?" the person on the other end of the phone asks. There is concern in the voice.

"Pretty much that. It sucks." I bend my head again, slowly this time, and I rest my bruised forehead on the bar. I can feel my chest tightening as I let out a quiet sob.

I don't sit around waiting for luck to drop by. I seek it. I look for it. *Goddammit*, I run after it. If I stay, it will only be a matter of time before I lose myself. I close my eyes trying to shake self-pity away.

Should I just run away? My entire body sags at this thought. *But where will I go?*

"Did they at least ask you to make some revisions?" This is said in a whisper, and I can sense interest on the other end of the line though somewhat vague. I want to hear more for comfort and I wait, but it doesn't come. This conversation has reached its threshold.

"No," I finally answer in defeat. "Now I have to pay that god-damn hotel room with money I don't have!" I scream silently, but I try to calm myself because my outbursts don't do me any good. They always go unheard. I should be grateful that someone is actually listening to my current state of despair.

I'm by myself in a crowded Times Square bar hoping that the loud noise will help numb the ache. It's 5:55 on a Friday night. I turn around and observe the weekend crowd loitering by the entrance and toward the middle of the restaurant. It's a damn fluke

I was able to grab an empty stool at the bar. No one drinks alone here. No one comes to Times Square alone. I, always the odd one out, am the exception. This is the story of my life.

"Stay the night anyway. You need it." The voice makes an effort to comfort. Again, I wait for more. There is none.

I'd like to stay forever.

I hang up the call, my pride in tatters. I stare into space as I try to deliberate on where to go and what to do after today. My stomach roils with anxiety. I lift the half-empty Stella Artois bottle and mindlessly roll the bottom on the bar. I stare at it, oblivious to everything around me, and then I slowly close my eyes to muffle the painful consequences of my life. In my mind, I enter a series of moments, fragments of happier times, of the person I thought I'd be, of the dream of my youth. I see the feisty girl from Jersey—beautiful but tough, a witty mixed-race girl full of hopes and dreams. Her smile is sealed with grit and uncanny sweetness. I like this girl. On her face, there is promise.

A glass shatters on the floor. I open my eyes in surprise, and I'm back in hell.

"Fuck it!" I finish my beer in one big gulp as if my life depends on it. No one is paying me any mind. The crowds make people here invisible. This is New York City—one of the most crowded places on earth—the place where you can certainly disappear and, if you so choose, can never be found.

"That's a lot of fucks," he says with a slight teasing chuckle. At first, I thought it was said to someone else—perhaps a friend on the other side. But when he chuckles again, I'm most certain it is directed at me. I slowly turn my head to where the voice comes from. I squint my eyes to demonstrate my distaste over the invasion of my space. He's sitting on the barstool next to mine with a pint of amber beer in hand. I should be furious, but his face is so unusually soothing that curiosity overrides my disdain. He looks distinguished. He is put together. He looks expensive, his stainless-steel watch shouting "big-ticket," but remarkably not in a vulgar way. His skin is smooth—olive in a lighter shade. Flawless. His hair is parted on one side, with its length almost covering his left eye, radiating mystery. I want to move his hair with my fingertips so I can see both his eyes. I frown at this flustering thought. He looks like a sculpture, chiseled jaws and high striking cheekbones. His facial structure is perfection and yet, somehow it seems, he's unaware of it. There is an air of nonchalance about him. Or perhaps he is aware but doesn't give two shits. I detect no vanity in his demeanor. I'm glad because New York City is sprawling with narcissistic dudes. To be quite honest, though I don't know him from Adam, he's unexpectedly easing away my internal madness. I scrutinize him from head to toe. He's tall—I can tell even though he's sitting down. But more importantly, after a thorough observation of his physical attributes, I can rightfully say that he is gorgeous. I shake my head. This is nonsense.

He chuckles louder, and this time, I glower, making my pretend irritation clear.

"Sorry. I heard you curse so many times, I thought it was funny." He's definitely not from around here. He's obviously of Asian descent—Korean or Japanese, maybe. Although I'm no expert on race or cultures of any kind, I know this because I'm a Korean drama, or K-drama, expert—a fan. This is a little trivia about me. It's how I spend my nights, my escape—usually on Netflix or Viki, two streaming platforms that are bursting with a good collection of Asian films. It's one of the few joys of my tumultuous existence. My best friend, Pam, introduced me to this world after she unexpectedly stumbled upon a Korean drama on Netflix one night that jump-started a beautiful fandom.

I continue to stare at this man, and I sigh, because what else is there to say? I see no malice in his attitude, for which I am grateful.

"Yeah, I think it's funny too . . . but not in the ha-ha kind of way though," I finally reply, accepting defeat. *Whatever.*

"Having a rough day?" His English is impeccable, though you can definitely hear a hint of an endearing, sexy accent. There is genuine compassion in his voice and a sudden gentleness in his eyes.

"No, a rough year," I whisper, and unwittingly I bow my head down in failure because I am one. *A rough life,* I tell myself. There is no denying the person I've become—a disappointment.

"Hey mister, can you give my friend here another round of whatever it is that she's having, please?" The bartender smiles, looks at the empty bottles on my side of the bar, cleans them up in a hurry, and drops one refreshing looking bottle of Stella right in front of me. I hope the bartender remembers to put this on *his* tab. I have a very limited—close to no—budget.

"You didn't need to." I give the stranger a weak smile and sigh again. I'm an obvious charity case.

"I was eavesdropping on your call. It's the least I can do," he says with sincerity. I nod in acceptance. This simple act of kindness means the world to me. I crave it.

"Thanks."

"My name is Eric." His voice becomes cheerful, and his eyes mirror his tone.

"Bianca." I give him a one-shoulder shrug as if to say I'm not a big deal.

"I can give you my Korean name, but it might be hard to remember," he says jokingly. He's making an effort to lighten the mood after the weighty exchange.

"Yeah, I'll stick with Eric," I joke right back, my sarcastic persona coming back to life. I welcome this. There is a certain kind of freedom in talking to a complete stranger. You can be whoever you want to be. Wonder Woman. Why not? Geez, I think I deserve to be called that—though I have no lasso of truth or magic bracelets to help me win my battles.

"Are you from around here, Bianca?"

"No. I'm from across the river in Jersey. And you?" I reply, trying to be as casual as I can be, like I'm okay, like I'm not going to start begging for food in downtown Manhattan very soon.

"On a much-needed vacation. One night only." He looks off into the distance as he reveals this. I can sense some underlying meaning, but I don't pry. He could be going through some troubles as I am, so I give him his space.

"Nice," I whisper. "I need a vacation." I take a drink of my new beer. I space out for a second, thinking again of the letter in my purse. The project I lost earlier today was supposed to be the answer, a perfect chance to get me out of my current slump, and now that it's bombed, I don't know where to go from here.

"What are you thinking?" His voice pulls me away from my dire thoughts.

"Are you rich, Eric?" I look at my new friend, who appears momentously taken aback by my bold inquisition. There is no room for propriety now that I've accidentally spoken my mind.

"I'm doing all right," he replies with a sly smile. I give him a sideward glance, trying to read his mood. He appears to be fine sitting next to a lunatic.

"Like, how all right? Like you have a house, two houses, maybe? A car? Retirement funds? Some savings for a rainy day? You know, that kind of rich?" I cross and uncross my legs under the tall bar in anticipation.

"Yeah. I plan well. I have guys doing that for me." He takes a sip of his beer.

"Nice." I sigh as I say this, feeling dejected. It's not like I don't plan. I plan plenty.

"You have to have a strategy, Bianca." I like the sound of my name on his lips. There is a strong syllabic divide between n and c.

"I know that. I do. Sometimes things just don't work out, you know."

"Maybe. But keep at it. Things will eventually fall into place." I look at this man again and can feel his shine, a positive brightness. I pull myself away slightly as I size him up. Wearing what looks like an expensive, crisp-white dress shirt and slim gray pants, he radiates influence, power. I notice the matching gray jacket hooked under the bar table, next to my purse that holds my imminent doom. There's something oddly special about him, something I can't quite place. I like him and feel instinctively safe talking to him. I can stay in this bubble for a long time.

I bend my head to look down at my clothes, an old black pantsuit over a white T-shirt and my most unfashionable pair of black flat shoes. I'm a total contrast to Eric's detailed, classy guise.

"Thanks," I say, giving him a weak smile.

"First, you have to smile wider and brighter. You shouldn't be half-assing things in life, you know. You gamble. Always all or nothing. That's how Americans say it, right? Half-assing? I like it." He laughs and, surprisingly, I find myself laughing along with him. His presence energizes me.

No one talks to strangers at bars anymore. People rely exclusively on dating apps to meet someone nowadays, and so this casual conversation of merry bantering is surprisingly pleasant. I don't feel the need to be defensive around him.

I hear the noise of tourists growing louder behind me. I turn around. The crowd has doubled in size now, and it's only six fifteen. I don't even remember why in the world I decided to step in here. I could have chosen to go to one of the smaller, quieter bars in one of the narrower streets around the area, but I chose to come here. Let's face it—it's so bright, so in your face, and because I'm so lonely, the allure got me. I'm too weak to argue with myself.

"Is it always this crowded here?" Eric turns and looks at the growing crowd as well.

"Yes. Tourists." I turn right back around, ignoring the noise and taking another swig of my beer.

"There are other restaurants here, but this place looks busier. Why do they come here?" I lean in to see him better. And as he speaks, there is such blissful innocence on his face that I almost reach out to touch it.

"Why did you come here?" I ask, gathering myself after a disconcerting impulse. I'm not being sarcastic. I'm genuinely curious.

"Someone booked it for me," he replies unpretentiously.

"Oh. Well, this place is, literally, just a few steps away from the Square, and it's good Italian food, so it's a popular spot. You should try their mussels, unless, of course, you're allergic to shellfish, and then I wouldn't recommend it. I always like their rib eye with mushrooms too. It's kinda stewy, but I'm half-Filipino, so stews are my jam." I shrug my shoulders at this.

"Aha!" he hollers, and I jolt backward, startled.

"What?" My eyes widen at his sudden outburst, an anxious smile pasted on my face.

"Now I see it. I was trying to guess your ethnicity. Not that it's a big deal. I was just curious." His smile is childlike and carefree.

Charming, even. If I were in a better headspace, I would have flirted some, or more. I smile slightly and for the first time, it feels raw. Real.

"Half here and half there," I say in an attempt at another joke.

"We're both from Asia." He straightens his back, excitedly clasps his hands and starts rubbing them together. This discovery is a treat for him, I can tell.

"We've got that going for us." I laugh, and he laughs along with me.

In a weird way, although he seems open and free, I can also sense control—his movements are calculated, like he's being watched. I shake my head to dismiss this thought. I don't really care. He makes me laugh, helps me forget, if only for a few minutes, the predicament that is weighing heavily in my purse, and for that I am indebted to him.

"Were you born in the Philippines?" He shifts on his stool to slightly angle his posture toward me. This conversation seems to excite him.

"Yes. My mom met my dad in Manila. He's American." I crook my head to face him sideways. I lean my elbow on the bar and I rest the side of my head against my palm. "How about you?" I ask. I don't really like talking about myself.

"From Busan, South Korea."

"Nice," I reply with a grin.

"Have you been?" he asks eagerly.

"No, but I want to visit Seoul someday." I do. I really do. These are the kinds of meaningless dreams I indulge in sometimes, though I have long conceded that the chance of them ever happening in this lifetime is close to zero. *Zilch.*

"Why?" He inches closer to me, which I welcome. His vigor is the perfect lightness to my dark side. If only I can bottle his enthusiasm, I will do so, and I will carry it around my neck like a talisman.

"Big K-drama fan here," I say proudly, pointing my index finger to my face. Then I wink at him.

"Really. . . ." He says this with a lingering drawl, and then a sudden flash of alertness appears in his eyes. I can't blame him. I would also find it oddly startling that a complete stranger could talk about my cultural background with such spirited zeal. I mean, what are the chances, right? He probably thinks I'm a freaking stalker.

"Yeah, like you would not believe." I wink at him again. He smiles at this, perhaps trying to gauge my level of crazy.

"So, when did you move to America?" It's a good call to change subjects on that. Even I don't know how to turn it around.

"My entire family immigrated here in the nineties. Like, everybody. My grandma and grandpa, my aunts and uncles, my mom, lots of cousins—so there's a whole colony of us in Jersey City."

It's true. Jersey City is a hot spot for Filipino immigrants. Every Filipino knows every Filipino in Jersey City, and mostly because they go to the same Filipino Catholic Mass on Sundays. I used to go with Mom when I was younger. Then I turned eighteen, and that was that.

"You're very funny, Bianca." He booms with laughter. I'm really not. No one has ever dared describe me as such. My life is not a comedy; it's definitely a great tragedy.

"I try my best to entertain. . . ." I try another joke. I enjoy Eric's company because he doesn't know who or what I am. I'm a mysterious blank canvas. *Freedom.*

"Mr. Park," the gorgeous hostess appears behind us and taps Eric's shoulder lightly.

"Yes?" We both turn to face her.

"Your table is ready. Let me lead the way." Eric gets up reluctantly and grabs his jacket from under the bar. He finishes his pint and stares at me with a curious, knowing smile.

"Goodbye, Eric. It was truly a pleasure talking nonsense with you." To be honest, I feel a little deflated that our night together is coming to an end. Something about this goodbye triggers a soft jab in my heart.

"Keep on entertaining, Bianca. It was a real great delight talking with you," he says, and with his curious attractive smile, he takes his leave.

Chapter 2

6:30 P.M.

I follow him with my eyes as he walks away, lusting over the way his behind sways with unabashed manliness. I laugh at myself, at the ridiculousness of where my mind has wandered. I cover my mouth with my hand to muffle a giggle, and I welcome this lightness because it's what I crave right now.

The thick crowd has finally swallowed him. I crank my head sideways hoping to catch another glimpse, but I don't see him anymore. Eric is an absurdly gorgeous male. I nod incessantly as I ponder on this. *Absurdly.*

I look at my almost depleted bottle of beer. Mister bartender notices and comes running. He's cute too. Blond, blue eyes, broad shoulders, and narrow hips . . . *I should stop there*, I think with an internal giggle.

"One more?"

I shrug, and then I nod with a slight pout on my lip. It'll likely be the last eleven-dollar beer I'll drink in a very long time. Splurge like there's no tomorrow, because tomorrow I break—both metaphorically and literally.

"Why not," I say as I veer my head to look outside. The sun is still up. After this drink, my fifth bottle, hopefully I'll drop dead and sleep peacefully in the hotel tonight, and my hurt forgotten, I pray. But my goodness, that hotel room is not cheap. Two hundred dollars plus tax wasted. I press my lips together into a straight line, suppressing a physical response to regret.

I inhale deeply, taking it all in, and then I exhale. This, or I will cry. Perhaps another interesting person will sit next to me and take my mind off my pathetic life. I look around for a prospect, but there are none.

Mr. Cute Bartender slides a beer bottle into my hand. I catch it just before it slides over the edge and onto the floor.

"Phew," I joke, as I wipe away nonexistent sweat on my right eyebrow. Though I react jovially to my surroundings, I know that my eyes betray a different mood. I just want to get drunk, black out, and forget—just for one night. One night. Unfortunately, I'm still very sober and wide awake. I can still hear the loud chattering, the clink of beer glasses, the dishes being set on tables, the bantering, and the laughter behind me.

I slowly put my beer bottle down on the bar and cover my face with both my hands. I let my head dangle forward.

Inhale. Exhale.

Inhale. Exhale.

And I do it again four more times. *Please don't cry here*, I urge myself, biting my lip and forcefully embracing the pain. I unexpectedly taste metal, blood. Then, I feel a light tap on my shoulder, but I don't budge. Slowly, after the next and more forceful tap, I look up and see Eric's smiling face behind me.

"Are you crying?" His expression suddenly changes as real concern appears in his eyes. He lightly touches my arm, but I clumsily pull back to wipe away pretend tears.

"I want to." I give him a weak smile and lift my head up higher to face him. "So, you didn't like your table and decided to come back and reclaim your stool. Here," I push the chair toward him. "It's still yours if you need it. I was saving it for you."

"Actually, the restaurant manager felt bad that I had a long wait, so he gave me a big booth all to myself. I thought perhaps you might like to join me. Looks like you'd be drinking here for a while anyway. It'll be more comfortable. Whatever it is, you can talk to a complete stranger, and he won't judge." I look at him in deep thought. He may be a stranger, but it sure doesn't feel like that. It's odd. I've watched one too many K-dramas, I think, that my reaction to any South Korean person now is familiarity.

"Sure." I wave at Mr. Cute Bartender, and he comes my way instantly. "I'm moving to his table. . . ."

"Hmm," he says with a quirky smile. Is he just flirting with me? I've gone mad, but you know what? I like it. I laugh out loud at this. Both men look at me like I've gone *loca-loca*—crazy—as my mom used to call me, a silly form of endearment during better, happier times.

"You can just add her tab to mine," Eric instructs the bartender with an air of authority. He's nice about it, of course, but I can sense that he's used to have people do his bidding. Maybe he's the CEO of a large tech company or something—the South Korean version of Jeff Bezos, perhaps. I angle my head to get a better look at his face. If I guess right, Eric could be in his late thirties—maybe, thirty-seven or thirty-eight, but not quite forty. The bartender nods, flirting gone, and does some clicking on the register.

"Is this yours?" He points at the big laptop bag and black coat hanging under the bar table.

"Yup." I start to reach for it but he beats me to it. He grabs my stuff and carries it in his well-toned arm. I take my tiny purse and jump off the stool. My legs aren't long enough to reach the floor with finesse.

"You're short," he says matter-of-factly, taking a step back to look at me. I give him a pretend angry scowl. Not only am I short, I'm also a bit out of shape, so jumping off the stool takes some effort. I don't say this to him, of course.

"Not everyone is blessed to be a giant," I say, looking at him from head to toe with one eyebrow raised. Geez, he's tall. Feet on the floor, with my flat shoes, I only come up to his chest. He starts snorting. I roll my eyes. "Whatever." But deep inside, I welcome his return.

Instead of leading the way, Eric walks next to me, guiding me to his table while also protecting me from the swarm. This place is getting busier by the minute. I feel his hand at the arch of my back. It feels decorous. Formal. I'm sure I've experienced this kind of protective stance toward me before, but tonight I feel significant . . . respected. He's mere inches away from me and I catch the scent of his expensive cologne—subtle but lasting. I close my eyes as the comfort of his presence embraces me.

The crowd thickens toward the middle of the room, the designated waiting area, where more people mill around expecting to be seated soon. He takes a step forward, lightly pushing me behind him, and takes my hand casually. Startled, my eyes widen. He looks around to me and smiles.

"I don't want to lose you. You're too tiny."

I roll my eyes at him again in pretend annoyance, yet I've never felt more secure. His hand is firm but soft. His grip is sure but gentle. In less than thirty seconds, we are at his booth where a silver bucket of ice is set on one side with an expensive-looking bottle of white wine chilling in it. I take the seat across from him.

He hands me the menu. "You should eat."

"Maybe I should. The last meal I had was a bagel and coffee this morning." I touch my stomach and hear it grumble at the thought of food. I calculate the money I have in the bank. Perhaps I can afford an appetizer. I scan the menu quickly. *Geez!* The prices in the menu are just outright criminal.

"You okay?" Eric has heard me gasp.

"Yeah, yeah." I wave him off, gesturing for him to go back to looking at the menu.

"You said mussels are good here?" He obliges and bends his head down, looking at the menu with pleasure. His hair is shiny, properly conditioned, and well cut. I touch the ends of my lifeless hair as if to compare.

"Your hair is really shiny," I blurt out, genuinely impressed.

"I don't pay attention," he says, still studying the menu, obviously trying to ignore me.

"To your hair?" I ask, flabbergasted. He lifts his head to finally face me. He scrunches his nose and smiles. This, surprisingly, takes my breath away, and I inhale slowly to steady myself.

"You're a very observant person, Bianca. Do you think I am so vain that I do stuff to my hair because I want it to be shiny?" he says. He's pretending to be annoyed, but his quirky half-smile gives him away.

"Don't we all? I mean, I totally wish I had time for it. You know what, no, I wish I could actually afford it!" I grab the ends of my dull hair to show him and to make a point. This time, his laughter occupies the tiny space we're in, and a few heads from the next table turn to us. He bows at them in apology.

"You're so funny, Bianca." His flat abs control a belly laugh.

"Yeah, funny is my middle name. Not." I roll my eyes. He's still laughing.

We both look at our menus in silence. I pretend to inspect mine. A twenty-dollar-flatbread with sprinkles of tomatoes and some cheese is not something I can either condone or afford.

After a few minutes, Eric lifts his head up to face me. His gaze is pulling, mesmerizing.

"So, what are your hopes and dreams, Bianca? What happened today that was so bad you were about to cry when I left you at the bar?" He folds the menu and sets it on his side of the table. He looks thoughtful now. All his attention on me—as if I am important somehow.

"Hmm . . . well, I'm a communications consultant. . . ." I begin.

"What does that mean?" He leans toward me.

"I draft campaign strategies based on research to help my clients push their messages to their target audience." I've said this to clients so many times that it now sounds more like *my* slogan.

"Like a PR person, a publicist?"

"That's part of the communications strategy, yes." I nod.

"And?" He puts both his elbows on the table, bends his head down, and rests his chin on his fists. I can now appreciate his entire face. When we were sitting side by side at the bar earlier, I didn't get the chance to see his full features. But now I can see that his eyes are expressive, and sincere, they draw you in. His lips are naturally red. His smile is so welcoming, warm, like it's meant only for me. His cheekbones are way too high to be normal. I smile at this.

"What?" He asks. His manner is childlike, and the muted lighting in this part of the restaurant makes his face look softer and more incandescent.

"You're so pretty." I say softly.

"Pretty?" He pulls back, sounding almost insulted.

"Yes. You have an angelic face. Like a model with great lighting."

"First my hair, and now my face, and though what you're saying are supposed to be compliments, they sound more like insults." He pouts slightly. I chuckle a little at this.

"I'm sorry," I say, pouting back at him. "Maybe, I don't want to talk about me."

"Araso." He slouches back on the faux leather seat with a pretend, but awfully cute, scowl.

"Hmmm?"

"I said, all right. I'll ask again later." He rolls his eyes as he says this.

"I kinda know that, I think. I hear it a lot watching K-dramas." I stretch both my arms in front of me, over the table. The table is wide, so I don't reach him.

"What's going on right now?" He points at my arms.

"What?"

"What are you doing?"

"Stretching." I stretch some more, the tips of my fingers almost reaching his face.

"Why?" There is interest in his smile.

"It's been a long day." I start wiggling my hands in front of him comically. I wiggle my nose along with it. He rolls his eyes again, but I see a glint of a smile at the corner of his supple lips. The beauty of being comfortable around him is not lost on me.

"Okay. Let's start with a drink. I have white wine chilling here." He grabs the bottle from the ice bucket and inspects the label.

"Maybe I'll have red."

He doesn't say anything but lifts his arm and waves at the passing waiter.

"Yeah, I don't picture you for a white wine kind of girl, anyway."

"Bold? Bloody? Strange? Dark? Sinister? So many layers?" I say this as I do a series of seductive poses. I like myself around him.

"I didn't say any of that." We chuckle together some more.

"What would you recommend for a bold and woody red wine?" he asks our waiter.

"There's always this." The waiter turns on his iPad, taps on the selection of red wines, and points at one. I see the price and gasp. I look at Eric in horror. It's way too expensive for me.

"We'll get a bottle," he says without blinking.

"Excellent. I'll be right back." And the gorgeous young waiter, who I'm sure is also an off-Broadway actor, glides away with a delighted smile.

"Finally, a conversation that led to an ending."

"Huh?"

"Most of our conversations start with one topic, but it never gets truly resolved," he says matter-of-factly.

"You're right. My brain is wired like that. Chaos. I apologize."

"For what? For being interesting?"

"Do you know that when you don't have anything good to say about someone, you call them 'interesting'?"

"Hmmm. I'll remember that for next time."

"Okay, fine. I'll tell you why my day was shit. I worked on this big proposal for a publishing company. One of the big five. My friend said she was sure I'd get the contract. She said they could no longer handle efforts in-house so they're subcontracting to freelancers like me. I walked in there this morning thinking it would be the beginning of the rest of my life." Eric moves closer to the table and looks at me attentively. "I'm halfway through my presentation when one of the younger executives, an attractive young blonde, gets up and leaves the room. I stop and I just look at her walk away. It's so insulting. Plus, she looks like she's ten years younger than me. And then, a few minutes later, the guy who called me in raises his hand to stop me and says that my concept isn't what they're looking for right now. But they gave me the fucking concept to work with! So there, I'm nothing but a big freaking loser. You may want to move away." I wave him off. "I'm not sure if it's contagious." I drop both my elbows on the table with a frustrated thud.

"I'm sorry." And I can tell that he means it. He leans back on the chair, stretches out one arm, unbuttons the sleeve and rolls it up. He does the same to the other. "Look, it's one bad incident. That's not a reason to think this is the end." Finally, the waiter comes back with two red wine glasses and a bottle of ridiculously expensive wine. He expertly pours us each a glass and hands them over gracefully. Eric winks at me.

"This red wine. . . ." he begins.

"Yes, which I can never ever afford." I stare at it like it is gold.

"Stop that. Don't interrupt me. Anyway, do you know the amount of time and expertise it took to put this here?" He raises the glass and swirls it around.

"I'm not a wine expert, so I don't know," I respond with a smirk.

"Well, let me tell you . . . a lot. A lot of time, and a lot of effort. This was not rushed. It shouldn't be rushed, or the result will be mediocre." I take a sip from my glass as he speaks, and its intriguing flavor takes me aback.

"Geez Louise, this is good," I gasp and savor every drop.

"Right!" There's excitement in his stare. A point he wants to make. He sounds almost like a child proving something of great importance. I realize it's who he is. He gets excited easily, finds most things of interest, and doesn't shy away from letting me know no matter how mundane it seems. I notice a small dent under the left side of his lip that makes him look younger.

I lean back, still holding my glass.

"Food?"

"Sure."

He looks at the menu again, giving me a perfect view of his impeccable, shiny hair. I relax and take a breath. I silently inhale and exhale. I finally feel a sense of calm. I continue to stare at this interesting man. I can't quite place it, but I feel that my body responds positively to him—comfortable, secure, calm—because I've met him somewhere before.

And then it hits me.

"Holy shit, you're Park Hyun Min!" I jerk upward, almost toppling the table and its contents. He immediately lifts his head with an expression of alarm and holds the table steady. I blink my eyes.

∞

Park Hyun Min is an insanely famous South Korean actor. Insanely. He's well-known not just for his great looks, but also for his legendary acting. An extremely private person, *GQ* Korea described him as kind, serious about his craft, and a prominent patron of the South Korean arts. *GQ* also named him most beautiful man in South Korea last year.

The last drama I saw of Hyun Min is *The Oasis*, which I have yet to finish. It's a story of a fugitive who escapes to the country-side, rebuilds his life, and falls in love with the town spinster. I think that was when I fell in love with him, figuratively speaking.

And he is sitting right across from me right here, right now, in a busy restaurant in Times Square, looking at me like an enemy. Eyes glistening in worry, lips curved into a frown, and face ashen with disappointment.

"Holy shit," I say again as I slowly sit back down on my chair with my hand over my open mouth, this time in a whisper.

Chapter 3

6:55 P.M.

We stare at each other for a good, true minute. Neither says a word. Both of us are in shock.

"What are the chances that the only person I decided to talk to in all of New York City is actually a Korean drama fan?" Displeasure is written all over his face. He still doesn't move, his eyes search for probable deception of some kind.

"What are the chances? Yes." I stare right back, not breaking hold of his eyes, and with mine beaming like headlights. My first instinct, of course, is to call Pam. But I don't move either.

Eric pushes both of his folded sleeves up his arms with gentle precision, like watching a television commercial. He doesn't smile, and I sense dread. I don't blame him.

"Look, I'm sorry I figured who you are. And I'm so excited about all this that I want to call my best friend, Pam, right now because we're both so in love with you. But I won't do that. You can relax. It's not like I'll be calling the South Korean press here or something. Hmm, I don't even know how to do that. I can leave if you'd prefer." I still don't break eye contact. He should at least recognize my sincerity.

He doesn't say a word. I lean backward in silence. He's looking at me like I've grown horns. Skeptical. Again, I don't blame him.

Our waiter is back with his overly optimistic grin, knowing full well that with the bottles of wine alone he is in for a hefty tip tonight just from our table.

"Do you want to order some food?"

Eric looks at him and smiles feebly. "Yes. Mussels for me. The red wine one." He then turns his head toward me.

"I'm fine," I reply.

"You should get something. You've only had a bagel today."

"Hmm. . . ." I don't know what else to say. "I'll get whatever he's having," I tell our waiter.

"May I recommend the white wine mussels for you?"

"That would be great," Eric answers for me, and I can tell that he wants to get rid of our waiter immediately.

"I can just leave, you know. I'm sorry." I gather my things, getting ready to go. He reaches for my hand from across the table and stops me. I turn to face him. We don't say anything. We stare at each other, frozen, both uncertain of what we want. It has been a good night until now.

"You don't need to be sorry. Nothing to be sorry about." Finally, the light in his smile is back. "I'm sorry I overreacted."

"For a moment there, you looked really terrified of me." I watch his face keenly, searching for something—I don't know what. Absolution? Trust? I want to say, *it's me, and you can trust me.* But who am I to him? I'm no one.

"Fame is terrifying. It's distressing. I didn't really sign up for it." Although the brightness has come back, I can still sense uneasiness. How one can be sad about fame is a mystery to me. But he's right here, talking to me in the flesh. He slowly sips from his white wine glass as the red wine glass sits on the table untouched. "It's a job, you know, what I do. Like you doing your presentation today. I don't go to work thinking that I'll be famous

or that I expect screaming fans to welcome me at the airport."
There is a lingering sadness in his eyes as he speaks. I nod my
head slowly at this. Screaming fans at the airport is a thing. I noticed that too.

"I believe that. But fame is a consequence of your job."

"Right. I started acting in high school. Then after college, I
auditioned for many acting jobs because I needed to survive. My
parents weren't thrilled that I decided to go that route. Then a
job came, and then another, and another. I didn't even have an
agent until my third drama."

"Please don't be sad," I whisper, staring into his sad brown
eyes.

"Now, I have to apologize." He bows his head in regret.

"For what?" I see no reason for it.

"For being unreasonable. How can one be sad about being
famous, no?"

"I get it, really." Not really. But I say it anyway to make him
feel less desolate.

"Thanks." He lifts his eyes warily at me.

"So, apart from all the stress, how does it truly feel to be famous?" I try to make light of the moment. I move closer to the
table, put both my elbows on it, and look at Eric with great interest. He finally laughs again. "Do you really get free stuff all the
time? Like expensive watches and skin care products and such?
Aha! That's why your hair is so shiny. Maybe you get advance
technology hair products that aren't available to mere mortals
like me." He laughs louder this time.

Seconds pass. Eric looks away at the distance, obviously deep
in thought.

"Fame is subjective. Some people chase it. Some people
simply want to evade it."

"Why don't you just embrace it—don't chase or evade, but accept."

I don't know where all my wise words are coming from. I've never been here before—on this side of a conversation.

"That's what I've been doing, actually. Sounds ungrateful, no?" He lowers his gaze in shame.

"Kinda." I answer before giving him a big teasing smile. We are both simmering.

"And yes, I get a lot of free things from advertisers," he finally reveals. Shame gone and hopefully forgotten.

"Have you received a Rolex yet?"

"Omega. I'm an Omega brand ambassador." He doesn't even blink as he says this, which to me sounds like the most insane thing I've heard in a live, in-person conversation.

"Someone saying this in front of me, in the flesh, is so surreal." I can't help being honest. "A fantasy happening in real life," I add thoughtfully.

"Julia Roberts said that in *Notting Hill*," he says, offering up this bit of trivia.

"She did."

※

In the ladies' room, I debate whether to call Pam or not. This is a once in a lifetime experience, and she'll definitely chop my head off if I don't tell her that the guy we were both screaming over on TV, and falling in love with in this show that we're so hooked on, is actually sitting across from me at a touristy restaurant in Manhattan. But I don't want to betray Eric's trust either. I'm in a very odd situation, and I can't help but jump up and down giddily. This is so surreal at every level.

I stop for a second and ponder this. I smile. This excitement is new to me. It's like being a kid again, shallow, and mundane. I've missed this.

I pull my phone out of my purse and search for *Park Hyun Min New York City*. Nothing current comes up. Instead, I see photo after photo of him from last year's Met Gala. He was alone in all of them. But my goodness, he looked like a gorgeous statue in a metallic blue-and-black tuxedo. He doesn't smile much in photos, I notice. He always seems so mysterious. I feel a little jolt of thrill in my center, but I shake it away.

The bathroom door hits me lightly when a young lady walks in.

"I thought I saw him too," she says to her friends.

"I've been following him and the Park Hyun Min fan group on Instagram, and they didn't say anything about him being in New York." I freeze hearing this. Then I start to worry. Eric should know by now that Korean pop culture has already reached Manhattan. Astro, the famous Korean boy band, was one of the featured performers at the Times Square New Year's Eve celebration. I feel a sudden need to protect him.

I move closer to the sink to get out of their way, trying hard not to look like I'm eavesdropping, pretending to focus on my phone.

"I heard this rumor that he and Suzi broke up," the other girl says. I may be a K-drama fan, but I don't follow the news very closely. I've got other things to do. "Heard he's greatly heartbroken." I touch my heart as I hear this. I can see that. He seems like the kind of guy who could easily get his heart broken. There is a gentleness in him, a trusting soul. His eyes give him away.

"I hate that Suzi girl anyway. Such a slut! Hyun Min deserves someone more his caliber," the first girl says as she puts on bright red lipstick.

I think it's time to drag him out of here.

I leave the ladies' room in a hurry.

⁂

"I think you should leave," I recommend. Eric squints his eyes at me as I slide back in the booth. I've seen that far too many times in the many shows I've seen of him. It's disconcertingly sexy. I slowly close my eyes and exhale.

"Don't do that!" I warn.

"Makes you fall in love with me even more," he teases. Honestly, I like that it makes me forget even for a second how devastatingly shitty my life is outside this dream bubble.

"Yes, but that's beside the point. Oh, and to be clear, I fell in love with the characters, not the person. Big difference." I raise one eyebrow and wag my index finger at him.

"Same difference, I think." His grin makes him even more handsome. I feel as if a breeze could knock me over as I stare at his absurdly beautiful smile.

"Ha-ha! Very funny." I wring my hands together under the table. All of a sudden, this man is making me nervous.

We devour our mussels quickly. Our wine bottles are both almost depleted.

"So, I guess you're more famous here than we think." I see that fear in his eyes again.

"Why?" he asks, and I tell him about the two girls in the bathroom stalking him on Instagram. "Were they Asians?"

"Actually, no. Surprising, right?"

"You know what, so what. Let's finish these bottles and not even think about it."

"That's fine by me. I'm not the one who's famous. Must be good, ha?"

"I told you it's not." There is hurt behind his eyes, but he masks it well.

"Whatever." I roll my eyes to make light of the situation.

"Do you need to be anywhere after dinner?" he asks.

"Yeah, mope in my room and wallow in pity."

"How about we walk off dinner? Just around Midtown. I can sit in the Square for a little while. Enjoy the jumbotrons."

"Why did you come to New York again?"

"To disappear."

"Well, I don't think that's happening."

"You didn't figure me out until like an hour or so of talking to me."

"True." I shrug in agreement. "Let's get out of here."

Chapter 4

8:35 P.M.

We walk side by side in silence. We don't speak. Instead, we let the din of Times Square comfort us. Eric is right. One can disappear here. I can disappear here. How many times have I dreamt of that, especially close to the holiday season when pain is so raw? The last one was only three months ago, and I can still remember the lingering, more penetrating loneliness that the Christmas season brought. Was it perhaps because of the cold weather—the absence of warmth and sunshine? Maybe I should move back to the Philippines where the weather is warmer. Too warm, actually. I sigh.

"Penny for your thoughts. That's what you say, right?" He turns his head to face me. Now that I know who he is, I can't help but feel both concerned and elated. He's more handsome in person, that's for sure, and I can't wait to tell Pam.

"Can we take a selfie?" It's the first thing that came to mind.

"That's what you've been thinking about?" he says, teasing me.

"No, I'm thinking about how I would break the news to Pam. She'll kill me. She's your biggest fan." This is partly true.

"So, you're not my biggest fan?" He turns around to face me and starts walking backward with his arms crossed in front of his chest and my laptop bag draped around him. He fits right in with the other guys in suits and messenger bags running around the city.

"A fan? Probably. The biggest? I don't think so. Be careful, you're going to hit somebody behind you. Geez!" I reach for his arm to guide him. I chuckle. He squints his eyes again. It's when he's cutest. And I'm sure he knows it. "Heard you broke up with someone named Suzi? Or she broke up with you?" He sighs and takes his spot again next to me, moving along with the crowd. I don't pursue the topic. Heartbreak sucks as it is. I'm sure it's suckier if millions of people are talking about it. The price of fame. I look at him. There is no gloom in his eyes—instead, I see the reflection of the magic of the city that never sleeps.

"I've been here once before. Actually, I've been driven here once before. I've never walked like this. This experience is new to me. I should explore cities on foot more often." As he circles around and soaks it all in, the child in him appears once again. I stare at this man who is bigger than himself, bigger than what he thinks of himself, and glances around like it's the most fascinating thing he's ever seen—when in fact, *he* is the fascination.

I pull my coat tighter around me. The March chill is still strong. I can't wait for the weather to get better. I can't wait for my life to get better. I stop myself. This is not the night for such thoughts. As Eric looks around, I walk slowly next to him, guiding him to make sure he doesn't hit someone in the crowds on Seventh Avenue.

"We have that in Seoul," he points at the Line Friends store with a giant brown bear at the door. There is a long line in front of it as tourists take photos. "Should we take our selfie there?" he teases. "And I will let you privately send it to Pam."

"I'll think about it," I say and walk farther on. I bet there are a lot of Asians in that store, and going there will likely give his identity away. I can feel the small space between us as he walks behind me. I smell his fresh scent again. I close my eyes and take it in. He rests his hands on my shoulders. I turn around to face him, and I see him still looking around, enthralled. Then, he grabs me by the waist. He has to bend down to do so.

"That's us on the big screen." A camera is right outside the American Eagle Outfitter store, pointed at passersby. He pulls me close to him. Tucked under his arm, we smile for the camera. A famous Asian actor is right in front of all these people, and nobody notices. We wave at ourselves on the screen and start laughing. I know we're not that drunk after finishing off two bottles of wine and five bottles of beer for me before that, but this is fun. The video of us freezes. Our photo is blasted on the screen in different frames and transition effects.

"What are you doing?" I ask him. "Didn't you want to be invisible?"

"You're most invisible when you're in the middle of a crowd. When you put distance between you and the crowd, that's when people notice." He walks to the center of the Square, climbs a few steps on the bleachers under the tower of screens where most tourists take their selfies, and finds the spot with the best view. I follow closely behind him. He pulls off my laptop bag and sets it next to him. I stand right in front, facing him. I'm tiny enough that we are face to face.

"Are you sad, Eric?" It's an idiotic question. It's the wrong place to ask. The energy here is palpable. It's a place of make-believe. Mascots and people in costumes—from Elmo and Cookie Monster to Batman and Iron Man—loitering around the Square add to the fantasy. How can one be sad here?

"Never!" He shouts this, and no one cares. He smiles ruefully because we both know that's a lie. In the past two hours we've been together, I've seen flashes of sadness in his eyes. He's terrific at masking it. It's part of the mystery that makes his public persona more captivating.

"Are you sad, Bianca?" It's his turn to ask me this.

"Always!" I shout right back. He taps my nose with his finger.

"You're like a kid, you know."

"And so are you," I mutter. "I just turned thirty-six years old, you know." I stomp my feet as I say this. I'm proud of my age. I'm not one of those who doesn't embrace time. I've waited all my life for people to take me seriously, and I only get a little respect whenever I declare my age. My Filipino genes make me look younger than I truly am, although I should be grateful and celebrate that; it doesn't always work to my advantage.

"I'm almost thirty-nine. And I'm not worried about turning forty. Time is irrelevant to men, I think, even in the entertainment business. There's always a role at every age."

"It's unfair to women, though, no?"

"Suzi fought for that. The age thing in the entertainment industry. She's almost thirty-five now and she thinks she's getting less and less interesting roles. And to answer your question earlier, yes, we just broke up over a week ago."

"Ah . . . is that why you're here?" I can't help myself. Curiosity overpowers my wish to be courteous. I have to take notes to share with Pam later. It's the least I can do after not telling her about Park Hyun Min in real time.

"No. I was in a meeting with executives at a television network this afternoon."

"Is this a scoop? Like, you're doing an American show or something?" I gasp in excitement. As if we're old friends, I put my arm around his shoulders and he shoves it playfully.

"Yes. But I trust you not to tell anyone until everything is final." His eyes widen in warning and he puts his index finger over his sensual mouth to silence me.

"As if anyone is going to believe me. This is exciting though. Like what kind of show."

"A detective drama."

"Are you guys going to film here?" I'm eager to learn more.

"Nothing has been discussed. Don't get too excited."

"Are you going to move here?" For some reason, this enlivens me. "Well, you have one commoner friend here now." He chuckles at this. I can sense his feeling of freedom, his anonymity, as he sits in front of me in this crowded place. Then he gently pulls me next to him. And I sit down. I put my elbows on my lap and rest my chin on my palms.

"Are you sure you're thirty-six?" he asks, observing my childish pose. If there is anything that tonight brings, it's all the smiles that we share—whether it's because we remembered something sad or found beauty in our conversation, there is an abundance of smiles. And when he smiles, he brightens the space around him. That's what movie actors are made of, charisma, which I don't have. I'm bottled sarcasm in the flesh. But tonight, I smile because for the first time in a long time, I can.

"It's a good time to be alive, Bianca. Look at all this, the energy of this place, people's excited faces, and you and I meeting like this." I appreciate that he thinks our encounter is a cause for enthusiasm.

"I know. I wish I were as excited as you are tonight." But I am. I just can't tell him this truth. I'm too embarrassed to admit it. So I look at my watch to avoid his gaze. It's almost nine o'clock.

"I promise things will eventually get better," he whispers, and I raise my head. We face each other, our lips mere inches apart, looking straight into each other's eyes. I turn away immediately. I look at my left hand and close my eyes in distress. "Anyway, Suzi and I broke up because she's ready to get married."

"Woah!" I rest both my hands on the metal bleachers, gripping them tightly.

"Right. It was good while it lasted. But she was really pushing for marriage. . . ."

"And you're not. Why is that always a reason to break up though? You know, I know this couple, and they've been together for twenty years. Not married. For a while we thought the guy was the scaredy-cat about getting married."

"Are you saying I'm a scaredy-cat?" He flashes me a pretend scowl, but his smiling eyes give him away.

"I'm not saying anything. Listen." I turn his face with my hand to look at me. "Then we found out it was actually the girl who loathed marriage. The guy accepted it, and they're still together. Twenty loving, happy years. Did she actually say she wanted to get married?"

"Yes."

"Okay. End of discussion. Wait, one question. Why didn't you want to get married?"

"This will sound like I'm the biggest asshole but. . . ." He hesitates. "I don't think she's the one."

"Okay. Well, that's important. When you find the one, there shouldn't be any doubts."

"How about you, what's your story?"

"Don't want to talk about it."

"I respect that."

"It's not a big deal. It's just that—"

"No explanation needed. End of conversation."

୨ଚ

We sit in silence. Silence is good in the midst of pandemonium. It is always the best time to pull your thoughts together, to balance your center, and to harness the art of deadening the noise in and around you.

I steal a glance at Eric. He's as mesmerized as I am by this place. Some would think this is hell on earth—the crowds can be pretty daunting —but Eric and I are of the same mindset. I grew up coming here. My mom is a big Broadway fan. When a new musical was out, rest assured she tried to get tickets for it, no matter how expensive it was. My dad? Well, he disappeared on us the first year after we moved to America.

I notice a group of Asian women looking right at us at the bottom of the steps. I discreetly nudge Eric with my elbow. He looks at me and I point at the group with my lips—it's a very Filipino mannerism, pointing with one's lips. Eric immediately turns around to look at me and pulls me closer into an embrace with his big, sturdy hands. Our faces are inches apart with his back to the curious spectators. His lips are lightly touching my eyelids. I almost pull back. Then I realize it's for the women down below, so I grab his arm and go with it.

"Are they still there?" he whispers close to my ear in a simulated public display of affection. I want to get lost in this. *Geez, what am I thinking?*

"One is trying to take a photo of you. Trying really, really, hard. I don't think she could get you, though, since all they can see is your back." I sneak a peek above his shoulder to check out the fans. "Does this really work?"

"What?"

"Public displays of affection?"

"Well, somehow it makes fans uncomfortable when they're faced with this situation. So I'm hoping they'll give our pretend smooch some privacy." I pull my head back and laugh out loud. "Don't do that," he snaps. You're attracting more attention."

"Sorry," I say. His face is on my neck.

"Are they still there?"

"They're slowly walking away. Slowly. Very, very slowly." A few minutes pass. "They've crossed the street to the Disney Store." Eric immediately lets go of me.

"I'm sorry," he says, embarrassed.

"It's okay. I don't think they were able to take a photo of you. Us." My heart is still pounding, though I know this means nothing. I'm acting with a famous actor. I laugh secretly at this bizarre joke.

"Will somebody be mad if pictures of you making out with someone surface on the internet?" he asks.

I stand up. "Let's go," I say. He looks up at me, questioningly. I brush invisible dust off my pants and stretch out my arms.

"Where?"

"Anywhere."

Chapter 5

9:45 P.M.

We take Seventh Avenue and walk away from the Square toward Forty-eighth Street. There are hordes of people crossing the street, but as soon as we take a right turn, it becomes miraculously quiet. Eric looks behind us.

"You wouldn't think it's only a few steps away, but it's pretty quiet on this street." He sounds amazed.

"It's late. People are in the shows. They don't let out until maybe eleven or so."

"Where are we heading?" he finally asks.

"The church." I can feel surprise in Eric's body language. I turn to him and chuckle. "You Catholic, Eric?"

"Yes, one of the ten percent in South Korea." It's my turn to look surprised.

"Interesting." I turn my body sideways to look at him and I nod in understanding.

"You don't have anything good to say about me?"

"Huh?"

"You said earlier when one doesn't have anything good to say about another, they say 'interesting.'"

"You listen. . . ." I place my hand on his arm for acknowledgment and immediately, I pull it away. He smiles at me. The glimmer in his eyes is apparent. I've only known this man a couple of hours, but I can tell, and deep down I can feel, that he's a good man. Considerate. Thoughtful. Present. We stare at each other for a while, not saying anything. I feel seen. Heard. And because all my life I've craved this kind of recognition, my eyes start to get teary—not from misery and pain, but from gratitude. The glint in his smile, all meant for me, offers me solace.

"Thank you," I whisper, my voice devoid of sarcasm and humor. I say this with sincerity. I've almost forgotten what sincerity feels like and the sense of calm and security that comes with it. My default setting the past few years has been to scream to be heard, to be sarcastic to get attention, and to be callous to get respect.

"You're welcome," he finally responds.

"Don't ever move to New York City." It's a statement of contradiction. I say this and yet I long to settle here. This is where the fight is. I want to move here to be in the fight, to actually have a shot at winning. I can't watch the action from a distance and think I can be a part of it, conquer it. But Eric and I are different. He is set. Made. He doesn't need to prove anything to anyone.

"But you want to move here, right?" he asks with confusion in his expression.

"Yes. In the process of doing so, I'm killing the few ounces of humanity I have left."

"You don't fight to be in the fight. You fight to win. And if you already know you're going to lose, then it'll be silly to go on."

"Then what does 'fight to the death' mean?" My humor resurfaces as I put my hand on my hip in pretend irritation.

"Only if you think you have a shot at winning, then yes, fight to the death! Do you think you have a shot at it?" He is emphatic as he says this.

"I don't know." I acknowledge my failures. There is no deny-ing this. The past decade had been a monotony of constant strug-gle in my path toward self-destruction.

"Bianca!" He pulls me out of my dark thought.

"What?"

"First, you have to believe that you do! People know when you doubt yourself and they will start doubting you. Your biggest fan should be yourself. You can't move forward if you don't have that." He scolds.

Eric stares into the distance ahead of us as we walk along Forty-eighth Street. His hands are linked behind him. He looks exactly how I remember him in *The Oasis*. I steal another glance at him. He catches me and smiles.

Our pace is slow and we take our time. I can see the lights of Fifth Avenue in the distance. Saint Patrick's Cathedral will hope-fully be waiting for us, though it's probably closed by now. It doesn't matter. We'll just sit on the steps and pray. I need some perspective, some guidance. A breeze touches my face and tou-sles my hair. I put both my hands on my head to protect my short black hair. It's unexceptional—a cheap haircut from Jersey City. I'm lucky not to be graying just yet, or I'll let it be—gray. Eric is right. I should be my number one fan.

"Piedmont Lounge? Is that a good bar?" Eric pulls me out of my reverie as he points to a dark restaurant we're walking by. It looks empty at this hour.

"I see it all the time, but I've never been there."

"Maybe we should drop by on the way back from church." He winks at me again as he says this.

The crowds on Fifth Avenue are thinning out. Stores are almost closing. It's dark where the church stands. Gentleman that he is, Eric guides me as we cross the street.

At the bottom of the steps of the church, we both stop. We look at each other and a transcendent understanding passes between us. He reaches for my purse, which I'm holding with both hands, and nudges me to go. I do. I climb the steps of Saint Patrick's Cathedral because I'm in dire need of solace. I can't cry my heart out at our church in Jersey City without starting rumors. I stand in front of the main entrance, staring at the intricate architectural detail, still in awe of the grandness and history—of how, in the middle of sprawling Manhattan, this has survived a hundred and forty years.

I turn around to look at Eric. Holding both my purse and my laptop case, he watches me. He gives me a gentle, reassuring smile. I sigh. My heart—a physical symptom is occurring. One that I can't describe. Full. Changed. Supported. Cheered on. Encouraged. Brave. I turn around immediately as soon as I feel my first tear is about to drop. I stand still in silence, controlling my sob until I can't any longer. I finally let myself go. I bend my head and put both hands over my mouth to muffle a cry. And then I pray in silence.

I make the sign of the cross. "Today's a bust. You know how much I needed that job. I don't know what else to do. I'm in the home stretch now. I don't think I can do this anymore. I can't be strong for someone else when I can't even be strong for myself. I tried. You know this. The battle is lost many times over. It's time I gave up. Please give me a sign, something, anything—that it's time to walk away." And then I start to shake. I bend my head farther. My heart hurts. I'm consumed with shame.

I feel strong big hands on my shoulders. I freeze, and immediately I relax. Eric. A stranger as an anchor is what I need tonight. Someone who doesn't know me or my sorrows; someone who will not judge; someone who will never ever know; someone I'll never see again, even in my wildest dreams.

"It's okay. You can cry. No one is here to see it. I'll be right behind you," he says in a whisper—light, almost like a chant, and so I give in and cry with all my soul. The anguish within me pours out in the middle of the night, in the middle of the city I crave, in the arms of a man I don't know. But I trusted, and I let go, and I poured my heart into mourning. I feel him squeeze my shoulders. I lean back against him, and he gently puts his arms around me and rests his chin on top of my head.

Chapter 6

10:30 P.M.

"Y ou deserve ice cream for your heroism."

We're sitting on the steps right out front of the church. My eyes are bloodshot after what seems like hours of crying.

"I don't mind ice cream," he teases. His deep voice soothes me. It's not boastful. It's not proud. In fact, for a famous celebrity, Park Hyun Min is remarkably down-to-earth. Pam will be glad to know this.

"I'm jotting down mental notes about what I need to share with Pam about you. She'll be thrilled to know that you're reliable." There is a quick, easy smirk on his lips as he hears this.

"I'm honored with that description." Our knees touch. On impulse, I pull away. He looks at me—I see a trace of hurt in his eyes.

"It's not you," I say in apology, putting my hand up to appease him.

"I know." He nods in understanding. I don't mean to insult. It's the last thing I want him to feel.

"Are you religious, Eric?"

"No. Are you?" Traffic is almost gone along Fifth Avenue. The shops are already closed. Eric and I are hidden in plain sight under the shadow of the cathedral. I pull my coat tighter around me. It's forty degrees tonight, and the wind chill doesn't help. I shake my head in response to his question, then feel a need to explain.

"I need to believe in something. I come here a lot. But I'm not religious."

"It makes sense. I was raised Catholic. I've been guilty all my life." He laughs. "And I don't even know what of." He laughs some more. I reach for his hand. I don't know why. I squeeze it.

"Thank you."

"You're welcome." No explanation needed. We just know.

꒰

Overthinking this will be futile. No matter where we go after this, or where our lives take us, I will forever be grateful that he's with me tonight. On occasion, the universe tries to make sense of circumstances, turning them into magic, and an unexpected spark of fate that changes peoples' lives forever.

"The first time I fell in love, I was fourteen years old." I sigh, trying to remember the exact moment when it happened. "To be honest, I don't even know if it was love at all. What did I know at that age?" I surprise myself by my sudden need to talk to him about this.

"That's young. But you know, love is at its purest at that age." He doesn't need to defend me.

"We were together for about four years before I got pregnant." I feel Eric tense up next to me then looks at me curiously. "I had an abortion. It was my decision. He begged me to get married and when I said no, I lost him. I'm still paying for that." He nods his head slowly. "I think that was when my relationship with the church ended," I add. I shift my position to look ahead into the darkness at the statue of Atlas across the street. "And yet I yearn to belong here," I turn around to look at the grandness of the cathedral behind me. "I need to believe in something, and I choose to believe that there is a God behind the bullshit of religion." I say this in a whisper.

He doesn't say a word. He nods in understanding, but it isn't clear whether he agrees with me or not. And for some odd reason, I need his approval tonight.

"The church didn't take me back. I was eighteen years old. I was brave. I took control of my life. But I needed a higher power to hold onto, so I went to church and decided to go to confession. The priest was probably scandalized by my boldness. I was not just a regular sinner. In his eyes, I was a murderer."

"I'm sorry," he whispers softly.

"It's been a long time—geez, two decades! Can you imagine that? And yet, it still defines me."

"It only defines you if you let other people get into your head."

"That's the thing, there are only two people who know about it—me and my ex. Well, three now. It defines me because it's how I define myself."

"Like you said, it's been two decades. You have to let it go and forgive yourself."

"I don't regret it. I don't feel guilty about it." My voice raises a level higher as I defend this lie.

"Even better. If that's the case, you simply need to forget." I know he's not buying it. He stretches both his legs forward and crosses his arms on his chest. He then brushes his hair off his forehead.

"Who the fuck am I kidding?" I bend my head between my

legs. "I'm a fucking liar." I pull my head up to face him. "I've been thinking about this for years. I've been thinking that maybe I can't get above water because someone needs to forgive me."

"Who?"

"Glen. I just disappeared and walked away. I ran as far away as I could and went to college without saying a word. I felt voiceless, and he didn't even try to understand."

We are quiet again for a little while.

"Where is he now?"

"In Jersey."

He sighs. This is probably starting to be too much for him. He came to Manhattan to escape, not to take care of some lunatic who can't even get her facts straight. "Did you see him again?" I nod slowly. "Is he with someone now? Happy?"

"I don't know. All I know is that he hates me."

"You know it's hard to speculate. The world is this way because people assume and act harshly because of those assumptions. I'm guilty of this too. If only people would start talking to each other, maybe we'll understand each other better."

"Some people aren't that brave." I respond.

"But you've already proven that you are. Sometimes we mistake pride for cowardice, and those two couldn't be any more different.

"That's very wise, Eric."

"No, that's a lesson learned the hard way." He snickers at this. There are so many layers to this man, and it saddens me that I will never have the chance to ever uncover them all. "I fell in love the first time when I was already in my twenties. My career was moving in the right direction, but I knew that my love for this girl was holding me back. I was such a late bloomer. I remember then that all I ever wanted was to just hang out with her, spend my days in her arms, and just forget that my career was important. Again, I wasn't thinking about fame. It's a job."

"Is she an actress too?" I ask. He gives me the look that says he will never ever reveal her identity to me, or to anyone else. I nudge his arm slightly.

"Then an agent found me, and I started getting a lot of work. Serious work. Good drama that helped my career to take off. She lives with her parents close to my parents' house, and so one day during a short break from filming, I visited my family and then went to see her. I planned to surprise her. Instead I got the biggest heartbreak of my life. I saw her kissing one of my best friends. They both saw me, and we were all traumatized that I witnessed their betrayal."

My eyes widen in disbelief. You see these famous people on TV, in their element, looking so put together and wonder if they ever live like we do. I put my hand on his shoulder to comfort him.

"It's a long time ago, but that night I was broken. That night, I assumed that she never really loved me. I assumed that they'd been doing it behind my back for a long time. Later, I heard it only happened that one night when he was trying to console her. She was opening her heart to him about her fear of losing me. But because this friend—this former friend—had always been in love with her, he jumped at the chance. I never spoke to her again. I thought it was fear of getting hurt that stopped me from seeing her. I was broken and scared. Obviously, now I know it was pride."

"Did they end up together?"

"No. She stopped talking to him entirely."

"Then, why didn't you try. . . ."

"Pride. . . ."

"Right."

"Later I found out that she despised me for not giving her the chance to explain. Our once beautiful love story turned into hate. It was sad."

"Was she . . . you know, did you think, that she was, somehow, the one?"

"I planned to marry her, yes."

"Woah! Do you still feel the same way?"

"We've grown up. She's married now."

"Shit!"

"Cursing comes so natural to you, ha?"

"Yeah. I'm taking medication for it, and it's still not working." He puts his big hand over my face and gently shoves it backward. "Stop it!" I can't stop laughing.

"We're basically the same age. We're still young. We'll make more mistakes. We'll learn from them. Wherever you are right now, know that this is not the end." He is somber again.

"It sure feels like it sometime, you know. The end." He nods in empathy.

"Well, it isn't." He reaches for my hand on my lap and squeezes it. "It's time, B."

"For what?"

"I think it's time for you to forgive yourself, and maybe . . . just maybe, you'd be able to move on." I don't know what to say to this. I search his eyes for more answers, clues, anything that can help me through all this. "How about that ice cream?" he finally says with an encouraging smile.

Chapter 7

11:00 P.M.

"Have you always had a high tolerance for alcohol?"

We are walking along Fifth Avenue toward Central Park. It's getting chillier, and the wind is picking up. Eric, still carrying my laptop case across his body, rubs his hands together for warmth.

"Yes." I rub his arm to help him warm up. He laughs at my response. "I had my first drink with Glen. I didn't get drunk until my seventh beer. Seventh! And everyone was staring at me like I was some alien from Mars."

"Yeah. We're beer drinkers too. And there's always soju to pair it with, so it doubles the fun!"

"I can drink soju." Soju is a clear beverage from Korea that has a relatively high alcohol content. "I doubt though if we can find it here anywhere. Oh, wait, I think we could, but in Midtown, maybe."

"For next time." And we both know there won't be a next time. "So, Glen?"

"What about him?" I try to avoid the topic, but I started it, so here we are.

"Did you talk to him when you saw him again?"

"No," I say curtly.

He nods and stops pushing. We walk quietly for the next few minutes.

"That's the Trump Tower, isn't it?"

"Yes."

"I don't think he comes here anymore, no?"

"I don't really follow politics these days." This is another defeat that I accept.

"Interesting," he says.

"Something bad to say about me?" I joke.

"I didn't think you were the kind to sit this one out. Women's rights and gender equality, climate change, and war. I'm sorry. I shouldn't get into American politics."

"I have a war of my own to win. But I was one of those who, together with Pam, marched in DC that day after his inauguration. I cried the morning when the world found out he won. I do my share in my own way. I donate ten dollars to Planned Parenthood every month. It's all I can afford right now."

"Planned Parenthood?"

"Yeah. They give girls free reproductive health services, and without them, I could have stupidly died in someone's basement twenty years ago."

"I see." We let the quiet linger between us. Sometimes words are not enough to best describe a picture. Sometimes silence is the best descriptor.

"I know it sounded like I was such an asshole for having an abortion and disappearing on the father. A lot happened in between. You see, he didn't ask how I was, or what I was going through. He thought getting married would solve everything. He was hurt, and I get it. But did he even wonder what I was giving up to go through with it? I was giving up a part of myself. I was giving up who I was. For the first time, I was afraid. I didn't have anyone to talk to. I was alone." I tremble at the memory. "He was the one who turned his back on me first," and I say this in a whisper.

"Bianca. . . ."

"No one will understand because it was never theirs to matter. It was mine, and I was not very good at explaining myself. And I guess that's the root of all my problems. I'm not the best advocate for me."

We walk again in silence.

"Maybe I should have listened to her when she tried to explain." It's an unguarded moment of contemplation, of saying something so personal out loud.

"Yes." We have our own ghosts, stories we are not proud of, and episodes in our lives that—unfortunately—define us today. "But, at least, you're still very positive about life."

"Did you not hear that I'm in Manhattan to escape?"

"Ha. Right. I guess we're both screwed up in our own little way." I snicker a little. I don't think I've smiled this much the past year, or the past decade.

"It makes us more *interesting* human beings." We immediately look at it each other and chuckle.

⁊౦

There is a line at the door of Serendipity. The place still has New York City landmark status years after being featured in a John Cusack film with Kate Beckinsale. I look at Eric to see if he's still up for it. He jerks his shoulders upward, nods, and falls in line. I stand next to him.

The darkness along Fifth Avenue served our purposes to remain unseen—and for most of the stroll, we were both quiet. Our revelations tonight about ourselves, the emotional display, and our realness and openness perhaps made us think more about the circumstances that led us both here—to find the need to talk, even to strangers—especially to strangers.

We are finally next in line and are both getting excited as we look at the menu of assortments of sweets. Suddenly, a black Suburban stops on the street next to us. A guy in awfully baggy jeans, white hoodie, and gold chains all around his waist, jumps out and runs around to open the other door for a gorgeous lady in a tiny, black sequined dress. I look at my watch. It's not even midnight, so this is not an afterparty kind of visit. I look at Eric, trying so hard not to make any kind of inappropriate face. He widens his eyes in warning. Instead of going to the back of the line, the newcomers walk past us and chat with the host, who's starting to look nervous. He then looks at us, and at them, and then at his list on his podium. We couldn't hear anything, but I see him shaking his head. I'm about to walk over and give them a talking to when Eric grabs my arm to stop me.

"What the. . . ?" I whisper in annoyance.

"Just be glad we're not those kind of people." The girl looks around shyly, and her eyes widen in surprise when her gaze lands on Eric. Eric turns his back to them and faces me.

"She knows you," I tell him quietly. "She's looking right at us."

"She's one of the women at the meeting this afternoon. Just don't attract any attention." Eric takes a step closer to me. His nearness is comforting. I inhale his scent again, which I'm starting to get used to by now. He bends his face to look at me, and I look up inquiringly.

"Do you want to leave?" I ask quietly.

"No. We've waited in line for nearly half an hour." He smiles and I feel my heart skip a beat. He pulls me closer, my face almost touching his chest, and then he puts his arm around me.

It's not a tight embrace, more of a protective stance. I slowly lift my head to look at him. He looks straight into my eyes, and for a moment, something oddly surprising passes between us. Thrill. Excitement. Attraction. I look away immediately. "We're getting you that ice cream whatever it takes," he whispers so close to my ear I can feel his breath on the nape of my neck. I feel a tingle down my spine.

"Eric?" His eyes widen and a pretend smile forms on his face before he turns around to acknowledge the voice. I'm left in the darkness behind his tall figure.

"Vanessa. What a pleasant surprise." His voice is different. He sounds businesslike, formal, but the charm is still there. He's an actor, I remind myself.

"Why are you standing in line out here in the cold? You should just tell the host who you are and the network you repre-sent." She flirts as she says this.

"I don't think he'll know who I am. It's fine. We're next in line. We'll wait."

"We?" She sounds intrigued. Then I feel Eric's hand search for mine behind him. I reach for it, and he gently pulls me out in the shadows.

"This is my friend Bianca."

Vanessa looks at me from head to toe with one slightly raised eyebrow. I smile at her. Eric doesn't let go of my hand. I'm freez-ing and his warmth is a welcome gesture. His nearness keeps this coldness at bay.

"Hi," I say.

"Hi," she whispers with a hint of disdain in her voice. All this time, rapper-baggy-pants here is looking at Eric with con-tempt. He pays me no mind. I am invisible. These three people here are the gorgeous kind—the ones that you see on the screen because they are meant to be there, because they are larger than life. "I guess there's no spot here for us, and I've been craving sweets." Eric just nods his head. I'm praying under my breath that he doesn't invite them to join us. He doesn't. I relax for a bit. "Anyway," she adds. "My friend is throwing a party downtown, and you should come join us later. Are you staying at the Lotte?"

"Yes. We'll think about it. My friend and I have a lot of catching up to do. A lifetime's worth."

"Okay, let me know. You still have my number, right?" And there it is, a little tiny clue that these two have a little bit of history. I feel a twinge of dismay.

"Yes."

Vanessa jumps on Eric and gives him a kiss close to the lips before turning around to face me.

"Prepare appropriately. This man is a handful." She says to me before walking away, laughing sarcastically, and giving me the evil eye. I don't understand the nastiness, but *whatever*.

"Do I want to know what went on there?" I ask Eric as we stare at the two figures getting into the Suburban and driving away.

"A lapse of judgment," he responds uncomfortably.

"When?"

"A few months ago."

"This is not the place to be invisible, Eric, when you have stuff like that lurking around!" I sound like a mother scolding his teenage son.

"I know." He bows his head in shame.

"You cheated on Suzi?" I ask harshly, but I lower my voice in a whisper so as not to let the people behind us in on the conversation. And with a scowl on my face, I put my hands on my hips in genuine anger.

"We were on a break." Eric looks at the people behind us. "She went out with other people too. I'm not trying to justify my actions or defend myself, but Suzi wanted to try this open relationship thing. I didn't have the energy to argue, so I went along with it. I was here for our initial project discussion. I was pissed off at Suzi, and Vanessa was a little too pushy."

"No judgment. I'd probably do the same to spite her." I do a one-hundred-eighty-degree turn there. I don't get that open relationship bullshit when you're supposed to be in a committed relationship.

"I'm a pretty level-headed guy. I get into what I get into because of the profession that I'm in. I don't deliberately seek attention or fame. That's the tiring part of my job, having to dodge people when all you want is some peace and quiet." I don't need to look at his face to understand. It's very clear in the tone of his voice.

"It's tough to be famous, ha?" I'm back to teasing on that.

"*Aish!*" He shoves me lightly on my arm. We've already reached this stage of our newborn friendship, and I already know I'm going to miss it when the night is over—I'm going to miss him.

Chapter 8

MIDNIGHT

"**A**re you kidding? I was the queen of lapse of judgment. I had a lapse of judgment every few days." I put a spoonful of chocolate and strawberry ice cream in my mouth as I say this. Eric looks at me with fascination. "I've had so many bad relationships that I'd rather forget." His eyes widen in surprise.

"Were you this chatty when faced with a prospect?" he jokes.

"Probably not. I'm sure I was oozing with mystery, very glamorous, and dead drunk most of those times." I chuckle. I reach for his ice cream, pistachio, and scoop myself some. He doesn't mind.

"It's New York. I was in my twenties. It was the time of *Sex and the City,* and everyone wanted to be Carrie Bradshaw."

"Who's that?"

"Sarah Jessica Parker."

"Honeymoon in Vegas?"

"Yes. If you think about it, I'm lucky to be alive. I could have met a fucking psycho and got murdered. I'm with you right now because . . . well, in theory, I know who you are." It's his turn to scoop some of my ice cream. "I bet this is not your thing?"

"Not really. I come from a very conservative culture. These are things that aren't discussed."

"I noticed that."

"But the Filipino culture is similar, no?"

"I moved here as a teenager. Apart from the many Filipino gatherings I attend, I don't really know much about that part of my heritage anymore."

"Have you visited the Philippines since you moved here?"

"No. I got busy living and screwing up my life." I smirk at him, though there is some truth to this.

"Stop talking about your life like that. I'm pretty sure there were happier moments."

"I'm sure." Sarcasm overflows in my response. I try to change the subject as I look around the restaurant. It's exactly how I remember it in the movie.

"What does serendipity really mean?" Eric asks as we both look at the sign at the center of the restaurant.

"I think it means like what happened by chance became some sort of a happy thing."

"Like us meeting tonight could be called a serendipity?"

"Yeah."

"Okay, then we came to the right ice cream place. I'm glad." He responds gaily.

"Didn't you see that John Cusack and Kate Beckinsale movie? They met by chance and they both looked for each other over the course of the next year because they felt they were meant to be together."

"How did it end?"

"You've got to watch it."

"C'mon!" He does the gorgeous squinting-eyes thing again. I shiver inside a little.

"It's Hollywood, of course they ended up together. Duh!" I roll my eyes at him, more so to cover the uncomfortable feeling his attractiveness makes me feel. He snickers at me.

"When I read scripts, I always look for a story that moves someone's life toward greatness. We already live in a very complicated world, so in my own little way, I want to leave something positive behind. Even if the story starts out dark, finding that light somewhere in the story matters to me." He turns serious now, leaning back on his chair after finishing off his sundae.

"I agree with you. I'm pathetic because, you see, no matter how broken I am, I still believe in fairytales."

"Like believing in God?"

"Yes." I nod at him as I wolf down my banana split. Eric steals the last cherry on my boat dish. "Hey!"

"You snooze, you lose." He laughs heartily as he says this.

I smile at him in acceptance and defeat, and he smiles right back. The kind of smile that holds a thousand meanings—but it's sincere, and I feel it. The lightness of our newfound friendship radiates from us both.

"So, have you finally found that fairytale magic you believe in?"

"No. I'll probably be searching forever. But that's the beauty of believing, right? It pushes you to find ways to get there." I stiffen at this. Do I actually believe this? I lower my head as I find the answer.

"So, what is that fairytale you're looking for?" He is dead serious as he asks. I look away immediately, afraid that he'd see the pathetic longing in my eyes for a fairytale that will never ever happen. A faraway dream that will never ever come true.

"I don't want to be Megan Markle, if that's what you're asking. I don't want to be someone's princess. I just want to be someone's joy. I also want to be able to love happily. I'm not asking for much. A true love that is calm and peaceful. That would be perfect. But no one truly gets what they want, what they really, really want."

"I think that fairytale fantasy of yours is doable."

"Believe me, it's not."

"Why?"

"Because that ship has sailed." And I don't offer any more information. I just want to be able to enjoy this, enjoy him, and engrave this moment in my heart forever.

❧

It is a stare-down. I know that he's trying to get more information by coaxing me with his gaze. I don't budge. I stare right back. We do this for a few minutes.

"Fine." He gives up.

"Talk to me about Suzi. I love showbiz drama."

"Nothing to talk about, really."

"Dude, you just told me that you guys were in an open relationship, and that you broke up because she desperately wanted to get married, and that she's not the one. I can come up with five questions just with that prompt." I laugh at him. He looks uncomfortable again. It's a great comeback, a perfect revenge, and I can't stop laughing.

"Ha-ha, you think it's funny." It's the first time I see him roll his eyes. I laugh some more.

"Did you love her?" He doesn't answer immediately; instead he pulls a napkin from the holder and methodically wipes ice cream residue from his mouth.

"Our agents got us together. They thought it would be great for us to meet, go on a date, and see where it goes. They said we looked good together. That was four years ago. And three blockbuster movies later, here we are." There is unhappiness as he reveals all this. I can tell that this is not something he's proud to disclose.

"So, it was more a business relationship with benefits?" I ask. Love has become an arrangement of sort.

"Sure, if you want to think about it that way." He bends his head to one side in an act of resignation.

"She must have really loved you if she wanted to get married, no?" We both look around as the lights start to dim. The restaurant is closing soon.

"Saved by the light." He throws both his hands up in satisfaction.

I look at my watch. "We have twenty minutes before they close. Talk, mister." I'm not giving him a way out of this one.

"Fine. I think . . . this is what I think, okay? I think our business partnership is going so well that she wanted to take it to the next level. Get married, have children, and then maybe get a divorce."

"You really think so?" This is a shocking reality to be faced with. That something this cunning actually happens in his world.

"Yes. Isn't that sad?" He can read me well by now. I'm very transparent.

"It is," I agree with great regret.

"I'm not being arrogant here, but if I leave this business behind, I'll be just fine. I've made good investments the past fifteen years. My parents helped me make wise money decisions when I was just starting out. I don't need to come up with publicity stunts to stay relevant. As long as good work keeps coming, I'll keep making them, but I can retire anytime I want and live in an island alone somewhere."

"Alone? Don't you want to be with someone you love, who loves you?"

"I think that reality is a rarity. How can people stay in love and be happy for years?"

"I totally believe that it's possible. Sure, when couples first meet it's all about the passion, the excitement, and the sex—the shallow stuff. Passion dies down after a few years, not because they fall out of love, but because they love deeper. It's no longer about the gorgeous eyes, but what those eyes actually say. It's no longer about those hot kisses, but how those lips comfort you when you need it the most. It's not about how those hands can excite you, but how those hands hold you so you stay sturdy and feel safe." I let my voice trail away softly. I speak of a faraway dream again. The pain hits me hard on my chest.

"Do you honestly believe that, Bianca? With all your heart?" The way he looks at me makes shiver inside. For the first time since I met him almost six hours ago, I can sense annoyance.

"Yes. . . ." I whisper this, and I bow my head down.

"Don't you think the tables have turned here, somehow? You were the cynic and I the positive fellow at the bar earlier."

No one speaks for a few minutes, both of us deep in our respective thoughts.

"I expect more from everything. I know it's not fair to everyone, especially to me. And when I get hurt, I stumble and fall. But you know what? Because I believe that there's a higher force out there, I continue moving forward like the characters in the films that you do. Isn't that what you want—for someone's life to move toward greatness, a positive thing you would like to leave behind?"

"Are you in love now?"

"I can't answer that," I look away again.

"Why not? C'mon, Bianca. You can't talk about love as if it's the golden ticket and not answer that?"

"Because I don't know. I honestly don't know. And I really don't want to talk about this right now." I can feel my heart break a little. Instinctively, I put my hand on my chest to calm my thumping heart.

"Love?" He is challenging me. His piecing glare is coaxing me. Trying to open me further. But it's not a place I can go to. Not now, not ever.

"Yes." I nod.

"Why?"

"Because it's important to me."

"Love is important to you?" His head is bowed down, and as soon as he says this, he lifts his eyes and looks at me from under his beautiful long black lashes. A dare.

"Yes!" I shout this at him. And we stare at each other for a long time. There are no apologies, only discoveries. And we let it simmer. Our friendship evolves way too fast.

I wave at the waiter for the bill. I pull my wallet from my purse and snatch my credit card out.

"Let me get this," he insists.

"You paid for dinner. Let me get this one."

"Bianca."

"Please. . . ." I'm pleading. I don't understand why I have a sudden strong urge to prove myself to him. It's disturbing. It comes straight from the center of my soul. The need to validate the equality of this relationship is physical, soaring and roaring from within me. I don't even check the bill. I just throw my credit card on top of the binder. This debt will hurt tomorrow, but I don't want to hurt my pride today, then so be it.

"I'm sorry if I've offended you, Bianca." If there is anything I learned about him, is that he says things with honesty. There is no bullshit, no need to pretend, because he doesn't have to—because he is who he is, and he is someone. I finally break into a smile, albeit an enigmatic one.

Chapter 9

1:10 A.M.

"Is it true that the Empire State Building stays open until two thirty in the morning?" Eric asks as soon as we step outside in the cold. I pull my phone out from my purse to check the hours. I nod as I scroll though the web page. "We should go!" The childlike personality is back. I stare at him questioningly. "Why not?" he asks.

"Well, because it's already way past my bedtime," I hear myself whine.

"Didn't you used to party in the city in your twenties, you said?"

"I've not been in my twenties for almost seven years now." I laugh at this, and he joins in. I think it's funny, and also frightening how life passes us by so quickly. One minute you're a hopeful twenty-something, and the next thing you know, you're almost forty and barely treading above water.

"Hey, we're Asians. We can still pass for being in our twenties."

"Ah, no. I hate to break it to you, sweetie, we don't look like we're still in our twenties. Heartbreaking as it may seem, I have to be true to you. But fine, let's go to the Empire State Building. We should get an Uber though. All this walking will kill my old legs tomorrow."

"Deal. So, how does this Uber thing work?" He pulls out his phone and starts playing with the App Store.

"You've never Ubered?"

"We don't have it in Korea."

"Really?" I live in a little bubble here in America.

"Yeah." He's still playing with his phone.

"Don't sweat. I have the app already downloaded. Let me do it." I plug in our location and our destination while he stands tall right next to me, still carrying my laptop case. A group of ladies coming out of Serendipity start to giggle loudly as they walk pass us. All of them eyeing this tall attractive Asian dude flirtatiously. I look up at him, oblivious to them.

"What?" he asks as I give him the stink eye.

"You really didn't see that?"

"What? See what?" He furrows his brows in confusion.

"All the flirting."

"Me?" He really is unaware of his surroundings.

"No. Them. With you." I point in the direction of the women, maybe a year or two younger than I am, walking away from us but still looking at him with tantalizing gazes.

"Are you jealous?" He takes a step closer, towering over me with a mischievous smile pasted on his face. His scent. *Geez.* I close my eyes and inhale heavily.

"Why would I be jealous?" I open my eyes with a comeback. "It's just infuriating that they don't even care you're with another woman. I mean they should at least assume that I'm your date. It's a little bit insulting. Now I understand how Captain America's ex-girlfriend felt, and it's quite reasonable." As I roll my eyes, he chuckles and puts his arm around me while staring down the women.

"Sorry, ladies, but my girlfriend is starting to feel really un-

comfortable here." They immediately turn the other way, humiliated.

"Stop it!" I shrug his arm off my shoulder. I hear my phone
ping. "Okay. The Uber comes in five minutes."

"I didn't take you for the jealous type." He finally lets go of
me, takes a step backward, and eyes me cockily. I don't want him
to see my vulnerable side that even I didn't know existed until
tonight. I couldn't say for sure if I were jealous, but it did make
my blood boil that those women had the audacity to openly flirt
with a man I'm with.

"I'm not. I normally don't care. I'm a stone. Rock."

"Normally is not today. So maybe you weren't particularly
jealous that they were flirting with me, but you know what's yours
and want to make sure that everyone knows it." He gets it.

"It's been a long time since I had anything that was mine.
That includes time and money. That includes me."

I stare away at a distance and move my gaze upward to the
stars. It's a hazy night, but you can still see tiny little twinkles up
there. To my surprise, Eric gently pulls me in for a hug. I don't
dare look at him, but instead I give in. I don't fight this because
my soul needs it. I didn't need to shout, I didn't need to be sarcastic, but he heard it, he heard me. It's a shame that I will lose
him after tonight. I don't aspire for romance. I'm not even going
to go there. He's an insanely famous, gorgeous celebrity who can
get any girl he wants. But I do want his friendship. I want his
arms around me like this when I doubt myself. So before I lose
this—before I lose him—I will let myself indulge into a fantasy
that no one will ever believe actually happened to me.

℘

The Uber stops right in front of the Empire State Building entrance at exactly one thirty. We have an hour left to go through the entrance, the elevator, and the maze that they call a museum before making it to the top to see the city. So we run.

Eric pulls my hand as we sprint into the building. We're out of breath by the time we reach the security guard at the turnstile. He looks at us oddly, but lets us through anyway. We get our tickets and line up for the elevator. For a Friday night, the crowd is surprisingly thin. Mostly couples, like us. But unlike us, they all look like they're on a real date—not that Eric and I are even on a fake date.

Inside the elevator, Eric pulls me closer to him to make room for the other visitors to get into the car. He puts his arm loosely around my neck. Our nearness provides warmth—inside and out. I'm probably trekking in dangerous territory here now.

No one speaks in the elevator, and all we hear is the swish of our ascent. The couples are holding hands, looking into each other's eyes, whispering sweet nothings to each other. And here's us, who just met.

"I think we're a better-looking couple than any of these guys," he whispers so close to my ear that I feel goose bumps on my arms. I elbow him lightly in his ribcage. "Ouch," he chuckles, pulling me into a tighter embrace.

We are the last to get out of the elevator. He guides me forward and then reaches for my hand and takes the lead. I let him. I like taking control like everyone else, but I also like it when someone takes care of things for me. I crave the attention of someone making plans to please me. I miss feeling like a woman. The past few years, I was merely a survivor, surviving. I still am.

"Are you interested in reading all these?" He's referring to the historical boards as we walk around to get to the next elevator.

"Not really," I say, shrugging my shoulder. He's still holding my hand, and I don't pull it away. I want to stay in this bubble for a little while longer. I know midnight has passed, but as soon as first light comes, Cinderella will go back where she truly belongs— in Jersey.

Finally, we make it to the top. The wind hits us as soon as we open the glass doors. As I step out, I think of all the beautiful love stories ever told that happened here at the Empire State Building. *Sleepless in Seattle* is the first one that comes to mind. Can strangers truly fall in love like that? Eric pulls me to the rails, and we stand there, looking at the glorious lights of the city that never sleeps. He finally lets go of my hand and rests both his elbows on the wire rails.

"Isn't this place something?" he says without really addressing anyone.

New York City is breathtaking. It's one of the reasons I want to move here. From the moment I first came to visit, I knew this is where I belong. Unfortunately, life isn't that simple.

I move next to Eric and join him, leaning on the rails. I let the wind brush my face. I don't cover it. I don't close my eyes. I take it all in. I want to remember this moment for the rest of my life. As I think this, I slowly look at the man next to me and I beam within. The wind has tousled his well-styled hair. I reach for it and I touch it gently, moving it away from his face. He turns his head to face me. I don't say anything. I stare right back.

I shouldn't have done that.

I can't kiss him.

I just can't.

I turn my gaze back at the gorgeous city night. I feel him watching me. Finally, after a few seconds, he turns away, leaving me be.

If you can find someone in your life who not only hears you but also understands the very core of your being, you should grab him. But Eric and I are worlds apart—both geographically and in stature. He's a handsome, rich, famous actor, and I'm a poor jobless nobody from Jersey. We couldn't get any more different from that.

Eric walks farther away. He disappears at a turn. I don't follow him. I stay staring at the city. It's close, and yet so far. After college, I desperately wanted to move here just like Pam did. But my heart was too fragile. Going back home to Jersey suspended my journey again, thinking that I needed to pay for my sins before I could fully, truly live. Twenty years later, and I still feel undeserving of my dreams for reasons I don't even know anymore. I'm breathing the same air, standing on the same ground, moving along the same space—and yet I still don't feel I've earned a spot in this world.

I close my eyes and try to reach for my center, my calm. A place only I know, only I can go to.

I hear a click. Opening my eyes, I turn around and see Eric taking a photo of me with his phone.

"You looked very peaceful; I couldn't help myself," he explains. There is coyness in his stance. I gather it's probably from getting caught—taking a picture of a *nobody*.

"How about that selfie you promised?" I ask as I pull my phone out of my purse. He comes right next to me. I angle the phone where there is light—but it's still way too dark. I can only see our eyes in the shadows. I take it anyway. I look at the photo. Eric is not facing the camera. He's looking right at me.

"Can I ask you now about your hopes and your dreams, Bianca?" He hasn't taken his eyes off me since the picture.

I don't answer him for a few minutes. This is not a question he's letting go. I pull my head back and look up in the sky. The little twinkling star has almost faded out. Perhaps, it's too late to make my wish.

"I wish to be able to walk away. I wish to be able to give up. I wish to be free." I don't add anything more. If at church earlier this evening, I was still uncertain about what I want out of life, well right this minute I don't feel guilty anymore—I want to be free. I can sense that he's still watching me, waiting for more, but I can't give more than I already have. I don't want to ruin this evening. It's perfect.

"And free you will be, B. I promise."

"And free I will be," I whisper into the night, hoping the universe will find some sense to this request and grants it.

Chapter 10

2:35 A.M.

We were kicked out of the Empire State Building's top level five minutes ago. The security guards weren't too happy when they did that. I had to pull Eric away from the rails, lost in time.

"What's next, B?"

We finally get out of the building. A big part of me doesn't want this night to end. But it's ending, the night is fading, light will emerge soon, and all the magic—the illusion—of this evening will disappear. I will go back to the dump I live in. Eric will jump right back into the luxury he's accustomed to. This could be a premise for a good movie. I see Eric pulling his phone out without waiting for my reply. "It turns out Piedmont Lounge is still open." I look at his phone. "What do you think, B?"

"Fine," I say, pretending to be annoyed, but deep inside I want nothing more than to spend more time with him. I pull my phone out and order an Uber.

While we wait, Eric and I stand side by side next to a lamppost. The lights overhead cast shadows that lurk like the unknown, like my inexplicable ferociously beating heart.

It's pretty quiet along Fifth Avenue now. You can still hear distant life happening in the big city, but where we are is still. I like it. This is what makes New York City special. It also provides space for quiet where you can stroll hand in hand, in our case wait for an Uber, in peace. There is magic in the chilly night that envelops us.

"The city is falling asleep on us," Eric articulates my thoughts.

"It's resting . . . as we should at some point."

"It's great to be alive. We should conquer this. Sleeping on a night like this is for cowards. We only live once, B." I nod at this and smile at him affectionately. His expression changes suddenly. I see fear as he stares at me unblinkingly.

There are so many emotions that can be mistaken for love. Destiny or serendipity—when you want to find a reason why things happen, most times it's because we're looking for that spark and believe it's the power of love moving the universe to suit us. But that's not always the case. Sometimes we trick ourselves into believing it can happen because we want it so bad.

We continue to stare at each other. Unspoken words have my heart beating triple time. Lust, maybe. It's been a while since I felt desirable, wanted, yearned for. In my life, those things are inconsequential. There is no space for such luxury of self.

"Bianca?" A white Toyota Camry stops in front of us. We don't move for a second as we try to ponder what is happening between us.

"I think we're in trouble." He leans toward me when he says this. The words linger. His voice is uncertain, from both excitement and fear. I shake my head. I don't want him to explain this statement. I don't want him to make me understand.

We sit in the car in silence. Thank goodness the Uber driver isn't chatty either. I feel Eric's hand on mine, and I let it stay there. We turn our heads at the same time. We look into each other's eyes—there are questions, so many of them. Most I will never be able to answer. He has the extravagance to be bold, which I don't. Here, I can feel the distance of our differences. I turn away first. I'm not brave. He lightly tugs my hand, asking me to look right back at him. If I don't control myself, I will end up crying again. I look the other direction, out the window, at the night that I'm wasting because I'm a coward. Or a saint.

When the Uber stops right outside Piedmont Lounge, I feel anxious all of a sudden. Our connection has shifted. There is tension between us now. The easy banter, the jokes, and the sarcasm have vanished. The way we look at each other carries an unknown dynamic. Eric jumps out and opens the door for me. I step out. He offers his hand for assistance and squeezes mine gently as he takes it. I look into his questioning eyes, and I can't help but stare at his mouth. I feel the sudden urge to touch it, to feel it on mine. I bite my lower lip in frustration. I see Eric stare at me with more questions in his gaze than I will never be able to answer. I turn away immediately.

At the door, the hostess looks at us doubtfully. Let me rephrase that—looks at me, me, suspiciously. She is in full smile when she turns her gaze to Eric. Eric turns on his charisma automatically and engages her with a precision of an expert charmer.

"Table for two. Quiet. Far from the crowd." He winks at her, making her beam radiantly. She then turns to me, and glares in dismay. I roll my eyes. *I get it. Geez.*

"Sure. Right this way, Mr. Park." I don't remember him telling her his name. And so we follow along behind the beautiful hostess. He reaches for my hand and holds it tight—there's something oddly uncertain in his grasp this time around. He turns to me with fearful eyes and moves his gaze toward our clasped hands.

In this place, I feel like a fraud. Everyone in the room is dressed to the nines and in their glittery best. The only glitter I have is probably the one strand of gray hair I found the other day while I was brushing my teeth in front of my bathroom mirror. The seats here are interestingly short and tiny, which makes them look more like decorative fixtures than actual chairs you're supposed to sit on. Most of the guests are standing, with drinks in their hands, or walking the tiny hallways in slow motion like they're on a runway.

It's particularly uncomfortable for women with their high heels and tiny skirts to even try to take a seat. The fashion statement here tonight is just that, short skirts and high heels, and for the love of God, I can't quite fathom how boys these days think tight, low-waist pants are attractive. My opinion is probably dated, so I shouldn't generalize. Thankfully, I see some smart-looking men in three-piece suits and women in long dresses that look like *Oscar de la Renta* or *Carolina Herrera*. I may be penniless, but I know fashion.

At the far corner, there is a DJ playing chill house music, much to the patrons' liking. Some are swaying and tapping their feet trying to look cool without going into full-on dance mode. It's sure a place to be seen and to mingle, and I can't help but remember the days of my youth. Surprisingly though, I don't crave loud nights anymore. I've used up all my energy by merely surviving.

The beautiful hostess shows us to a *normal* booth far away from the hustle and bustle of the young crowd. I slide into it slowly—and to my surprise—Eric slides in next to me. I don't complain, but my heart is in shambles, and beating violently, knowing there is more to us now beyond our initial connection. Or perhaps I'm deranged and taking all this out of context. A guy like him will never hook up with a girl like me.

My apprehension is interrupted by the arrival of our waiter, dressed in a sequined vest that makes him look like a chorus girl. He hands us tiny menus in wooden bindings. I struggle to read mine, and the lack of lighting here doesn't help. Bless his heart, the waiter then pulls out a small flashlight and points it at the menu.

"I'll have a cosmopolitan," I say, because it's the first item I see. The waiter then looks at Eric expectantly.

"Beer. Heineken, if you have it." I can detect exhaustion in his eyes and in the hoarseness of his voice, sparking a desire to tend to him, to hold him. This is dangerous. I close my eyes in the hopes that all these unwarranted feelings disappear before I lose it altogether.

"Thanks. I'll be right back with your orders."

"What's going on?" I have to ask. It's a form of self-indulgence, if I'm being honest with myself.

"What?" he asks right back.

"Why are you acting strange?" I should have asked, *Why are we acting strange*? I don't correct myself.

He looks at his watch. And I look at mine. It's three in the morning. There is sadness in his expression all of a sudden.

"I had a good time tonight. One of the best," he whispers to me.

"It's not over. We just ordered our first drink." I try to make light of the moment. It's what I'm good at. I hate confrontations, confessions, and goodbyes. Especially goodbyes.

"You're right. I'm just tired." Eric covers his face with his hands and rubs it lightly, trying to pull himself out of the gloom that's hit him. He then rests his arm at the back of the chair behind me. I feel a tingling down my spine. Not fear. Excitement. I turn to face him, head on, our lips mere inches apart.

"So, what's next for you Park Hyun Min?" We are nearing the end of this night. I turn on my fan-girl mode. It's time to ask fandom questions. For Pam. Of course, it's for Pam.

"Sign this new TV show. Move here, maybe. What do you think I should do?" He's serious.

"Is that going to make you happy, Eric?"

"Tonight makes me happy." I don't know where this conversation is heading. As much I would like it to go where my heart wants, my brain is smart enough to step away from this territory. "Does it make you happy, B?"

My heart wins. I nod because it's the truth. Our faces are too close, and I can't help brushing my fingers lightly on his cheek. He leans into my hand, welcoming the gesture, and closes his eyes. He reaches for my other hand and brings it to his lips. I should snatch it away, but I don't. I ask the universe to let me indulge. Just this, I promise, and nothing more. I bend my head. Our foreheads touch. I turn my head sideways to avoid our lips colliding. I can't. I start to take my hands away from his face, but he keeps them and rests them in his lap. My heart doesn't have the will to stop him.

"From here on out, I will remember to start believing in love again," he says as he searches into my eyes for something I can't give.

"I'm glad. You deserve to have it in your life. I hope you find it."

"And I wish the same for you."

"Thank you. Let's hope the universe is listening to our whispers tonight."

"Will I see you again, B?"

My heart pounds violently under my shirt.

"Eric Park in the flesh!" The booming voice comes from behind us. Eric and I both turn around in surprise. A big, burly Caucasian man in a dark suit, with hair brushed neatly to one side with slick gel, is walking toward us, holding a tall cocktail. I move away from Eric, who gets up and greets the man with outstretched arms. They hug and pat each other's backs.

"I didn't take you for a party animal, Eric," the man says. Then he turns his gaze on me, sitting in the booth, willing myself to disappear.

"Not partying at all. Nothing else is open in the city at this hour. We just came from the Empire State Building. By the way, this is Bianca. This is my friend Robbie, from the network."

"Hi," I wave at him, and then I get up to join them. He offers his hand to shake, and I take it. Firm grip. This man means business. But his smile is genuine and warm.

"This is our man," he tells me. "We're so excited with this project. The entire network is abuzz over it. His last Netflix show was the biggest Netflix original drama in North America. Obviously, it's huge in Asia."

"*The Oasis,*" I offer. Eric, looking surprised, turns to check me out.

"Yes. Pure genius. We are getting the best writers in the business to do your show, Eric. The best. Cost is not an issue." Robbie's voice signals power, and he knows it.

"Are you guys also getting Korean creative teams?" I surprise myself with this question. "I mean, we should study their storytelling skills. What's most interesting about their style is that it always starts with something conclusively impossible, and yet finds its way to redemption. I'm obsessed trying to follow the scenes and see where it bends." Robbie looks at me curiously. Eric snickers behind him.

"We have an ultimate Korean drama fan right here," he says.

"Is that right?" Robbie eyes me curiously. Now, I'm no longer just a bystander.

"But what do I know. I'm no filmmaker. Just an avid TV watcher." The three of us laugh at this.

"Can I join you guys for a drink?" Without waiting for an answer, Robbie slides into the seat across from us. Eric and I take our same spots, but the physical distance between us is wider this time.

"So, as an avid audience of Eric's shows, what do you think makes them click?" I can sense his real interest here. I'm a top audience mark for them—my age, my race, and my interest. "You are not Korean, are you?"

I shake my head.

"They don't rush things. They simmer through every scene. I mean, maybe there are business implications to this here in the US, you know airtime costs and all, but with Korean drama, time is irrelevant. When I started watching a couple of years ago, I wondered why they spent so much time with reaction shots. Then I realize it's because these scenes take the audience into the character's journey through his or her feelings. It becomes a ride, and not just someone's life we're witnessing. You start feeling with them, and like them. And I guess that's the secret recipe to its success."

"Holy shit, that's good stuff you're saying here." Robbie looks at me with a fresh pair of eyes. He sips his drink and squints at me with frank admiration.

"Hey, I'm saying this as an audience and a fan, not as an expert. I'll leave that to the creative people."

"What do you do for living?"

"I'm a communications consultant. Freelance communications consultant." I turn to look at Eric. I expect him to be embarrassed. Instead, I see pride in his eyes. And it's toward me. I beam within. He reaches for my hand under the table and squeezes it lightly.

"It's exactly what I was saying yesterday at the meeting. I loved the concept and all, but we can't do this like a Jackie Chan movie. Don't get me wrong, I love Jackie Chan movies, but it's not what I do. Before I did action, I did a lot of drama." Eric is supporting my stand.

"You're right, you're right. And we need her demographics to make the show work. They are the hottest audience, and we want the share of that. What else? Any more tips, Bianca?"

I look at Eric first before I speak. "I think he should do his own stunts, if they're not terribly hard."

"Why?" Robbie asks.

"His fans love seeing him do manly stuff. I know stuntmen give the illusion of the actor doing the hard stuff, but my friend and I would scream and swoon when we see his face do the manly action scenes."

"Exactly what I said yesterday as well," Eric adds.

"Interesting observations. Do you work for Eric here?" Robbie teases.

"No."

"So, he didn't ask you to say all this?" Eric and I laugh together in perfect harmony. We don't tell him our backstory. I relax a little. Although this is unknown territory to me, I can actually contribute to this conversation. I lean back in the chair. Eric does the same, and our shoulders touch. Finally, our drinks arrive. I get my cosmopolitan and I take a sip like a lady. Eric takes a quick swig of his beer.

"Robbie, do you need another drink?" Eric asks the newcomer. His formal persona has returned. The waiter stops when he hears this.

"Sure. Another Long Island tea for me please, and put it on my tab," Robbie instructs.

"Nonsense," Eric says. "Put it on mine."

"Certainly," says the waiter, walking away.

※

Robbie is deep in thought, and Eric and I don't interrupt. I get it. The creative types get their imagination all hyped up in the wee hours of the morning. Now is that hour.

"I think I'm attacking this the wrong way," Robbie says to no one. We let him be. "No offense, Eric, but I thought it's always been about star power—but Bianca here is right, we should also consider the creative treatment." I see Eric smile and nod at this. Where am I? This world is my parallel universe. People are actually listening to me in this reality. Sadly, this will all disappear at first light. "What's your last name, Bianca?" I look at Eric, confused.

"Pierce. My full name is Bianca Pierce. Why?"

"I just like to remember the names of the people who give me good advice."

"I'm glad to be of help."

The waiter comes back with Robbie's drink. He immediately downs it straight. Eric and I look at each other.

"Am I costing you a job?" I lean in sideways to Eric and whisper this.

"It's exactly what I told them yesterday, but they didn't listen," he replies quietly. I have to lean in closer to hear him speak. The chill music is overwhelming the ambience. "He needs to hear from people who get him the profits, audience like you. You know they spend money on tests and focus groups. You just saved him thousands of dollars."

"Let's take this to my place," Robbie says, rising. "This is really good insight, Bianca. Can I invite you for another drink in my suite at the Lotte?" Eric and I look at him, bewildered. "With you, Eric, of course. I'm inviting both of you." I see Eric exhale sharply and I look at my watch. It's almost four in the morning. In two more hours, I'd have been up for an entire day. Eric looks at me questioningly.

"I don't know, Robbie. We've had a full night. I think it's time to rest."

"One hour. I promise."

Minutes later, Eric and I are ushered into his black limousine waiting outside the bar. The three of us are squished in the backseat, with me in the middle. Eric, still holding my laptop case, puts his arm around my waist to make sure there is a good distance between me and Robbie. I lean my elbow on his lap and he holds my arm affectionately. Why I'm allowing this is because I'm a mere mortal. I'm human. This, right here, is the most amazing experience of my existence, and I want to own it. It's mine. I'm letting myself live it, even the parts that are surreal and would likely contribute to my already complicated life. But this is just for tonight.

"Do you trust this guy?" I ask silently. We're walking behind Robbie in the grand hall of the Lotte. If you've seen *Gossip Girl*, you'll know this place by heart. I look around the hotel like an idiot. I then look at Eric, who he gives me an affirming nod.

Robbie's suite opens to a large living and dining room area that's three times the size of my house in Jersey. I secretly look around in awe. I've never been in one of these suites before. Upon walking in, Robbie goes straight to the bar and mixes himself a drink. He looks at Eric and then at me. Eric asks for a beer. I shake my head. I think I've had enough.

"How about coffee?" Eric asks.

"Yeah, I can do that."

"There's a Nespresso machine right there," Robbie points to the mini kitchen behind us. Eric goes and fixes me a cup.

"Cream and sugar?" he asks.

"Two packets of sugar. Black."

Chapter 11

5:10 A.M.

We're in the lavishly decorated living room space. I love the combination of black and gold, which are perfect colors for a king. Robbie is a big man, and his presence even bigger. All he needs is a crown. I smile as I envision him on his network throne. As he sips his drink, I can tell that the wheels are turning in his head. He is deep into his process.

"This will work," he says to himself and immediately looks at me for approval.

"It will work," I agree, suppressing a yawn. "I've been watching Korean drama for almost two years now—religiously. In fact, it's probably the only thing I watch on Netflix these days. You don't take the actor out of his comfort zone, change the rules, and expect him to win fans. Take the formula that's working and improve it—don't change it."

"This is a smart woman right here, Eric. She's a keeper."

"I know." We're sitting next to each other on the large black leather sofa. His arm is resting around my shoulders. It feels good to have his fingers lace gently on my arm. I no longer feel guilty, nor do I question my value as to why I'm here. I plan to enjoy what's left of this fantasy. He relaxes his hand on my arm and softly pulls me closer.

"What's your cologne?" I whisper close to his ear. I turn my head toward his face, and I can feel heat coming from within me. There is a pull between our lips. A slight movement can send me to that one place I know I can never go. I suck my breath in, intoxicated by the notion that I have the power to choose here.

"Chanel Homme. Why?" His eyes lazily take in my face, finally stopping on my hungry lips.

"Nothing, just curious." When I miss him, all I'll need to do is smell his scent, and hopefully that will be enough to keep me going. I bite my lower lip, not to tease but to restrain myself.

"Yours is Kelly Caliche, isn't it?" He asks. A gift from my mom every year on my birthday. I jolt away to regard him in astonishment.

"Do you know many women who wear this?" I demand. I feel bold to even ask. Like I have the right to react this way.

"No. You're the first, and I'm glad."

"Then, how do you know the scent?"

"I've smelled it somewhere before. But not on someone, thank goodness." He then moves his face on the nape of my neck. I close my eyes because I might lose all the self-control I've been trying to muster. There is no reality anywhere in which I will end up with him. None. I should just keep my place in this dream and move on, move forward, move anywhere as long as it doesn't involve hoping for more.

We hear a loud snore and turn our heads to look at Robbie, smiling. He has finally fallen asleep, with his drink still in his hand. Eric gets up and carefully moves his glass on the table.

"I think it's time to get going," he says. I stand and gather my things. I don't let Eric carry my laptop case anymore. It's safer that way. We tiptoe out of the room, careful not to wake Robbie. I can see a glimmer of light outside the window before we close the door behind us. *This is it*, I whisper to myself.

"I'm upstairs. The penthouse." I don't say anything. Instead, I walk silently next to him. At the elevator, I push the down button. He looks at me questioning and I avoid his glare. "Hey, hey, look at me." He caresses my face with his cold fingers and gently turns it toward him. My eyes stray away. I can't bring myself to tell him that this is the end of this dream. "Is everything okay?" I can't cry again in front of him. "Bianca?" he gently coaxes. "Please look at me." His gentleness is what I will miss the most.

"Eric, I have to go." I look at my watch. It's 5:37 a.m.

"Why?" There is pleading in his voice. I hold onto my purse, where my judgment awaits, as tightly as I can.

"I have to go," Tears are forming in my eyes, and a painful sob is trapped in my throat. My chest starts to tighten as I silently will myself to be strong—all I need is a few more minutes, a few more steps, and a million drops of conviction to walk away.

Finally, the down elevator comes and opens for me. I step in. He reaches for my hand and doesn't let go. He steps in with me after realizing I can't be dissuaded. The elevator dings as it closes. The silence is eerily heartrending. I'm facing the door, avoiding his questioning glare. He puts both his arms around me in a tight embrace from behind as if our lives both depend on it. He's making it harder for me to do the right thing.

"I can't. Not yet," he whispers close to my face. I can feel the warmth of his breath. I sense desperation. The kind that mirrors what I feel inside. There will be more sorrow and pain and tears if I stay. There is no part of this story that will end with a happily ever after. My dreams are mundane and simple, achievable. He is not a simple dream. He is an impossible one. I can feel my heart breaking into pieces, but I have to walk away.

"There's light out now. I have to get going." I still don't look at him. I can't breathe as I hold myself together.

The elevator door opens at the lobby. I step out. The place is empty. Eric is still clinging to me. Then, I gather all the courage that I have and face him.

"I have to go. You have to let me."

The boyish face is here again. The man, who is around six foot three, but looks like a little boy, with his begging eyes, is asking me to stay. I reach for his face because I want to remember how it feels in my hands one last time. He gently takes my hand and lets it stay where it is.

"Why?" he asks in a whisper. We look at each other for a very long time. Goodbyes are hard, especially goodbyes that have no path to a hello. I try to remember every aspect of his face—every dent, every arch, and every angle.

"Know that for the first time in a very long time, I felt heard and seen and respected. Thank you. And if you ever doubt yourself about anything, always remember that I think of you as a good man—no, the best. I hope you find that love—the one you still don't believe in—and when you do, please think of me and thank me in silence. You may not see me, but I'll know. I'll make sure to check in on entertainment news every now and then." I smile a little.

"Give me one good reason why you need to walk away." He takes a step closer, and this time, I take a step back. His eyes are waiting for an answer.

"Because that's what a good married woman should do."

Slowly, his hands release mine. He doesn't say another word. I turn around and walk away, slowly at first. Then my pace quickens, and I don't look back. And with all of my aching heart and all of my dying soul, I weep.

It's 5:55 in the morning.

PART 2

Chapter 12

The sun is beaming brightly. The air is chilly, but the morning is filled with beautiful rays of sunshine that bounce around where I stand, outside the station, waiting for my Uber driver to come for me. Although I recognize the beauty of the morning, a dark cloud looms above my head and over my heart.

"It's better this way," I say again under my breath, convincing myself that it was the right decision. It still is.

The train ride back to Jersey is the longest, most harrowing journey of my life. And believe me, I've been in more difficult situations than I can count. My eyes are weary and bloodshot, and my head is a mess. I look at my watch, which says it's ten o'clock in the morning. I have not slept a wink, and it has been more than twenty-four hours. I'm exhausted—physically, mentally . . . and no, my emotions don't get a reprieve either. For a moment, as I was dragging myself out of the hotel this morning, I was almost tempted to run back to him—I was Meryl Streep to Clint Eastwood in *Bridges of Madison County*. I'm only human. But I'm also a married woman, I remind myself again. I made a promise. I'm keeping my vows.

It's perfect timing that my Uber stops right in front of me, just as I spot a busload of weekend tourists heading to New York City getting dropped off not far from where I stand. I need to get out of here before traffic jams up the entire area. It's only a ten-minute ride from the station to the house that I share with Tommy, my husband of twelve years. I don't plan to get stuck here for a half hour. As the Uber driver expertly swerves to get out of the busy street, a loud wailing and the arrival of a fire truck take us to the side of the road. Not far behind is an ambulance.

Five minutes into the ride, the emergency vehicles are still right ahead of us. And we seem to be heading in the same direction. Google Maps says we'll reach my house in another three minutes.

"It's like we're following them," my Uber driver jokes, eager as I am to escape this convoy.

"I know, right? And they're very loud." The blaring sound aggravates my pounding headache. I feel a jolt in my chest, a sudden worry about facing my husband this morning. I hope he has already left for the day when I get home. I provided him the gist of what happened on the phone last night anyway, and he even suggested that I spend the night in the city.

"Are you on Avalon Street?" The driver asks, pulling me out of my reverie.

"Yes." Head bent down, scrolling mindlessly through my phone, I respond without looking up at him.

"The ambulance is stopping right out front. Is that your house with a red door?" I immediately look up in worry.

"Yes. What's going on?" I jerk forward to see the commotion in front of the car. "Stop." I've been here before. This scene is not new to me. The car abruptly halts and I jump right out, running straight to the ambulance. "This is my house. What's going on?" I ask one of the EMTs with a tight knot in my stomach.

The door opens, and my mother-in-law, Celeste, comes out in tears.

"Celeste, what the hell is going on?" She has a tall beehive hair, as if we're back in the '60s, and she gives me a furious glare. We don't like each other very much.

"While you were out last night, Tommy looked like he OD'd! Where the hell were you?" The pang of guilt hits me hard. I sigh, but I don't respond. Instead, I run into the house and find EMTs busy rattling their equipment around. There, in the living room, sits Tommy in his favorite recliner chair, barely breathing.

"Tommy! Wake up!" I drop to the floor next to his chair and scream his name. He doesn't respond and so I push his chair and shake his arm. Nothing. "Tommy! Wake the fuck up!" I'm losing it. The volume of my voice reverberates in the room and for a quick second, everyone stops and stares, perhaps weighing the need to sedate me. I stay glued to the floor, anger building inside me. I just can't deal with this shit right now.

"Ma'am, please make way. We'll take care of it from here." One of the technicians takes me by the shoulders and moves me to the side while the others check on Tommy. It's always about him. When will it ever be about me? I bend my head and cover my eyes with my hands. I want to cry. I should cry. I'm exhausted. *I need a fucking break.*

"Is he breathing? Can someone please tell me if he's breathing?" I scream again. The chaos in my tiny living room is making me woozy. I'm trying to hold myself together. Celeste is standing on the other side of Tommy bawling, her mascara-stained tears running down her cheeks.

"Yes, he's breathing. We need to get him to the hospital as soon as possible." When I hear this, I start to sway. Everything is a blur from here on out. Then I black out. I don't remember anything else.

He had the bluest eyes I'd ever seen. They were luminous and fluid, and they could take you somewhere serene. He was standing next to my cousin Mike, outside my mom's house the day I came back from Washington, DC, after graduating the previous week. He was wearing a Pearl Jam T-shirt, low-waist Levi's, and a pair of navy-blue Chuck Taylor Converse sneakers. His hair was short, a buzz cut, offering a better view of his handsome face. He didn't smile much, but when I opened the door of my car, I saw him beam, his chest expanding with his breath—like he was actually waiting for something to happen, like he was waiting for me. He was known as the bad boy of our neighborhood, and the girls my age were all fighting to get a piece of him. His reputation as a bad boy was just that, a reputation. But his drug addiction, that was real.

"I love you, baby. . . ." When he said those words for the first time, I was on top of the world. He chose me. Among the many girls who wanted to be with him, he picked me and loved me. We were sitting under the stars by the beach, holding hands, just the two of us. "Let's get married," he blurted out. We were both twenty-four.

"Yes!" I said impulsively, and I put my arms around his neck and kissed him from the depths of my heart. There was no doubt in my mind, back then, that I wanted to be Mrs. Tommy Pierce.

Tommy was a sweet, gentle, and considerate young man who was often misunderstood. It also didn't help that his mother, Celeste, had been in and out of rehab for most of his childhood.

"I want to be a better man for you," he whispered close to me as we enjoyed the beauty of the starry night.

But addiction is an illness. And by the time I felt I had to walk away, the battle had been lost many times over. *How can you leave someone who is sick without everyone judging you?*

On one fateful night, I walked into our dark living room feeling an unexplained distress. It was a regular day, and he had promised to be home early to prepare dinner. I just got back from the city after an event, and I was exhausted. When I turned on the lights, there he was, splat face down on the floor. It felt like the world had fallen. His body was twisted, and I knew something bad had happened. I dropped down next to him and started sobbing, shaking, as I rummaged through my purse for my phone. That was when I saw him overdosed for the first time. We'd been married for three years.

The second time it happened, it was Valentine's Day. I wanted to surprise him, so I rushed home earlier than planned. It was also a rough week because he'd just lost his fifth job in construction, which had paid handsomely. We had planned to go to dinner; it was our way to try to reconnect as a couple, as a team. I had committed to him no matter what.

But I knew that something was amiss from the silence that greeted me. Normally, Tommy would have music blaring when he's at home. I looked down at my feet and saw water on the floor. It was coming from the bathroom. Dropping my things on the sofa, I rushed toward it. I hit the door hard with my fist, and inside I found Tommy in the tub, naked, after a hit, with water still running from the faucet. From the looks of the damage, he had been in there for hours. His wrinkled fingers also gave him away, after I touched him to check if he was still breathing. I turned around and went back to the living room to call 911, but even as I did, I had become apathetic. I knew I was in the wrong life. That was almost seven years ago.

❧

When I wake up, I feel a tiny prick on my arm where a needle is impaled in my vein. I'm in a hospital room, on a hospital bed, attached to various machines that beep in sequence. *Am I dying?* My throat is dry, and my head is heavy, the pain making itself immediately known with a drilling sensation on my temples. Slowly, I turn my head to inspect my surroundings. I see Mom on the chair next to my bed, and she rushes to my side as soon as she sees me open my eyes. Pam is here too, standing next to Mom. She reaches for my hand and rubs it gently. I smile at the sight of Pam because she reminds me of the *dream* I had the night before. It's deceitful that my mind wanders somewhere it shouldn't go. She smiles weakly back at me. Pam, with her gorgeous blond hair and smiling blue eyes, is a complete contrast to my dark hair and big brown eyes. She has always been the positive side of my life, but today I notice dark purple circles under her eyes, and the sore redness of her nose reveals that she's been crying. Weakly, I reach out to touch her, a furrowed question on my forehead. Without warning, my mother buries her face in my hair and bursts into tears.

"How are you feeling?" Pam asks gently, ignoring my mom.

"I'm fine. Just tired," I assert with a croak in my voice. "How's Tommy?" I ask. I no longer feel the need to exaggerate the situation. It has become a norm. He gets bad drugs, takes them, and puts his life in danger. Some days, he gets good drugs, and he's out for days, missing work, and then good as new as soon as he comes out of it. I don't think love is the reason why I stay. It's mere survival now. *I'm done. I'm leaving him.*

I slowly turn my head to face the window, not waiting for Pam to respond. It's already dark outside. *How long have I been asleep?*

"I'm sure you're hungry. Let me get you some food at the

cafeteria." Pam wants to get away, I can sense it. She turns around and heads for the door.

"He didn't make it this time, did he?" She stops in her tracks. My mom, clutching my arms tightly, begins whimpering. Shaking her head, Pam confirms what I knew was going to happen sometime soon. Part in anger, and part in sadness, I burst into an excruciating howl. A flood of pain escapes my body, and I shake uncontrollably. Mom stares at me in panic, holding me down, kissing my forehead, and comforting me the best her tiny little frame can.

"Pam, call the nurse for help!" Mom screams and starts pressing the many call buttons next to my bed.

"Help! There's something wrong. Please. . . ." I hear Pam's frightened voice pleading outside the hallway.

Then I hear hurried steps, a herd, as I howl. I hear machines beeping as I scream. I can't stop myself. I'm trying. I want to run away. I want to disappear. I don't want to face any of this. I feel myself getting hotter, and I hear myself screaming louder. I'm trapped. Claustrophobic. Falling. Someone touches my arm, trying to calm me down, giving me a shot, a tiny painful prick, and then I black out again.

✺

"She's in shock but she will be okay," someone's soothing voice says.

"What is happening to her?" Mom. From the sound of her quivering voice, I can tell that she is terrified. I'm not dying, I want to tell her, but I can't manage to speak. I can't even get their attention. My eyelids are too heavy. I just want to close them forever. I don't want to hear anyone speak for a long, long time.

"Is she pregnant?" my mom asks.

"No, she's not. We checked that already." I exhale. And I black out again.

❧

"Celeste is working on the funeral arrangements, and she wants to know if Bianca has any money for it." I want to scream and shout at the person who's speaking, but it's as if there's a heavy brick pinning me to the bed. It's Tommy's uncle Pete.

"I don't know anything about their money, Pete," I hear Mom say politely.

"Look, if Celeste doesn't want to wait until Bianca is better to make decisions about that, there's nothing we can do. I don't understand why she's in a hurry." Pam is angry.

"We just don't want people to start poking around." Pete sounds apologetic.

"Poking around about what? That he overdosed? Everyone from Jersey City to Hoboken knows that Tommy overdosed."

"We're not saying that. . . ."

"If you ever blame this on Bianca, I swear to God, Pete!" Pam couldn't help herself any longer. Then I don't hear anything more. I black out again.

❧

"She's been living this hell all these years and no one even noticed?" I know that voice. I've not heard that voice in a very long time, but I'd recognize it anywhere because it holds a piece of me. *Am I dreaming? Am I stumbling into my past? I'm losing my mind.*

"Dad?" I hear people rush toward me. I try to open my eyes but can't.

"Baby, I'm here." It *is* my dad. I don't know what he's doing here. He didn't show up for my graduations, either high school or college. He didn't respond to my invitation to walk me down the aisle at my wedding. I don't understand why he's here now.

"Mom?" I sound like a child lost.

"Sweetheart, I'm here." She didn't know anything about Tommy. I kept her in the dark because I didn't want her to worry, and I don't want her anywhere near this man now. I need to protect her.

"What is he doing here?" I hear contempt in my voice. And then, just like that, I'm out again.

ॐ

This time, I wake up in my mom's house, in my old room, surrounded by familiar things—my Jon Bon Jovi poster livening up my dull purple walls. There are a few trinkets of my past on the banister next to my small desk, reminding me of that beautiful promising life I once lived. I'm alone. It's still dark outside. I look at the clock on the bedside table that says 2:15 a.m.. I try to get up, but I wobble. I try again. Holding on to the chair next to the bed, I finally make it to the window. My mind is in shambles. I stare at the darkness outside, trying to focus—at the lamppost illuminating the street, my mom's old red car down below pinched between two large SUVs, and the green trash bin right out front the neighbor's door.

I hear a light tap on the door. Mom.

"Come in," I smile weakly as she walks in, and seeing the worry in her eyes, I smile wider.

"How are you feeling?" Are you hungry?" In this house, in our little family, food is a quintessential response to everything—

celebration or grief, birth or death. It's a very Filipino coping mechanism.

"I'm okay. It's two in the morning, Mom. I'm fine."

"I can scramble you some eggs quickly. Or, make you some French toast the way you like it. It's easy to make." I wish I could bluntly tell her that what happened, that Tommy dying was a good thing. But just to listen to my thoughts articulating this makes me shiver. I cannot admit this to my religious mother.

"Mom, why are you up?" She walks in and sits at the bottom of my bed. I sense her uncertainty.

"I heard you get up. This is an old house that creaks with every movement. I can't sleep anyway. I worry about you." She puts both her hands on her lap tentatively, as if not knowing what else to do with them.

"I'm fine. I'm alive. It's not me who died." She gasps.

"Bianca," she warns.

"You think it's heartless that I speak of Tommy like this?" I'm not being sarcastic. "This is not the first time it happened, Mom. But this time, he wasn't so lucky." How can I explain the pain when I was so good at covering it up? No one knew, except Pam, that my life with Tommy was a hellhole.

"What do you mean?" There is confusion in her eyes.

"I've lived with a drug addict for twelve years." I sit next to her and reach for her hands to stop her from wringing them. They are cold and clammy.

"Oh, Binky." It's a name she calls me, a form of endearment, when no one's around.

"This happening was not an *if*, Mom, it was a *when*." My chest tightens as I reveal this. I promised myself a long time back that I would never pull her into my complications because she unquestionably deserves to have a quiet life after my father walked out on her, for working hard and for being a remarkable single parent to me for so many years. I have failed.

"Why didn't you tell me? I heard stories about Tommy from other people, but I didn't believe them because Tommy is . . . was . . . such a sweet and respectful boy. I always said that someday his luck would get better. I couldn't quite understand why he kept losing his jobs."

"It was because there were days when he couldn't go to work because he was high. Then he would sleep for days to get over it. I'm so grateful we didn't have any children." I whisper this. Mom had been nagging me for grandchildren for years. Now she knows why I never gave her any. She nods at this, finally understanding.

"I pray every day for your happiness, Binky."

"I know, Mom." It's the reason I couldn't tell her about all my pain, because it would have only devastated her.

We're both quiet, simmering through the shock of this revelation.

Jersey City is no quieter than Manhattan. I hear sirens at a distance, garbage trucks backing up, and dogs barking loudly in the neighborhood. I take comfort in all this because it means I'm alive, I still appreciate the textures of my life, and I'm embracing Tommy's death so things can finally turn. I bend my head down in shame.

"I'm sorry I wasn't there for you."

"You were there for me plenty, Mom. You didn't need to be part of that dark life." She had her own time of suffering. I didn't need to add more to it.

"Twelve years is a long time to live in darkness, Binky."

"It was all right. Tommy and I had happier times. I just don't remember them anymore." I pause, trying to evoke memories of those happier times, but I can't think of any. "I should get the funeral arrangements sorted tomorrow. I'm sure Celeste is freaking out."

"Poor Celeste."

"Celeste is Celeste. For her, everything is about the theatrics, the drama, and her story." I despise her as much as she despises me. For some reason, she thinks Tommy could have done better than me. "I'm sure she loved Tommy. But she loved Tommy the way she knew how. It's not the kind of love you give me." Mom reaches out to hug me, and I hug her right back.

My life is not all bad. I have Mom, I have Pam, and I have that sliver of a dream so far-fetched no one would believe it was once lived—for one great night.

Chapter 13

I'm wearing white in contrast to everyone's black attire. In the front pew, I know I stand out. Today, I don't disappear, and ironically, in church, I want the world to see me at my most selfish moment.

On the other side of the aisle, Celeste eyes me with contempt, accusing me of not mourning her son's death enough. I stare right back, challenging her gaze, because I honestly no longer give a fuck. I mourned for the past decade, and I was robbed of a life I feel I deserved. It ends today.

I feel my mom's hand on my arm, rubbing it gently, silently telling me to let Celeste be.

"Bianca, she just lost a son," she finally whispers softly into my ear. I break free of our stare-down only to appease my mother. I specifically told her earlier today that I didn't want Celeste sitting with us at church. Finally, she's no longer family. I don't have any reason to acknowledge her existence after this display.

The church is eerily quiet. There are no murmurs of greeting. No one even dares come to me to offer condolences. I wear my face devoid of expression. I don't cry because this is something we should celebrate. Tommy is at peace now, resting, and hopefully enjoying the freedom that he had been searching for. The crowd is also thin. Tommy doesn't have many friends, and the few friends that he had are not the kind who turn up at funerals of people who overdosed. It's like looking at their future. As I turn around, I see most of my mom's side of the family—my grandparents, my aunts and uncles, my cousins and their spouses, my nieces and nephews. Then I see him, at the far back. I do a double take. Dad. He smiles at me weakly, which sends my heart into a painful tumble. I don't return the gesture but instead, I immediately look away.

"Mom, is that Dad at the back?" She turns around and right back again.

"Yes," she replies without further explanation.

"What is he doing here?"

"I'll explain later."

I turn around again to look at the man who abandoned me, us, years ago. He's still a handsome man in his sixties—tall, well built. He's wearing a dark suit, and even from a distance, I can tell it's not from Men's Warehouse. It looks new, expensive, well-tailored, and on-trend. I give him a questioning glare, to which he responds with a compassionate nod.

In this universe, as I sit down in numb silence, I am between the two men I despise the most.

℘

Waves of colorful sunlight shine through the mosaic glass window directly above the cross. Below it, right in front of the altar, rests Tommy's body inside the mahogany coffin Celeste insisted that we get for him. Tommy and I lived paycheck to paycheck. In fact, most times it was hard to make ends meet, but Celeste wanted that goddamn mahogany coffin, so I let her wipe me out. A big picture of him stands next to it—Tommy Pierce as a young boy, with a beautiful smile that drove girls crazy. But in his eyes, there was darkness.

"This is not me, baby. This is not me," he begged me to forgive him after the last bad episode. He was crying like a broken child, which in truth, he was. He was kneeling on the floor, clutching me tightly, tears flowing down his cheeks like a waterfall. "I need you in my life. Without you, I am nothing, Bianca. Nothing." In my head, I said, *Without you, I could be everything.*

The priest walks in and looks right at me, but I don't budge. I sit, unmoving. Finally realizing he's not getting anything from me, not even a weak sad smile, he starts the funeral service.

"Brothers and sisters, we are gathered here today to celebrate the life of our son, our brother, our friend . . . a husband, Thomas Anthony Pierce."

I zone out for the most part.

⁊◌

It's over. I heave a sigh because finally this chapter of my screwed-up life is coming to an end.

I didn't do a eulogy. Tommy's uncle Pete did, and it was a disaster. He was probably high on something. I didn't want to be part of the show. There were no tears shed in the room except, of course, in Celeste's loud performance.

I don't move from my seat. I need this time to be alone, and Mom and my aunts and uncles have been efficiently blocking people who attempt to come talk to me and offer their condolences. I can't face anyone just yet.

The church empties out quickly. We're finally alone again—Tommy and I. But I don't go to him anymore. I said my goodbyes years ago—to the Tommy I knew and once loved. That person in there is not the man I fell in love with. That body is a stranger. I remain in my seat. Now it's time to mourn the woman that I was with him.

"Are you going to Celeste's?" Mom asks as she walks back to me after talking to a few of the guests.

"No." I shake my head. "I don't plan to see her or talk to her ever again after today." I still don't show any emotion.

"I should go. One mother's respect to another mother."

I nod at this. It's but a fitting gesture from our mothers, I suppose. "Just tell her I need to lie down. I don't feel well."

"You're staying with me, right?"

"Yes." I nod again. I'm not ready to go back to my house, the house Tommy and I bought together. I'll put it on the market first thing tomorrow morning before the eviction notice goes into the mail. I don't ever want to step foot in that house again.

I see Pam hurriedly walking toward me after herding away some of our high school classmates. I feel bad that I have nothing more to offer them other than my stoic face, but it's best that I don't speak to them at this time. I don't have the energy to be polite.

"Do you want to get drunk with me today?" I ask Pam in a monotone.

"I thought you'd never ask!" Pam grabs my arm. Mom, hearing this, pushes me up and out the church in encouragement.

❦

Pam grabs a table from a departing family like an expert bar-hopper. The two children, both teenagers, stare at her as if she has lost her mind, and she gives them a massive eye roll as if to say, *I don't give a shit.* That's my Pammy!

We're at Carlito's, a local favorite, which in my opinion, serves the best authentic Mexican food in the tri-state area. This place is not just any restaurant to me; this is home, as Carlito and his son, Miguel, are like family. The bar is its most famous attraction because it showcases a glass window that reveals the kitchen where customers can see how Carlito's amazing chefs grill their famous taco meats. Being here comforts me. There are ghosts of the past here too, but here is a lot better than the cold, dark house sitting empty on Avalon Street.

"Stay put; I'll get us drinks." She pushes the chair toward me and disappears into the mob around the bar.

I watch the crowd, not paying particular attention to anything or anyone amid the boisterous noise that occupies the place. My brain is a medley of tumultuous images. In and out, little snippets of the past twelve years flash before me. Varied emotions come with them. I try to search for the happy ones, but even our wedding day, which back then was supposed to be the happiest day of my life, couldn't come close to the joy I'm searching for today. *Have I changed?*

I'm a widow now, and that, for me, sure does sounds strangely false. I'm here, but I'm not. I exist, but a part of me doesn't anymore—the part of me that was once married.

I'm free. I gasp as I realize this, covering my mouth with both my hands as this new reality finally dawns on me.

Did I will this to happen? Did I ask the universe to kill Tommy? I look around the crowded room. I sigh in relief that there are no strange glares from anyone blaming me. *I'm losing my mind. I fucking need a drink.*

"You good?" Pam asks as she comes back from the bar with shots and beers in hand, balancing them like a pro. Before the tequila shots even hit the table, I grab one from Pam's hand and glug it down. I grab the beer as well to chase the tequila down. "Geez, you need another round already? It took me forever to get that." This is the Pam I know and love. She's glaring at me. She's back. I'm glad. I don't want her to be walking on eggshells around me tonight.

"I'll get the next one." I get up, grab my bag, and push my way toward the bar. I'm tiny enough to make it unscathed, and then I see Miguel, and immediately I feel a surge of safety envelop me. I'm glad he's here tonight. He spots me, his head veering sideways as if to ask if I'm all right. With glistening eyes, his face softens in sympathy.

Miguel knew Tommy well because this place had also been his safe space. On occasion, when things were getting out of hand, Carlito or Miguel would call to make sure I took him home before he got into any more trouble. Miguel walks around the bar, pulls me away from the crowd, and gives me a big hug. I melt in his embrace, my body sagging heavily, finally letting go.

"Sorry I couldn't make it today," he whispers as he holds me tight, holding me up.

"I didn't want anyone there today, anyway. I wanted it over and done with. I wanted that part of my life to end." I bury my face in his chest. The heat coming from his body is a comfort to me.

"It's the reason why Papa and I stayed away."

I cry in his arms quietly, the rowdiness of the bar as the backdrop to mask my pain. No one gives us a second glance.

"You are a good person. You were a good wife. He was lucky to have you. I saw you give it your all. It's over. You can breathe now." I hold onto his shirt tight, pulling it as I try to bear the pain in my chest. Carlito appears next to us and guides us to the quieter part of the bar. Carlito holds me in his arms. This father and son duo has been another lifeline to me.

"Where's your table?" Carlito inquires, and I point to where Pam is sitting, staring at us, perplexed. Her blond hair glows beautifully under the muted lights coming from the chandelier above her. "Miguel, take her there. I'll get some food and drinks ready, okay, *mija*? You're going to get through this. I've seen you at your bravest. You've got this, Bianca."

Miguel and I walk side by side toward Pam, who's staring at me with a creased forehead. Miguel, ever the gentleman, pulls a chair out for me and takes the seat across from Pam.

"Hi, I'm Miguel."

Miguel is a handsome Mexican American man who's currently doing his MBA at Princeton while also working in finance downtown. He's slightly younger than us, in his early thirties, and like the great son that he is, he comes home every weekend to help his dad with the restaurant. He offers his hand to Pam, which she cordially shakes with absolute curiosity.

"Pam," she says coyly, obviously enamored. I smile at both of them despite my tear-stained face and stuffy nose. "How do you and Bianca know each other?" She looks at me sideways as she says the last bit.

"Tommy used to hang out here a lot. He got into trouble a lot here too. They'd call me when he couldn't be helped and needed to be taken home. I've done it so many times that they've become like family." I look at Pam, embarrassed. I have far too many secrets I'm too ashamed to share.

"How was the service?" Miguel asks.

"It was quick. It was something that needed to be done," I say. Pam takes a drink of her beer. I see that the tequila shot has been consumed.

"Are you driving, Pam?" Miguel asks, eyeing the two empty shot glasses in front of her.

"Are you telling me to stop drinking already?" she protests. "Plus, this one is Bianca's."

She pushes the other empty shot glass toward me.

I smile at this. "I'm only asking because I'm happy to be your designated driver, if you'll let me. That way, you ladies can enjoy yourself in a safe space." I reach out to touch Miguel's shoulder in gratitude. I have cried in his and his father's arms far too many times.

"Great! But we also need food. Can we order something?" Pam asks Miguel.

"Papa is putting something together for us. It's taken care of."

"Wow, Bianca. It's like another set of family that I don't know about."

"Yes, they've been very generous and kind to me and Tommy." I give Miguel another sideward glance.

℘

"Come, come, *mija*." Carlito comes out from the kitchen and invites us to move to another table, this one holding a lavish spread of Mexican food and drinks. The steaming fajitas and tacos, with lots of fresh tortillas and salsa, make my mouth water. I'm hungrier than I thought. A bottle of tequila and a big bucket of ice filled with a good selection of Mexican beer are also chilling on top of the table. I see that the table is set for four. I'm glad they are joining us.

"Jorge, can you man the restaurant for an hour or so? We're having a simple celebration of life with Bianca tonight." I know Jorge very well too. On occasion when Carlito and Miguel were not around, he has called me about Tommy. Everyone in this restaurant knows who I am, but not once have they ever asked me to never come back. "It's better that Tommy is here, in a safe space, *mija*." Carlito's fatherly voice has always comforted me.

"Okay, let's take a seat. I tried to get us the quietest table in the room."

"Thanks. You didn't have to do this."

"But we are family. We do this for family. I didn't attend to-day's service because I didn't want to be part of Celeste's spectacle. I will pray and honor Tommy's name in my way here, tonight, with you and your friend."

"Pam," Pam offers.

"Yes, Pam, Thank you." Carlito's Mexican heritage is in full view in his big personality. His mustache makes him a popular person in the restaurant scene here in Jersey City. And, of course, his food is phenomenal. His restaurant has been around for almost forty years, way before Miguel was born. "Let's hold hands." And we do. "Tommy, son, I hope you found the freedom you deserve in heaven. You were a great boy—generous and kind, vulnerable and softhearted. Your heart was too fragile for the harshness of this world—and so as you leave us, we will forever remember the tenderness of your soul. Be free, my son. Be free. Amen."

"Amen," we all say in unison.

"*Mija*, this is not the end for you. This is just the beginning. Tommy has been a big burden for you the past few years. You deserve to take care of yourself now. You deserve to soar high and leave all these painful memories behind. Okay, *mija*?" I nod my head because I can't speak. If I do, I'll only end up in tears again. "In the meantime, let's fill our stomachs. You've lost weight. Here, have some of my *camaron* fajitas." Carlito prepares a plate for me—he knows shrimp are my favorite—and Miguel helps Pam with hers. One of the waiters, Raymundo, opens the tequila bottle, pours all four small glasses full to the brim, and hands each of us a shot.

"To Tommy," Carlito says as he raises his glass. And we all drink at the same time.

To Tommy.

❀

I never liked tequila, but I'm drinking it tonight. It's the only alcohol that can knock me out. I think that's a brilliant goal for this evening. Get as drunk as possible, head to bed, and forget about this phase of my life. I know the positive that can come out of this. This means I, too, am free now. It doesn't change the fact that pain is here. Death is still cruel. Goodbyes are still difficult. And moving on is still hard. Where do I even begin? I say here, with family and friends.

Chapter 14

I hand the keys to the new owners of my house. A young couple—the way Tommy and I once were—but I don't tell them the story of my life, or how the love that was once sheltered here died years ago. I smile at them, the pretend-happy kind. Both giddy, I can see true love emanating from their souls.

"Congratulations," I say wholeheartedly.

The young woman clasps her hands together and looks at the knight in shining armor next to her. The young knight, with his dashing red hair, puts his arms around her in a tender, possessive gesture. It's an inspiring vision of young love. To my surprise, they both give me a hearty bear hug. Red-haired knight then lifts me off the ground a little. We stay like that for a while, and I can hear within our tiny circle their quiet giggles. Finally, the hug loosens, and I'm able to extricate myself from their embrace. I take a few steps back in case they decide to do it again. I brush invisible creases from my jacket and hook my purse properly over my shoulder again. I don't make eye contact, lest they see the pessimism in my soul.

I turn and I take a few steps down the street, the two of them following close behind me. I'd like to say that they don't need to. They can go inside the house now, enjoy it, own it. I just want to take one last look alone but I can sense that they will not indulge me.

"Where are you heading now?" the young woman asks, curious. It's the sympathy stare from a woman with so much love to one who is empty. She touches my arm lightly.

"I'm going to my mom's for a couple of weeks to get everything sorted. Then, I'm moving to the city." It's the first time I say this out loud. No one has actually heard any of these plans before.

"Like, New York City?" I hear the mesmerized excitement in her voice, the hint of a dream she probably once had as well, and an invisible understanding passes between us—woman to woman. I give her a weak, knowing smile.

"Yes. I'm finally crossing the river." I walk toward the car and she trails close behind me.

"That's so exciting!" She clasps her hands together again in genuine delight, looking behind to see where her knight is. Red-haired dude is no longer listening, but walking to the trailer next to my car that carries their belongings. I donated all of mine to the Salvation Army, so I don't have anything. I wanted to burn Tommy's recliner but decided against it in the end. I don't have a space to do it—definitely not in the weedy backyard of this house that could have started a major fire in the neighborhood.

"So, this is it," I say as I walk around toward the driver's door of my car. "Again, congratulations. I seriously hope you enjoy the house."

"Thank you," she says. "Good luck in New York City!" And she finally leaves me alone. I open the car door slowly as I stare at the house I called home many years ago. It has not been home to me for a while. It was my prison. I get in the car, and I take my time. There is nowhere I need to be. I don't have a regular job to go to and, miraculously, I was able to finish all my writing projects a week in advance. I didn't want to be left thinking about Tommy, his death, and my life, so I jumped into work and got it all done soon after the funeral. I sit in my car, pretending to be looking for something in my purse to avoid the lovebirds walking by to get to the house. When they close the door behind them, I stare after them.

"We're going to have five kids running along this pavement," Tommy once said. I was a blushing bride, full of love and hopes and dreams. I kissed him on the lips with my heart beating triple time. "I love you, Bianca Pierce."

"I love you, Thomas Anthony Pierce."

That love was real. But we lost it along the way. I don't love him anymore. I don't even remember how loving him felt. I don't even remember why.

Mistakes are inevitable, I know this. I've made two big ones so far. Sadly, both involved men. Because of my first failed relationship, I decided to work extra hard to make it with Tommy. Somehow, I was convinced it would redeem me from my past sins with Glen. In my heart, they were connected. I had to stay with Tommy; otherwise it will mean I was weak, a quitter—like my dad.

I didn't kill Tommy. I need to remember that. Whether or not he was happy with his life, that was his responsibility and not mine. I tried the best I could to be a good wife, a friend, and a partner—no matter how hard it was for me, no matter the agony. I close my eyes as I think of this, finally blocking the vision of the house where all the suffering happened. I bow my head in silent prayer—and it is selfish, because it's all about me.

I hear my phone ringing inside my purse. I pull it out slowly, not particularly ready to interact with the outside world again. I see Pam's name.

"Is your house sold yet?" she asks as soon as I answer. I nod, though she doesn't see me.

"Yeah." I pull out the check from the folder in my purse. I sold the house on my own. I couldn't afford to pay a realtor for this. Fortunately, my aunt, who is a real estate broker, helped me with the process. It kept me busy and gave me purpose. "I'll drop by at the bank by noon to get this all taken care of. I need to pay the house in full and see if there's anything left for me to start over."

"I'm glad. Do you need any help with anything?" She asks that all the time, and some days I wish she would stop, not because I don't appreciate it, but because it reminds me of my current state of slump.

"Nah. I'm good for now. My mom is cooking dinner. Her entire family is coming again. It feels like they do this every week now. Do you want to come to Jersey?" She doesn't speak, and I can sense hesitation. I laugh and say, "You don't have to." I laugh some more.

"I'm so happy to hear you laugh, Binky-doo!" She is the only other person who knows about this nickname. "If I go there and my parents find out, that's my entire weekend out the window. Well, how about you come stay with me this weekend? Since Amy got engaged, she's barely in the apartment. I have a feeling that she's going to bail soon and leave me here alone. Holy shit! How about we move in together? Which reminds me the real reason why I called you in the first place. Marco called with some good news."

Marco is Pam's best friend from college, whom I adore.

"Yeah?"

"Well, he told me that there is a junior public relations associate position open on his team at the network and that they haven't advertised it yet. They were just told that it's open and were asked for recommendations."

"Are you serious?" I like this news. I like this very much. "Did he say he'd help me out?"

"Yes!" Pam screams, and my phone almost falls out of my hand.

"Stop!" I laugh, holding my phone tighter to my ear.

"That's the reason I'm calling. So, this is what I did. Please don't be mad."

"What did you do?" Pam is the most innovative human being I know. She doesn't take no for an answer and jumps right in. She's brave like that, like I'm not, or at least not any more.

"Do you remember the CV you sent me for one of your clients? You asked me to print it for you while you were in the city a few months ago? Well, I added some other stuff to it. Put my name, Marco's name, and Bridgett from Wells and Honey PR as references and emailed it to the HR person at the network. Marco gave me her email."

"What email address did you use?" This is so typical of Pam. Waiting is not something she tolerates.

"I created a new email address for you with your maiden name. biancamariacurtis@gmail.com." I can imagine her twirling around with pride wherever she is. I can definitely hear it in her voice.

"Pam. . . ."

"Please don't be mad."

"I'm not. I'm grateful. Thank you!"

"And there's more!"

"What?"

"You have an interview on Tuesday at the network at ten thirty! I just got the email a few minutes ago before I called you."

"Holy shit, you're a miracle worker!" And she is, and also the best book editor in all of Manhattan.

"So, go home and put your writing portfolio in an impressive file. Make a list of all the clients you've worked for and projects you've worked on, print it on a nice expensive paper at Kinkos, and buy a nice clear file folder, okay? Also, it's been a while since you experimented with your look. You need a change—cut your hair, dye it, get a facial or something. Buy yourself a nice interview outfit with that check right there, and come stay with me in the city."

"Oh, my god, Pam! You are magic!"

"Oh, I know!"

"Thank you. Thank you." I start sobbing as I say this—silently at first, and then it becomes one of those loud, ugly whimpers. My heart is full. Hope is inching back into my life again. If there is that, I think I'll be just fine. I'll be just fine.

"Are you seriously crying right now? Stop that! Let's stop the pity party already. Today is the beginning of the rest of your life. The fucking life you rightfully deserve."

Hope. It's the catalyst to moving with purpose.

It starts to rain. Today, the universe has decided to purge me of my past. Tomorrow, I welcome my new life.

"Thanks, Pam. Thank you."

"Hey, chin up, baby, and get ready for a fucking wild ride! I'm so excited for you!"

I exhale.

Mom's house, located in the middle of a narrow busy street at the heart of Jersey City, is quiet when I walk in. I expect people to be drinking and laughing on the porch, but no one seems to have arrived yet. There is a fancy car out front, parked in my usual spot, which kind of irks me. I have to drive around in circles and park a couple of blocks out because of it, and it's such a hassle with this rain.

"Mom? Where's everybody?" I wipe my wet feet on the mat and brush water off my jacket as soon as I walk in. The smell of adobo, my favorite Filipino dish of pork and chicken in vinegar, soy sauce, and garlic, lingers in the air. I wrinkle my nose in delight.

"Right here, in the living room," Mom calls out.

That's strange. Mom never spends time in the living room. The living room is for visitors that aren't family. We normally just hang out in the kitchen or in the backyard.

I drop my purse and my car keys on the table by the door. I was just at the bank, which had been a surprisingly successful trip. I can't wait to share the good news that I actually took home almost forty-five thousand dollars of equity. I can now pay her back the down payment she lent Tommy and me a decade ago, as well as the many times I borrowed money from her to pay the mortgage.

"Mom, you would not believe. . . ." I stop abruptly at the French doors that divide the living room and the tiny foyer.

I stand there in shock as soon as I see Mom's visitor. The three of us stare at each other. There are no words to describe the rage I feel right this minute. Mom's expression softens. My dad, on the other hand, is fidgety. He looks anxious. *My dad.*

"Sit down, Bianca." Mom waves at me to sit next to her, and I do as I'm told. Slowly, I position myself opposite the man who abandoned us more than twenty years ago. He doesn't take his eyes off me. He smiles nervously. I don't remember that smile anymore, despite longing for it for most of my life.

"What is he doing here?" I say this with controlled fury.

"This is probably not the best time to tell you this, but you are brave, Bianca, so here it is. Your dad wants to be around for you." My mother says this is so matter-of-factly that it's a little unsettling. She doesn't show any emotion. It's hard to tell what all this means to her.

"Why now?" I quietly reply, my tone dripping with sarcasm. My mom's normally bright living room is ghostly and quiet. All you can hear is the rain still going strong outside. My dad comes closer, but I jerkily pull away and avoid looking him in the eye.

"This is all my fault," my mom says. I turn to her instantly. How can she blame herself for this man's sins?

"How is this your fault, Mom?" I can't believe what I'm hearing.

"No, it's my fault, Nina." The man, who is no more than a stranger to me, interrupts her.

"Can someone please explain to me what's going on?"

Mom turns to face me. I can finally sense nervousness in her stance. I search for answers in her eyes, something that only the two of us can know and understand—how we've communicated all these years—but I can't read her. She's blocking me. Somehow, I feel, they are both in this together—a team—and I am a mere spectator, which angers me even further.

"Your dad didn't abandon you." She takes a long pause. "I asked him to leave. You see, he was already married when I met him in Manila, but he didn't tell me until we moved here."

I've heard this story before. Grandma said something to me when I was young, but I didn't really take it seriously. I didn't need to hear reasons as to why the father I trusted disappeared. My hatred for this man is not about his past, but about how he left Mom and me behind. "He didn't want to go back to his wife, and his family, his kids. But I made him. I was so angry that I didn't think of you. When I realized my mistake, it was already too late because you already hated him so much. I didn't know how to fix the relationship anymore. But he begged me to be part of your life, even in secret. He paid for you to go to college. He gave me the money for the down payment of your house as a wedding present. When you were short, he told me to make sure I paid your mortgage." Mom is in tears now. "Your dad wanted to be in your life, and I was too selfish to let him. I'm sorry, Binks."

I'm speechless. How can my parents impose this on me now while I'm still trying to put myself back together after the death of my husband? Do they think that because I'm already hurting, another source of pain won't make any difference? This is bull-shit. Heat flushes through my body.

I don't say a word, but I stand up. My dad stands up to face me. I raise both hands, protecting myself, gesturing for him to back off. My dad takes a step forward. I take a step back because this hurts too much—much more than the funeral I had to endure to bury a piece of who I was. This, right here, is my entire life blown up into a big fat lie.

"Binky, I'm so sorry." My mom looks at me with tears in her eyes. She holds my arm, but I brush her off. And then I run.

Chapter 15

To go to the city on a Friday afternoon is the worst possible idea. And so, in anger and annoyance, I groan loudly as I endure my bus not moving—stuck in a horrendous traffic jam as we make our way to the Holland Tunnel—for the past thirty minutes. Thankfully, I have a seat by the window. I stare out into the distance. The rain is still coming down in full force, pounding heavily on my tattered soul. I didn't grab an umbrella when I ran out of my mom's house, and the jacket I'm wearing is not enough to shield me from this downpour.

I've been trying to hold it together most of the time, and this being piled on my plate is just harsh. But I know that I have to keep moving because to stop means to break; to stop means to give in; to stop means I lose. *I'm done losing.*

It's been more than four weeks since Tommy passed away, and I've not been to the city since. Guilt. There is a part of me that doesn't want to go across the river because the city now holds a different memory. I pull my soaking jacket more tightly around me, as if doing so will shield me from all the cruelty of my world.

My last twelve hours in Manhattan feels like a lifetime ago.

Park Hyun Min.

He crosses my mind every day. *Every. Single. Day.* I still feel his arms around me sometimes. *All. The. Time.* I constantly remind myself that it happened. *It did happen.* And I have proof—a blurry photo on top of the Empire State Building locked securely in my phone.

My phone vibrates in my back jeans pocket again, pulling me away from beautiful thoughts of a distant dream. I'm almost certain that it's Mom, but I'm not ready to talk to her—them—yet, and so I don't answer. I just confirmed not even an hour or so ago that my entire life has been a lie. My childhood. My marriage. I should also add that because of my own doing, who I am today is murky as well.

Finally, the phone stops.

I lean my head against the foggy window, feeling the damp, cold glass against my cheek. I try isolating the sound of the rain from the rest of the noise around me—the honking of the horns, the firing of engines in traffic, and a baby crying at the back of the bus. The rhythm of the rain comforts my broken soul somewhat. I close my eyes, and let it cradle me. And then I see his face, and I feel safe and calm and loved. Eric. I stay there for as long as I can. There, with him, though only in my mind. I think about the little quirk of his smile, his lingering stare that holds so much meaning, his laughter that is so open and free, and most of all, his heart—and how he shared it with me that night.

I love him. I knew this the morning I left him. It's the reason I had to leave. His face is still vivid in my mind as anger and confusion hit when I told him I was married. I remember clenching my fists as hard as I could as I walked away to stop myself from running back into his arms, which had sheltered me for twelve amazing hours.

I open my eyes and laugh at myself after recognizing the absurdity of all this. I bet he has long forgotten about me. Perhaps I'm not even the first stranger he spent a night like that with. While I found our time together meaningful, perhaps to him it was an ordinary encounter. He can talk to any stranger he desires, and know that at the end of the evening they are his for the taking. And that's okay. I don't intend to have him. I can't even dream it. I'm fine with fragments of memories.

I know it seems silly that I refuse to even speak his name for fear that pieces of him may escape from my heart. I want to hold on to him as Eric, not as Park Hyun Min the actor, for as long as my memory can.

❧

I take shelter under a platform along Broadway and Thirty-fourth, where the bus lets me out. I don't tell Pam that I'm in the city yet. I want to walk around for a while. The rain has stopped. The city is wet and dreary, but it's still as beautiful and mysterious as ever. I stand on the pavement, letting people pass me by, just like everything else in my life.

On these streets, in this city, I walked my fairy tale.

❧

"You're here!" Pam screams as soon as she answers my call.

"Yes. Do you have plans tonight? I can just hang out in your apartment, if that's okay. Are you still at work?" I'm walking toward her office in Midtown, where the noise coming from all directions is overwhelming—tourists walking in swarms heading for Times Square.

"Where are you?" she asks

"A couple of blocks from the Square," I tell her as I soak in my surroundings, observing the motions of this big city as if I've never been here before. But today is a different day—my heart is not as heavily laden, my soul is not as pained, and though my life has become more complicated, for the first time I actually have tangible choices.

"Perfect! Meet us at Pig 'n' Whistle in Midtown. Marco and I will be there, and we can strategize for your interview on Tuesday." Yes, the interview. I'd almost forgotten about that after my face-off with my parents. A different excitement, of a different height, consumes my center. I almost skip in glee.

"Okay, but I have a problem." It's a good problem in comparison to the many I had over the years.

"What?" There is panic in Pam's voice.

"I just ran away from home. Literally. Don't ask. I don't have any clothes with me. We need to go shopping!" I smile widely as I reveal this, holding on to my phone tightly as I walk the busy streets of Manhattan, knowing that a full-on scream will follow suit.

"Oh, my god!!" And there it is, the scream that I'm expecting. "I thought I'd never hear that from you ever again! Yes, we'll go shopping first thing tomorrow morning after brunch!" And we hang up.

I've been to Pig 'n' Whistle a few times before, and all those times I've been with Pam. As I walk toward that direction, away from Jersey, I can actually feel heavy loads being lifted slowly with each step. A sense of optimism is gradually rising within me.

My phone rings again. Thinking it is Pam, I almost answer, but it's Mom. I don't answer. Seconds later, when it finally stops ringing, I receive a text message.

"When you're ready, please call me. Mom."

"Not today," I whisper to the wind. "Not today."

I order a cosmopolitan like the old days. I'm not wearing a sequined miniskirt, but I'm enjoying the youthful taste of the drink I once so enjoyed with abandon. I'm sitting at the bar where the bartender is looking at me funny. He's right. No decent middle-aged woman should be drinking a cosmopolitan at five in the afternoon. But you know what, right now, I don't give a fuck. I feel light and free today, considering, and no one can stop me. The city has quickly and magically transformed me. I smile at him, a little annoyed.

Then suddenly, not even a couple of hours since I landed here on my magic island, it hits me. I heave a sigh. The temptation is coaxing me with power so strong that I pull out my phone from my jeans pocket. I finally give in. I look him up.

Park Hyun Min.

Thousands of search results pop up. I click on images.

I smile as I see the first photo of him from *The Oasis*. His hair is longer. In that drama he had facial hair. He's wearing a white linen shirt. It's a photo I've seen before. Then fear hits me as quickly as my need to see him. I click my phone to sleep immediately. *I'm losing my mind.*

"Hey, Bianca!" I hear Marco's voice echo as he walks in the door. I turn to the voice immediately. I'm grateful for the distraction. He struts his way toward me, owning the hall like a runway. Gorgeous, green-eyed Marco. I've known Marco a long time, and I hung out with him and Pam quite a lot before I got married. On occasions that I need to be in the city for work, we try scheduling a quick lunch or drink when we can. For a while, Marco was dating this gorgeous Haitian guy who was on an educational exchange program at Columbia. It was the longest, most dramatic, and most painful goodbye Pam and I have ever witnessed. I don't think he's ever recovered.

"Marco!" There are air kisses.

"My condolences, Bianca." He puts his hand over his heart. I put my hand on top of it.

"We don't need to do this. I'm fine. Thank you." He then gives me a hug, which is totally contrary to what I just asked him to do. But I let him, and I hug him right back. He's going to help me get a job in the city, so he can do this all night if he wants. When he finally lets go of me, he asks the bartender for a cosmopolitan. The bartender's look of disdain is back.

"Make it two," I say to him with squinted eyes. "I sold my house today. I'll get this one."

"Congratulations!" Marco raises both his hands up in the air and freezes in a dramatic pose like Evita Peron. There is no dull moment with this one.

"Thanks." I honestly don't know what people say to people who just sold their houses. I shrug at this thought.

"So, the job. Are you ready for it?" Marco brushes the stray hair off my face. He's motherly like that too.

"More than you'll ever know." I sigh at him. "Marco?"

"Aha?" He looks at me with pouted lips.

"Can we just skip the part about my recent loss?" I don't want to take this story with me. I want that memory to die in Jersey, in that house that I no longer own, on Avalon Street that I will never ever drive down again.

"In this town, that never happened to you," he declares. I already asked Pam not to tell anyone about the funeral service, including Marco. It was best no one witness it. We smile at each other and a promise passes between us. I touch his arm lightly in thanks.

"So, how have you been?" I change the subject immediately.

"You know," he responds coyly. Marco's playful personality is what makes him endearing. He is not an easy character, by all means. He can be snotty and sarcastic and a straight-up bitch, but he's a lot of fun. He doesn't beat around the bush, but he'll tell you the truth because he means well. He is loyal and real and there is no second-guessing with him. "My life is all about work, and I need a little excitement, Bianca—a love affair, maybe. I don't know. I need to spice things up a bit. Come move here in a hurry! Pam is always on dates and such, and I'm always left alone doing nothing." He pouts a little as he says this. I don't know why he doesn't date very much. He's flat out gorgeous—yes, in a model, tall, skinny, and stylish kind of way.

"We'll find you a hot date soon!" I say, though I've not been on a date in more than a decade myself. "Wait, I don't even know how the dating scene works anymore," I blurt out in alarm.

"Yeah, a lot has happened in that realm, my friend. Nobody meets people in person anymore."

"So I've heard." I roll my eyes in disbelief. Then my mind wanders toward a memory of meeting someone spectacular at a bar recently. I immediately brush it away.

"Anyway, enough about that. First, we need to get you a job in town," he says pointedly. I sit straight in attention and turn to face him.

"Let's do that," I say.

"You've worked freelance PR, so this is nothing new to you. The bad part is you'll do the eight-to-five routine inside an office and in meetings most of the time. The good, you get medical, dental, and paid leave. Oh, yeah, the 401K is awesome too." Marco uses a lot of hand gestures as he speaks, so I follow along as he points out the good with his fingers one by one. I've never had medical insurance before, or paid leave, and certainly not retirement savings. These are all very new to me. Don't ask me about

Tommy's medical expenses—charity works in mysterious ways.

"Sounds great! I'm really excited. Thanks for doing this, Marco."

"I'm just the messenger. The interview, you've got to nail that one down. Our director is not the sweetest person. She's a stern woman in her late forties. Single. This job is her entire life. She wants us to treat it the same way. Not going to happen. There are so many gorgeous men running around town after six o'clock. I have to be out of the office by then." He slaps both his hands on his knees to emphasize his point.

"Okay. Noted. Stern. I mean it's likely I'll devote a lot of my time to working anyway. I don't have anything else to do."

"Duh! Hang out with me after six o'clock and hit the bars. You don't want to be stuck in that office with Cruella Deville."

"Okay."

"Wait, you've met her before." Marco clasps his hands together as he recalls this, which I don't.

"Pam and I were at Jamba for my colleague's birthday party. You came to meet us there. It was awkward because Diana was there too, having dinner with a friend by coincidence, and no one had actually invited her to the office party. Whoops." He makes a face at this.

"Oh shit, the Ice Queen?" Now I remember.

"Exactly. You were even trying to make small talk with her while the rest of us were shaking our heads trying to stop you. You were oblivious." We both laugh at this.

The door opens, bells chime, and a gust of wind enters. Pam, tall and striking, walks in with her miniskirt and long legs. She's wearing a pink suit jacket over a black sheath dress. Her shoes are to die for—a black high-heeled Chanel pumps with gold studs. On her shoulder is a Celine canvas white tote that holds the

manuscripts she takes home to read. She waves at us as she folds
her rain-drizzled umbrella. Again, air kisses are given all around.
Marco moves one stool over to let Pam sit in the middle. She puts
all her things on the floor. The bartender, eyeing her apprecia-
tively, comes up immediately.

"Drink?" he asks flirtatiously.

"Whatever they've having," she says and points at our glasses.
Yes! I want to say with an air punch in victory. But I don't. Instead, I
give the bartender a pompous look to confirm I'm no loser.

"Got it," he replies to Pam sweetly and turns to me quickly
with a look of disdain before returning his attention back to our
girl in pink. "Do you want me to put your stuff on the bar rather
than leave it on the floor out there?" the bartender offers. Pam
bends down, gathers her things, and gives them to the guy.

"Thanks, Rod."

"You know him?" I ask.

"She knows every bartender on this side of the island. Don't
ask why." Marco rolls his eyes to tease Pam. A year older than me,
at thirty-seven, Pam embodies the very essence of a hard-working,
successful woman. She bought her apartment when she earned
her first million five years ago. She tried living by herself for a
couple of years before putting her guest bedroom up for rent.
She had just broken up with Luke, her boyfriend of three years.
Marco couldn't move in with her because he had just bought his
apartment, and I was a struggling married woman in Jersey. She's
a lot better now. Amy, her roommate, with whom she has a
strong, respectful friendship, is very good for her.

"Oh, I forgot to tell you that Miguel is coming too," Pam says
nonchalantly.

"Miguel. My Miguel? I mean, Carlito's Miguel?" I don't know
why I said *my*.

"Yes," Pam nods.

"Why?" I'm a little bit confused. I know that Miguel works in the city, but I didn't know that they're in touch.

"We exchanged numbers at the restaurant, and since you're in the city, I thought I'd invite him."

"Oh. Okay. I think that's cool . . . I guess."

"Is this Miguel straight?" Marco asks.

"Yes," Pam and I say in unison.

I think my dear Pammy has a little crush here, and I'm a little uncomfortable about this because Miguel is a softhearted, level-headed guy and I don't want her breaking his heart. Since she broke up with Luke, she has floated from one casual relationship to another. Most of the time, she does the walking out . . . without a trace. Ghosting is the new breakup, she reasons. I don't agree, but I don't judge her choices either.

A few minutes later, Miguel enters in an attractive three-piece suit, looking fetching and beautiful rolled together in extreme Latino manliness. I don't remember seeing him looking this professional before. The Miguel I know is always in jeans and a T-shirt, the graphic kind—Pearl Jam, Metallica, or Jon Bon Jovi. This is a good surprise. I smile widely at him as soon as he sees me. He beams in return, in a way that's different from the smiles he used to give me in Jersey.

"Hey, Rod, can we move to the booth at the back?" Pam asks, swinging her gorgeous gold locks toward Rod and almost hitting Miguel in the face. Rod nods his head eagerly like a bubblehead figurine. His eyes sparkle with worship. Gathering our things, we all walk to the quieter spot. I slide in first and notice Pam secretly pushing Marco to slide in next to me. Smiling brilliantly, Pam moves in across from us and without any other options, Miguel sits next to her. Miguel's olive skin is a gorgeous contrast to

Pam's snow-white complexion. They are different, but somehow they blend. I don't understand my indifference about this. Well, actually, I do. I worry for *my* Miguel. *He's not yours, ding-dong!* I scold myself silently. Noticing Miguel looking at me funny, I shrug my shoulders in defeat and just smile at him.

"So, Miguel, how do you know these two?" Marco asks while putting his elbow on the table and brushing his invisible long hair on one side in a comic pretend. Pam and I start chuckling. There is no stopping Marco from confirming Miguel's identity.

"My father has a restaurant in Jersey that Bianca frequents. But I guess, not anymore." He eyes me questioningly.

"I was just there with my mom a couple of days ago. They finally met for the first time." I raise both my eyebrows with pride. "We're friends. Tommy used to hang out at their restaurant," I add casually. Marco nods his head slowly. I know I said I wouldn't talk about my past here, but it can't be helped when someone from that world suddenly appears.

"Are you finally moving to the city?" Miguel seems different here—and although I have seen concern in his eyes before, his apprehension feels more potent right now. *Is there an underlying message to this?*

I let my heart settle into a calm space with a long pause while I notice that Miguel, Pam, and Marco seem to be waiting intensely for an answer. "I don't know yet."

"I can help you look for an apartment. I can inquire in my building." Miguel offers this like the brother I never had, which he had been to me for the past five years. And yet, now that Tommy is gone, I don't know how to navigate this new relationship.

"I got this," Pam says, shoving him on the shoulder. "Bianca is staying with me. My roommate, Amy, just got engaged, so I'm expecting her to move out anytime soon."

"I haven't really decided yet." There is no reason for me not to. If I use Mom as an excuse for staying behind in Jersey, it's only because I'm nothing but a coward. There is no stopping this now. "But yes, I guess. . . ." I feel good saying this. Makes it more real. "I don't know if I even want to go back to Jersey to get my things. I mean, I gave all of my stuff away, but I still have some of my clothes there at my mom's." I came here into the city today with nothing but my heart and my soul and my will to move forward, my will to finally live.

"Don't go back for now. Stay with Pam. Do this interview. And then decide." Marco sums it all up neatly for me, and I like it. I'll do just that.

Chapter 16

Today is interview day.

Pam and I are up early this morning after spending a good chunk of last night practicing my talking points. We're not taking this lightly—we are in it to win—and I couldn't be more confident having two brilliant professionals holding my hand to take me to the finish line. The amount of time, energy, and effort Marco and Pam dedicated to me over the weekend were extraordinary, and I'll be forever grateful.

There is a fresh pot of coffee in the kitchen, which Amy likely left for us earlier this morning. Over the weekend, she kept dropping hints about moving in with her fiancé soon. What she doesn't know is that Pam and I have been trying to find subtle ways to get her to move sooner, so that I can officially take over her room.

Pam's apartment is in Midtown. It's a gorgeous two-bedroom apartment with two full baths. It's quaint, and it perfectly reflects Pam's fashion-forward personality—sunshine-yellow walls in the living room, orange in the kitchen, and dark cream along the foyer that pulls the eclectic colors together. The bedrooms are large and can accommodate king size beds with enough room to add more furniture. I took a peek of Amy's room yesterday and started jotting down mental notes on how I will rearrange it to my taste.

"Are you ready?" Pam asks sleepily. We're both in her bathrobes, lazily plopped on the floor in the living room with our steaming cups of Amy's coffee. I nod my head in reply and lean back on the sofa behind me. "Your clothes are laid out? You've ironed your white shirt?" Pam asks.

"Check and check," I say, making the check hand gesture twice.

"Good. What will you do between now and then?"

"I'll hang out here and study my spiel."

"That's good. Make sure you remember your lines exactly like we rehearsed them."

"Yes, of course." She's acting like a nagging mom, so I make a pretend annoyed face, but she knows how much I appreciate this. I've not been home since Friday night, and she took me in for the entire weekend, excited over the prospect that we're finally going to be roommates. We went shopping, walked around the city, and just hung out. It was a relaxing weekend because I didn't need to rush back home to Jersey. I took my time and strolled with friends like I belonged here. We even met Miguel again for brunch on Sunday.

"Do you like Miguel?" I ask Pam point-blank.

"Why do you ask? Are you guys a thing?" She is wide-eyed.

"No!" I say. My heart belongs to someone else, someone who is impossible, I want to add, but I don't. I'm not ready to go there.

"Actually, I kinda like him. Strong but quiet, tough but sensitive." There is a dreamy look on her sweet angelic face as she lists Miguel's obvious attractive qualities.

"Yeah. You can describe him that way, for sure." I give her an encouraging smile although I'm not one hundred percent comfortable about the idea of the two of them together—their personalities are like night and day.

"Does he have a girlfriend?" she asks. I shake my head.

"You know what, I take that back. I honestly don't know. It's actually strange that I'm seeing Miguel socially like this. I'm not saying I don't like it. It just feels a little odd. You know how you see a person in one part of your life and never imagine them in another? This is how it is with Miguel. Not that I don't want him here, it just takes a little getting used to."

"Well, it's good to make new friends," Pam says with a slight smirk.

"He *is* my friend," I confirm.

"Whatever, just focus on the task at hand when I leave for work. This is really important."

We're both quiet for a few minutes, enjoying the silence of the morning and the smell of coffee in the apartment. New York City is like a mythical, magical place for me, somewhere I can live my fantasies and push myself to be part of the whole creative atmosphere. I'm not going to lie that I had my share of New York City walk-of-shame stories, but moments like this are what I crave at this time of my life—the quiet in the middle of a dream.

"Pam?" I whisper.

"Hmm?" She answers me with her eyes closed, enjoying the ray of sunshine coming through the window.

"Do you remember when I didn't get the contract with Ambrose Publishing last month?" I sit still on the floor. Nervous. Afraid. Happy. Uncertain. I am a ball of mixed emotions. Four weeks is such a short a time to turn my life around. This feels like a joke, like I'm on a prank television show. The drama with my parents also doesn't help. I'm tired of being a constant train wreck.

"Yes, and I know where this is going. So, stop." She shifts her body to face me. The concern in her face is obvious, though I know she's trying to conceal it. "We're not going to quit. If you don't get this job, you will apply for another, and another, and another until you find the perfect one."

"What if—?"

"Bianca, don't. You're one of the hardest-working people I know. This is just the beginning. In fact, we should be excited because for the first time in a long time, your options are limitless." There's a change in her aura as she says this, because I know she believes it. It appeases me somehow.

"We're almost forty, Pam."

"Shush. It's a fucking number. We're barely in our late thirties. Plus, forty is the new thirty. People live longer these days." Pam moves next to me at the bottom of the couch, shoulder to shoulder, looking at the big bold pink art on top on her TV in her yellow living room. She shoves me a little. I put my head on her shoulder. "You're going to be fine, Binks. This, I promise."

"I'm so glad you're in my life," I tell her this softly. I don't have many friends and I don't need a lot, but I need this one right here.

"I'm glad you're in mine too."

⁊

I look expensive. The bright pink suit that Pam insisted on buying last Sunday actually works. I smile at my reflection on the mirror in front of Pam's dresser. I've never looked like this before—I am channeling Jessica Alba, in a way. Well, Pam and I stole her look from a Pinterest post. I can't help but twirl.

I hear my phone ring from inside my purse. I reach for it and see Miguel's name on the screen.

"Today is the big day?" He is lively. Miguel is normally a quiet man, so I truly appreciate this. He knows how to cheer for me when I need it the most.

"Yes. And I'm nervous," I say because I am. I don't know what to expect with everything moving so fast.

"It will be fine. You'll be great. I can feel it." Today, right now, I'm glad that Miguel is close by. He's been my anchor for many years as I navigated a darker life, and so he deserves to see my light.

"Thanks."

"What time do you need to be there? Are you on your way?"

"Putting my makeup on. I'm still here at Pam's."

"Don't put too much makeup, Bianca. You don't need it. You're prettier without makeup." I'm a little taken aback by this comment. But coming from Miguel, I don't really mind it. Again, he has seen me beer-stained, tear-stained, and at one point I had to get Tommy out of the bathroom, and yes, I had urine all over me. I don't need to feel self-conscious around him.

"Ha! But I actually look really professional and expensive. Pam taught me well."

"I'm glad." He laughs on the other end. "Anyway, I need to get back to work. Just went down to get coffee and call you to wish you good luck. I'm rooting for you, Bianca!"

"Thanks, Miguel. I'll call you if I get the job."

"No, call me whether or not you get the job, okay? I can probably get to you, and we can grab a quick lunch."

"Or how about I head your direction when I'm done. Where do you work?"

"I work close to the World Trade Center. Let me know. I'll text you the address."

"Perfect, and thanks for calling, man."

"Of course. Okay, I'll be waiting for your news. You can do this, Bianca."

❧

As I stand outside the CWS building at exactly 9:55 a.m., I feel my heart doing somersaults under my nice bright-pink suit. On my arm is Pam's Celine mini-luggage purse in nude, which is probably the most expensive accessory I've every carried in this lifetime. She lent it to me because it matches my new trench coat. I take a deep breath and in my nude high heels, I walk in with confidence. Fake it 'til you make it, as they say, and I'm faking the shit out of this interview.

There's a line at the guest registry. I pull out my phone from my expensive purse and send a text to Marco to let him know that I made it into the building. I'm already next in line when he shows up. He does look very casual in jeans and an emerald cashmere pullover. His green eyes match it beautifully. He stands next to me as I hand my driver's license to the lady at the counter. A few minutes later, she hands me a badge with a lanyard that says *V*.

"You can get your driver's license on your way out," the lady says, and I nod. Marco pulls me to the turnstile, shows my badge to the guards, and we both walk toward my future. The elevator foyer is tall and massive, and it's one of those where you punch in your floor on a kiosk and it tells you which elevator to take.

"This would have confused the hell out of me. Thanks for meeting me."

"Oh, believe me, I'll do anything to take a break from work." I lightly nudge his shoulder as we wait for elevator F to pick us up. He looks at me, rolls his eyes, and we both chuckle. "You'll do brilliantly, I'm sure. Just remember what we talked about, okay, and you'll be fine."

Elevator F arrives with a loud ding. We step in. There are more than ten elevators in the hall, so we are the only ones in the car. I wring my hands and Marco reaches out to hold them. A few minutes later, we land on the sixteenth floor.

"Here we are," he whispers. He gets out first, and I follow close behind him. There is a large waiting area, and beyond the glass window that separates the reception area and the offices, you can see and feel the hustle and bustle of the morning. Behind the reception counter, it says Communications Department with clocks under it that display every US time zone.

"Van, this is my friend Bianca Curtis. She has an appointment with Diana at ten thirty." I look at my watch and it says 10:17. I'm early, but not too early.

"Hi," I say to Van.

"She's early, but I'll leave her here under your care, Van. Okay?"

"Sure. Hi Bianca. You go ahead and take a seat, and once Ms. Diana is ready, I'll come get you."

"That sounds perfect. Thanks." I turn around and Marco walks with me. "You can go back to work now."

"Are you going to be fine?" Marco asks gently.

"I'll be fine. I'll be right here." I walk toward one of the big, comfortable-looking leather sofas in the middle of the reception area.

"I helped choose that," he points at the sofa. We laugh together. "Call me when you're done."

"I will." He turns around to go back to his office. "Marco," I call out.

"Yeah?" He looks at me curiously and I mouth, *Thank you.*

I close the door behind me and stand motionless as I savor the moment of victory. The carefully carpeted hallway is empty and quiet. I put my hand over my mouth, and I bow my head. And then I cry. For fuck's sake, I feel like crying has been my default setting lately. But I cry quietly anyway. This time I cry because I am joyful.

I got myself a job in New York City that pays sixty-five thousand dollars a year. I don't think I have ever seen, let alone made, that kind of money in my life. As I walk slowly toward the end of the hall, I can feel my hands shaking. I pull my phone out of my suit pocket and see that I already have a dozen calls from Pam, Marco, and Miguel. When I turn the corner to the exit, I see Marco waiting for me with anticipation. His eyes widen as he sees me walking toward the door, and rushes to me.

"I got it," I whisper, trying to prevent a croak. He pulls me toward the elevator hall and gives me hug. I look for Ms. Van and wave goodbye. She mouths *Congratulations* to me.

"I knew it!"

"Holy shit, Marco, I got myself a job in the city! Thank you!" I try to keep my voice low.

"So, what's the next steps, did she say?"

"Well, I need to drop by human resources on Thursday to sign some paper work. I need to wait for my official offer by email this afternoon. There will be instructions for medical tests and such, and I guess I can do that tomorrow. If all goes well, I start Monday!" I jump up and down while trying to be quiet as Marco plays with the elevator kiosk.

"I have a meeting at twelve thirty, so I can't go to lunch. Let's catch up later for drinks," he says.

"Yes!" I say, and I hug him again. "Don't escort me down. I can handle it from here. You've done a lot. You're magic, Marco! Thank you from the bottom of my heart. I owe you so much."

"Let me tell you something, sweetie. You don't owe me shit. You did that interview alone. There's nothing I could say or do to get you that job. This is all you, girl." The elevator dings, and I step in. As the elevator closes, I blow Marco a kiss and bow my head in gratitude. When the door finally shuts, I start crying again—the sobbing kind—because I can slowly feel my chains snapping off one by one.

୨ଓ

I try to keep my composure the entire way out of the building— leaving the elevator, walking to the receptionist to claim my driver's license, and getting out in one piece without causing a scene because I can no longer contain my excitement. When I'm finally outside in the April noon air, which is thankfully a little less chilly, I let go. I jump up and down as high as I can. I don't care if people are staring at me. This is a defining moment of my existence. I will look back at this someday, after many years, when I'm finally able to live my life with a little bit of happiness, and I will remember how this moment changed the course of my destiny.

I wish I could call him. He wished this for me that night.

I call Pam instead. And when I tell her my great news, we scream and shout and then do it again.

"And get this," she adds as she tries to catch her breathe.

"What?" I ask, rocking back and forth like a lunatic.

"Amy is moving out! She called me this morning on my way to work!"

"What? Oh, my god!" I jump up and down again, hoping that my new boss, Diana, doesn't come out the building and see me. "When is she moving?"

"This fucking weekend." There's more screaming at both ends.

"Oh, my god! I'm going to live in New York City!"

"And because she really feels bad leaving on such short notice, she is paying the rent for the next two months. You, my friend, are going to live in New York City with the first two months' rent free!"

"Is she sure?" I pin my phone between my ear and my shoulder and clasp my hands together in gratitude. Finally, my fucking luck is turning. *Finally.*

"Yeah. She knows your story, and she's fine doing it for you. Her fiancé is loaded. She'll be fine. Where are you heading now? It's past noon and I can't get off work right now."

"It's fine, I'll give Miguel a call and see if we can meet for lunch."

"Really? You'll go all the way downtown?" There is a sudden change in Pam's voice.

"Yeah, what else would I be doing? And after lunch, I'll do all the New York City touristy stuff. Because you know what? I can!"

"Okay, once you're done, meet me at Pig 'n' Whistle around five thirty. We can head home together after."

"Sounds perfect."

Home. Finally, I'm heading home.

Chapter 17

Though she is teeny-tiny, my mom gives the tightest hugs. I hug her right back because I have missed her greatly. It's been three months since I left home, and finally, and to my great relief, we made up a couple of weeks ago.

As I pull away from her, I see that her quirkiness is back— she is no longer the nervous woman she was a few months ago. She actually looks happy, and light, in her stylish denim jeans, a peasant blouse under a red cardigan, and Birkenstock sandals. Yeah, my mom wears Birks. Her hair is cut short now, a bob, and it looks really cute on her. There is also something different about her, a good vibe that I can't quite place.

"How was your trip?" I ask with a wide smile. I want her to see that I'm finally okay.

"It was a pleasantly easy ride. I was asleep the entire time." I grab her duffle bag and carry it on my shoulder.

"Do you want to head straight to dinner?"

"Yeah, I can eat." My mother has the best appetite in the whole world, and with that, the best metabolism. She doesn't gain weight no matter how much she eats. She says it's genetics, but I don't believe her. My hips and thighs are magnets to fats but my boobs, which could use a little fat, are forever flat.

"Korean?" I ask.

"Why not." We love all Asian food. Chinese food. Thai food. Indonesian. Korean. And it goes without saying that we love Filipino food the most. No matter how bad my situation was with

Tommy back in the day, I always made time for Mom and our Saturday lunch dates. "Is it close? Let's just walk. I could use some stretching." And so we head toward the heart of Midtown, and it's my favorite destination for beauty products too. It's where I buy those fancy-but-affordable facemasks that are the craze. They actually work, so it's worth the trip to that part of the city every once in a while.

"Geez, this place is still spectacular," Mom says under her breath. "I'm glad you made it here," she adds as we walk side by side on the busy pedestrian walkway.

"Mom, it's too early to assume that," I whisper.

"That what? That you made it? You have. You live here. You pay rent, and you have a job here. You've made it to New York City, Binks." I guess if she puts it that way, then yes.

I shift her from side to side to make sure she doesn't get accidentally hit by the crowd, or worse, mauled deliberately. Summer in the city attracts more crowds from all over the world than any other city, or at least, it seems like it, with the swarm of tourists from June to late September. When we finally reach the restaurant, there is a long line from the second floor, down the stairs, and out the street. Mom and I agree to wait. I've been here before and the long line speaks for itself. This is a famous spot even for the locals. It's your standard Korean BBQ—and since Mom and I are meat eaters, this is definitely the perfect choice.

"Look, I know standing in line like this is not the best time to ask you this, but do you think you'll ever be ready to see your dad again?" This startles me. The sudden mention of my father is like a punch in my gut, but I pretend not to hear it and I move pass her in front of the line so I don't need to look at her. "Hey, yes, he made a big mistake. But not being around you was my fault. I was so mad that I stupidly took you away from him." My mom is fierce and persistent if she wants to be, and that's obviously what's happening here right now.

"I don't know, Mom." I shake my head slowly, feigning disinterest. I still have not processed any of this, and to be honest, I don't know how I feel about the lies and deception. I just want to enjoy this weekend with her without having to deal with my tainted past. I moved here to escape that.

"Hey, listen to me. You're almost forty, and—"

"I'm thirty-six, Mom," I roll my eyes as I cut her off.

"Fine. But you shouldn't act like a wounded teenager anymore. You've been through a lot worse." I can hear the scolding tone in her voice now. She means business. "He lives in the city, your dad."

"What the f—" I turn around to stare at her. She gives me a stern warning look, and I stop before I say it. "Mom!"

"Blame me. He didn't abandon you. Let me make that clear." The line moves. I drop her duffle bag on the ground and kick it a little. We don't say anything to each other for a good five minutes. She's on her phone texting someone while I scroll through Twitter. The amount of time I spend on social media these days is excessive. It's addictive, to be quite frank—but I have a perfectly good excuse. I run the network official social media accounts, and I follow influencers who are relevant to us.

"He's coming here," my mom announces.

"What?" I don't understand at first. My eyes widen in comprehension. "What? Mom!"

"It's been three months since you found out. I know a lot is going on in your life right now, and they are great strides so don't keep this one hanging. Let's close it up so good karma will just keep on coming, okay."

"This is emotional and spiritual blackmail!" I whine.

"Call it what you want, Bianca Maria, but you are going to talk to your father tonight and start a relationship with him. Are we clear?" I roll my eyes in frustration.

"Mom, do you know how tight this restaurant is? I mean serious. This is an eat-and-go spot. We won't be allowed to linger. Talking is not an option here."

"He's coming here, and then we decide where we go next."

We finally reach the bottom of the stairs in the line. The restaurant is on top. People going up and down the stairs make it really tight and uncomfortable. Mom sternly stares at a young girl who almost hit her in the face. It's loud upstairs too. The grill sizzles. How does Mom think we'll be able to talk here? I turn my back to her, and I face the wall as I wait for the line to move faster. When it's finally our turn, my mom has already taken control of the situation.

"We need three seats," she tells the Korean *ajumma*. She turns her head, shouts something in Korean to the young men busing the tables, and leads us to the farthest table with four chairs and a big grill in the middle. The smell of barbeque makes my mouth water. I only had a fruit salad at lunch with Marco today. Once we're seated, Mom looks at the menu, points at a couple of pictures, and the *ajumma* leaves us alone. I feel nervous all of a sudden. I don't really know how to feel about all this. Well, I do. I don't like it. It's confusing, and I hate being confused.

"Bianca, again, let me repeat. I threw him out of the house. He begged me to take him back for years. But I felt cheated on, even though I was technically the mistress." She makes a disgusted face at this. "He said he would only stop bothering me if I let him be part of your life, in the background, and I agreed."

"I don't get it. What was he doing in Manila? Why did he leave his wife?"

"It was a very complicated time. His parents are business partners with Elaine's parents."

"You know her? Have you met her?" She nods at this. I smack my forehead with my palm in disbelief. "Like how and when? Goodness, Mom!"

"Your dad and I loved each other greatly. We still do. But he can't run away from his responsibilities to Elaine. After they got married, he left her and went backpacking all over Asia. She was pregnant at that time with twins. Your dad didn't go home to her for fifteen years. When I found out about her, I was so mad that I kicked him out. Because your dad is from money, your grandparents took care of Elaine and her kids. Your siblings."

"Why are you laying all this on me now?"

"So you can fully move on." I understand what she's getting at. I really do. But I don't know if I have the emotional capacity to welcome all this right now. Thankfully, our beers arrive, giving me a few minutes to wrap my brain around all this new information. She takes a big gulp from her bottle. I stare at mine, raise it, and tip it lightly on my lips. I knew my dad. It's not like I grew up without him. He was a great father. The best.

I remember us flying kites at the park in Manila. I remember us buying ice cream from the *mamang sorbetero*, the Filipino ice cream man, every day after school. He helped me with homework more than Mom ever did, and he would kiss my feet at night before I go to bed. He used to call my toes "little piggies." I remember those times vividly. That's why it hurts much more because I didn't get any explanation.

"Binky, it's my fault. I wanted to hurt him so bad that I took you away from him. He said it was the most painful part of our breakup. Losing you."

I can feel my chest tightening. In the grand scheme of

things, this isn't a life-and-death situation. I know this, but it doesn't hurt any less. I just need to understand them both so I can better deal with it.

Suddenly, Mom waves at someone behind me. I tense up but I don't look around. I continue playing with my beer bottle on the table, rolling it from side to side. I sense him standing next to me.

"Go sit down, Charlie," my mom says, and my dad obeys. We are probably five inches away from each other. I don't have a choice but to face him, so I give him a weak smile, and he beams with glee. With that one look, I melt, and my heart swells, and I almost cry.

"Hi, Binky."

"Hi, Dad."

❧

After dinner, my parents and I walk to Bryant Park without really knowing what to do next.

"I'm getting ice cream!" Mom blurts out as we settle on a bench facing Seventh Avenue and hastily rushes off, leaving Dad and me awkwardly uncomfortable. Dad put Mom's duffle bag on the bench, filling the space between us.

"How's your new apartment?" he asks.

"It's okay. It's my best friend Pam's apartment. I'm renting a room." I don't intentionally plan to be mechanical, but I do sound cold.

"I'm glad you're staying with a friend. Also, I'm not far away. I live on the Upper East Side."

"Okay." I can recognize the beginning of my collapse, but I'm holding on to myself as best I can. This man hurt me—the memory of him, not because he was a bad man, but because he was a great man. He loved me, and I felt it, though I was too young to realize, and so when he disappeared, a big part of my soul was lost.

"I didn't mean to hurt you, Binky." I can feel his sincerely as I control a sob. "You and your mother are the best things that ever happened to me. To lose you both broke my heart more than you could ever imagine. And it was my fault." I turn to look at the first man I truly loved, and the first who broke my heart.

His head is bent down in extreme remorse. He's still a good-looking man, I can still see his ebullient traits though there is sadness in his eyes. He's still the best friend a little girl ever had. He's still my dad, whom I remember so well—he was proud of me, spent most of his waking hours with me, running in the park, taking me to school, holding my hand when I needed it the most.

"I'm sorry, baby. . . ." Finally, my tears start to roll down my cheeks. The pain is raw and present, like I've pushed it way down for years, and now it comes bubbling up inside me unrestrained. He wipes his face with his arm and I can see tears dripping on the pavement. "There was not a day I wished I could be with you again, to be your dad again."

"But how about your other kids?"

"Though the twins were born earlier, I didn't get to experience it. And it was my fault, I know. So to me, you were my first child. You were the one I saw from birth and watched grow into a feisty teenager." He lets out a sad little chuckle at this. "That doesn't mean I love my other children any less, but you were my first baby. Made me realize how much I loved being a dad—your dad. How taking you to school in the morning and picking you up in the afternoon were the highlights of my day because I was able to be a kid with you. You were funny, and smart—very sassy,"—he chuckles for a second time—"and our lives were full of laughter." He brushes his arm across his eyes again. "When I lost you, I thought I had lost everything. It was unfair to my other children, and so I gave them as much love as I gave you. Unfortunately, I couldn't love their mother, and the best thing a father can do for his children is to love their mother enough. Without that, I failed them."

We let the silence envelop our hurting hearts, muffling the noise of the city on a Friday night. I lean back and slouch on the bench as I try to find comfort in this—the revelation, finally, the truth that my soul has always craved. Dad does the same. I can feel the pain in his heaving chest. A grown man is crying, baring his heart and love to my mom . . . and by connection, to me. *My dad.*

"Thank you for telling me." The word *Dad* still feels alien to my mouth, so I don't say it again. But I do feel him—the regret and the remorse on our parting. It seems odd that I am now a grown woman and yet, inside me, I am still that fourteen-year-old girl ditched by her best friend.

"Not a day goes by that I don't think about you and your mother. There is no reason for you to forgive me or to make me part of your life again, but I really want that—if you'll have me as a father again, Binky, I really want that." He doesn't turn to me, or move me to look into his eyes, or to plead baring his soul, but I feel it all. I feel his heart. He is my dad, after all, and I will love him forever and always, no matter what.

I exhale again.

Chapter 18

I'm exhausted. But at least my weekend had a good ending. Or beginning.

I had an eventful weekend with my parents, which included visiting my dad's apartment on the Upper East Side after our tearful conversation at the park. He lives there alone in a massive apartment that is suitable for a family of ten. He and Elaine have been divorced for over fifteen years now. They tried to make it work when he came back, and they had another child, but eventually, after more than seven years, Elaine gave up, packed up, and left. As it turns out, I have three siblings, and Dad is so excited for me to meet them. I'm not. Well, at least not yet.

I look at my bedside alarm clock that says it's almost midnight. I need to be at work at seven thirty tomorrow morning. I jump into the shower and purge the weekend drama away. If I'm being truthful, I'm actually warming up to the idea of a complete family—a mom, a dad and me. And for some weird reason, I also sense a new fondness between my parents. *Can love really stand the test of time?*

Pam is on my bed when I walk back into my room wearing my new favorite pink fluffy bathrobe. She's already in her pajamas and looks as exhausted as I feel.

"Why the long face?" I ask, concerned. Pam almost never shows sadness except when Tommy died, which was totally understandable.

"I have to tell you something," she begins. The uncertainty in her voice makes me nervous. Pam is never uncertain. She bends her head as if she is about to confess the biggest sin of all time.

"What?" I'm now near panic.

"I think . . . well, actually, I know."

"Okay?" I sit next to her on the bed and I hold both her hands.

"I like Miguel."

I exhale upon hearing this. "My god, I thought it was something serious."

"But that is serious!" she wails and widens her eyes to emphasize her point.

"Why? Why is it serious?" I shake my head and give her a questioning glare.

"Because I think. Well, no, I know. . . ."

"Okay?" I'm waiting for her to say more.

"That he's in love with you." She bends her head as she says this and looks at me from under her beautifully fashioned eyelashes.

"For fuck's sake, Pam!" I get up immediately and look at her in disbelief. She lifts her head to face me. I back away in disgust because I think it's the most ludicrous thing I've ever heard. "It's like telling me that Marco likes me!"

"Why, is he gay?" There is surprise and fear in her eyes.

"No! But you know what I mean?"

"I think you're just blind. That man will do anything and everything for you with a snap of your fingers."

"Let's not do this to Miguel, Pam. Let's not taint our friendship with malice. He's like a brother to me. That's all he is."

"I'm sorry. But all I'm saying is, if you're not interested, then can I make a move?"

"Pam, he's not just anybody. Look, I might not be romantically interested in him, but he's my friend. And I don't want him getting hurt."

"What does that mean?" There is hurt in her eyes, and I immediately regret my words. Who am I to talk to her this way—to judge her, or to make assumptions?

"I love you with all my heart and soul, Pam. But you are also known to be breaking boys' hearts," I say lightheartedly.

"I do not." She pouts and plunges backward onto my bed with outstretched arms and starts making duvet angels. "I've been trying to avoid these feelings, you know. I tried going out with other guys. And all of them end in disaster. He's all I think about. How he makes me laugh in certain situations, or how gentlemanly he is to us, or you know, how smart he is and how great a son too." These are all true about Miguel. "But he's only got eyes for you." She pulls my duvet over her face and makes pretend crying noises.

"Look, I'm not going to stop you if you really like him—if you really, really like him. But as your friend, I need to protect both of you. How about let's see where these feelings go in the meantime?" She lifts the duvet off her face and stares at me grimly.

"Fine! But the first sign that he's interested, I'll pounce on it."

"Yes. Pounce away!"

❧

My lights are out but I've been tossing and turning for two hours now. It's past two o'clock in the morning.

"Argh!" I softly scream. It's also infuriating that, I think, the cause of my insomnia is Miguel . . . and the idea that he might be into me. I've known him for more than five years now, and he's always been that reliable guy who was constantly saving Tommy. He didn't do that for me. He did it for him, for Tommy. I mean, any woman would be lucky to have Miguel, and everything Pam said is true—he is caring, gentle, smart, and a great son.

I should also add that he's a very attractive young man. "Argh!"

And out of the blue, flashbacks of the many kind things he has done for me come rushing into my head—like running to see me at work during lunch hour when he could only stay for twenty minutes; or that time when I got stuck in Chelsea in a torrential downpour and he appeared out of nowhere in a cab to rescue me; or the many times he cooked dinner for me at his apartment, and the movie dates that to me weren't really dates but two friends going to the movies together. I think of those moments and see them differently now.

I don't think I can do relationships right now. I don't think I can do love, even if I try. There's a part of me that's still broken. There's the other part that is in love with someone who doesn't exist. And these two are very hard situations to recover from. I just need to stay still. My mind wanders to that person who doesn't exist in my universe. I still refuse to succumb to the urge to look him up online, but I can still feel him, smell him, and see his brown eyes—all in the magical conflicted place that is my brain.

❧

Pig 'n' Whistle is a thing every Tuesday now. Marco and I get here first, Miguel is on his way, and Pam is running late as usual. Rod, the bartender, has accepted that I drink a cosmopolitan on weekdays, and he's preparing one right this minute. I give him my teasing wink, to which he responds with an eye roll, as if to say *whatever*. Thankfully, he's in love with Pam, so I'm quite confident that he will never lace my drink with poison—or spit in it.

When Miguel walks in, all tall and handsome in a perfectly tailored suit, I am caught off guard. If not for the conversation I had with Pam on Sunday, this would have been a regular Tuesday night out with friends. Now I start thinking about the many ways Miguel supports me. He sits next to me, gives me a light peck on the cheek, and reaches out to Marco for a lazy high-five.

"You look fancy today, Miguelito," Marco teases and gapes at him. He cleans up well. Think of a beefier and taller Diego Luna of *Star Wars* with the same boyish smile and atypical shyness. Miguel waves at Rod who immediately comes up with a bottle of Corona beer with lime.

"I swear that guy has a third eye or something," Marco says as he squints at Rod strangely.

"I've been ordering the same thing for the past three months," Miguel reasons.

"Still. Also, Bianca, do you think he's into me, or Miguel, maybe?"

"No. Geez, he's so into Pam," I say as Marco and I look at him dreamily. Young, buff, blond, and gorgeous.

"Eek!" Pam walks into the tiny narrow bar and screams as soon as she sees us. She's a sight to behold in her gold jumpsuit with black strappy sandals, carrying herself with grace and style notwithstanding the nasty screaming. Her hair is parted on one side with a big clustered-pearls clip on the other. Her lips are red as an apple. All three of us stand up to receive her with concern. She immediately waves us all off and bends her head to read something off her phone.

"You will not believe this, Bianca. Park Hyun Min is engaged!" I squint my eyes and furrow my brow because I don't quite understand what she's saying. The mere mention of his name, in whatever context, confuses me. I stare at her with a blank expression. "Hyun Min is getting married!" she says to my face.

Then it hits me.

Eric is getting married. *My Eric.*

I suppose he finally found the love I wished him to find. My heart plunges. Both fear and pain, present here—almost choking me—and I can sense the blood draining from my face. I should be happy for him, but instead, I feel like a bucket of ice-cold water has just been dumped over my head. "This bitch is one lucky chick. Suzi whatever." Pam shoves the phone in my face to show me a picture of the happy couple. My heart skips. No, it's breaking. I see Eric's face split screen with Suzi. The photo is not of them together. "You look pale, Bianca. I know, right? I'm pissed off, too."

"So, they've finally confirmed their relationship?" I croak and swallow hard.

"Let me read. Hold on. It says here that Hyun Min was in New York four months ago while he was on a break with Suzi. Upon his return, the couple confirmed their relationship of three years and secretly got engaged. They officially announced their engagement yesterday." I start to feel sick. It's coming from the center of my core, spiraling upward toward my head, and releasing intense anguish. The effect is physical. I start hyperventilating.

"Are you okay?" Miguel leans in to ask.

"Yes," I jerkily reply. "Sorry," I reach to brush his hand lightly. "This is disturbing news," I add and pretend to laugh a little. I almost topple his beer bottle.

"Bianca and I have been in love with this guy since *The Oasis* came out last December. It's a television drama on Netflix. Since then, we went back in time and watched all of his previous shows. He had plenty," Pam says dreamily, recounting the many sleepless nights we had binge-watching Korean drama where Eric was the main act.

"He can't marry this woman," I blurt out. They all look at me questioningly.

"Yes, because he's meant to be mine," Pam adds with contempt before pulling a chair next to Miguel and plops on it.

"Whatever." Marco turns around to wave at Rod for another round of cosmos.

I jump off the barstool and head to the bathroom as quickly as I can. There is no way I can maintain my pretense. Once inside the tiny stall, I shove the door shut and lock it. I can't have Pam following me with more information about them. I don't want to have to explain my change of mood and why I feel sick to my stomach. I don't understand this reaction. This is what I wanted for him.

I look at myself in the mirror. I'm a changed woman. Everything I see today is a product of hard work and perseverance, and I should embrace this person, but instead I feel my chest pulsating with both pain and rage. I'm quite sure he doesn't even remember who I am. I'm a fucking idiot to think I mattered to someone as insanely famous as Park Hyun Min.

I close my eyes.

Inhale.

Exhale.

Inhale.

Exhale.

My breathing is slowing down. Then I see his face inches away from mine, smiling, teasing, and happy. And I calm down some more.

I may have guilt and regrets about that night, but no one can take away the truth that it happened—and it happened to me.

⁊◌

Park Hyun Min missed the ferry heading to the countryside. To travel by car, it will take him more than twenty-four hours. He stands there in distress, almost in tears, and in his posture, there is regret and dejection. He's wearing jeans and a white collarless shirt—tidy and clean. The wind picks up, and it sweeps his hair backward. He watches the ferry as it steams away. The anguish on his face is apparent. Even without words, you can genuinely feel his desire to jump into the water and swim after that moving ferry. Without another option, defeated, he bends his head down, his legs apart with both hands in solid fists. Then he hears someone call his name—a distant echo. He looks for it, sees it, and his face lights up. He sees Jin waving at him from the top of the ferry. She calls his name again, and her happiness is clear after discovering that he showed up. The music picks up, the excitement is palpable, and Hyun Min jumps into the water and swims to catch the ferry to be with Jin.

Marco, Pam and I are watching *The Oasis*—the last few episodes we missed.

"Holy mammoth, he is hot!" Marco screams and throws both arms up wide in the air to stress his point. The three of us, Pam and I in pajamas, are squashed together on the sofa, each with a tub of popcorn on our lap.

After realizing how absurd it is to ache for a fantasy, I caved in when Pam asked me to watch the episodes of *The Oasis* we've missed. Preserving our night together shouldn't mean I miss out on all the things that I like doing—like watching him at his best.

"Should we start another episode?" Pam asks eagerly.

"It's Tuesday, and it's almost ten o'clock. How about we do the marathon on Saturday?" I get up and stuff the rest of the popcorn in my mouth. Marco yawns and looks at his watch.

"Yeah, I better get going. We have an early thing tomorrow, Bianca." Marco gets up, puts his shoes on, gives Pam and me a hug at the same time, and runs out the door. "I love you, my darlings!"

"I'm tired!" Pam declares. I give her a kiss on the forehead, and I go to my room. I jump into bed, pull the covers over my head, and I think of him.

Tonight, I say goodbye to the fantasy. Tonight, I say goodbye to Eric. And I let one foolish tear roll down the side of my face.

PART 3

Chapter 19

It's been almost two years since I moved to the city, and today I turn thirty-eight. To be honest, I don't feel any different from when I turned thirty. In fact, because I'm in a different phase in my life, a happier and more peaceful phase, I've never felt more alive.

I got up early this morning, eager to face the next year of my presence in this vast world of second chances and countless possibilities. Pam was still asleep when I left the apartment. She had one too many drinks last night as we welcomed my birthday with Marco and Miguel—the two constant *Ms* in our lives.

It's only seven thirty in the morning, and I'm already walking into my favorite building in all of Manhattan. I stop, stare, and sigh. I didn't think it was ever possible to love a building, but I truly love this one. Tall, shiny, and silvery, and as the morning sun hits its stellar facade with inconsistent rays, a magical vision of sparkles appears. I love this building because it reminds me every single day of how my life has been totally altered. I sigh again as I enter, proud, with my brown platform boots clicking on the marble floor. Today, I also feel confident in my tight denim skirt, whose long slit right in front makes me feel a little saucy, and which I paired with a blue-and-navy Vineyard Vines oxford shirt topped with a brown leather trench coat. On my shoulder is my birthday present to myself—a Louis Vuitton Noe. It's an extravagance I felt so guilty to succumb to, but Pam said I deserved it in every possible way—because not every day does someone reach the milestone of changing her life 180 degrees. And so I bought it with her at Bloomindales last Sunday.

The crowd is light at this hour. There are no long lines as I walk through the turnstile after tapping my badge lightly on the access pad. I walk toward the elevator hall with big wide strides and I stop right in front of the kiosk where I punch floor number sixteen. The loudspeaker says I should take elevator C. I walk in front of it and I wait while singing a new pop song playing through my AirPods. I may be alone this morning in this quiet elevator hall, but I am not lonely. Nothing and no one can dampen my mood today. I'm thirty-eight, and I'm happy, alive, and I survived.

The elevator *ding* echoes in the hall, and elevator C opens wide. I step in and I lean sideways at the far back. I have the car all to myself, so I sing a little louder, immersed in the lyrics, closing my eyes. The elevator doors are slowly sliding shut when I notice hurried movements out the hall—a hand suddenly appears blocking the door from closing. The doors jiggle lightly until finally giving in, moving backward, opening the entryway wide. A throng of people walks in at the same time, and I move farther back to make room. The newcomers hold the door open until finally, someone who seems to be walking in a leisurely pace and is busily scrolling through his phone, steps in. They let go of the door. I know the type. Network stars. Maybe some big shot guest on today's morning show. I roll my eyes at this.

Then I freeze.

My heart pounds. I remove my AirPods from my ears—all my senses are on high alert.

A disconcertingly familiar scent takes me back to a place I long ago pushed further in my memory. Not forgotten or erased, but stored deep down where I can't easily access it. Curious, with my five-foot-two frame, I tiptoe to look at the person in the middle of the car. He's not hard to see since he's the tallest person in the box. Unfortunately, I can't see his face, or any of the others, as their backs are toward me.

What are the chances? I'd say zero. This has happened to me once or twice before, where I thought I'd seen him, and my heart started to pound, and my palms began to sweat, and I was both relieved and disappointed that my mind was simply playing tricks on me.

Someone says something in Korean, and the hairs on the back of my neck rise.

"Top floor," the person in the middle answers and arches his head sideways. I know that voice very well. I've heard that voice in my dreams far too many times. He turns his head nearer to mine. I see him and I immediately bend my head down. I push myself farther backward, hoping no one will notice that there is one other person in the car who is not part of the party. I slide sideways to hide behind one of the burly guys in front of me. I realize I take cover not because I'm afraid to be recognized, but because I'm afraid I won't.

In what feels like forever, the elevator finally stops on the sixteenth floor. I make my way out of the car with my hair shielding my face and my head bent so low it looks like I'm bowing at them. And of course fate is funny sometimes—I bump into him as he takes a step to the side to let me through. To be near him again is unsettling. To smell his scent is intoxicating. I get out as fast as I can and run straight to the ladies' room, which thankfully is only a few steps away from the elevator hall. I let the door close behind me with a loud thud. It's empty and quiet. I sigh and let my heart settle down. I stand right in front of the mirror and stare at myself. I know there have been many anomalous events in my life, but what are the chances of this run-in, really? After finishing *The Oasis*, I cut back on watching K-drama. I would get some tidbits of news from Pam, but I stayed away from his work entirely.

I rub my palms together in an unsuccessful attempt to calm down as I pace back and forth. Why is he in my building? And with a full entourage! I rest both my hands on the sink and bend my head. This should not be a big deal. Not a big deal at all. I doubt he even remembers me. I laugh at myself. We're talking about a global celebrity here, and I'm quite sure he's been through many of those nights with fans and more-than-willing friendly females. So there, it's settled. I should not make a thing about this. I sigh again. I turn on the faucet and splash cold water on my face. I pull some paper towels off the dispenser and wipe my face dry, not caring how rough they are on my skin.

He's in New York City, he's in my building, and he's also very engaged. Pam just gave me an update recently that there has been no new announcement following their engagement two years ago. I look at my left hand without my wedding ring.

It's been twenty minutes since I tried to calm myself down. I can't stay here the entire morning. Maybe a caffeine fix will do the trick. I look for my lip and cheek stain and dab some on my face. I tighten my bun on top of my head, and I put some stray hair behind my ears. I smile at what I see. I brush my denim skirt with my palms front and back and fix the collar of my shirt under my coat. If this is what being in my late thirties looks like, I'll take it. My Asian genes are at play here.

Finally, I bravely walk out of the bathroom convinced that today is just going to be another day in my improved life.

I stop. Then I panic, looking around for an escape. My chest pounds violently under my shirt, but there is no way out of this moment. This is not a dream. Not a nightmare either. It's a frightening amalgamation of both. Twilight zone.

He is standing in the middle of the foyer. Alone. Looking right at me. He looks even better now than the last time I saw him, more relaxed in jeans and a checkered shirt over a white T-shirt. He's wearing a ball cap that shades his eyes. He looks taller. He looks perfect.

We stand like this for a while, facing each other six feet apart, simply staring, and no one saying a word. I wish I could see him smile again. It doesn't come. He recognizes me, but I can't tell whether he's pleased to see me or not. It's not like we parted cordially. I still remember the hurt in his eyes. I still remember the anger over what he probably thought was my deception. I walked away that day with regret that I couldn't be that person I so wanted to be for him—someone who was free. He doesn't move at all. Not an inch. It's impressive, actually. He's staring at me like a statue.

A ding breaks our stare-down and a number of communications department employees step out of the elevator. Their chattering fills the empty space. I take a step back to let people through. Finally, a smile breaks on his face.

I exhale.

"Mr. Park?" Diana runs from behind him and he turns around to face her. "The meeting is in the executive conference room. I'll walk right up with you," she adds. He bows his head in greeting and Diana does the same. Marco then steps out from one of the elevators and sees what's going on. He does a double take and sends me a questioning glare. Not every day do you see me standing by the elevator hall in an extremely confused state with Diana and one of our clients at eight o'clock in the morning.

"Marco!" Diana welcomes him with a hint of panic in her voice. I've worked with Diana long enough to know her many quirks. Still, she looks totally put together in her lilac pantsuit and bright pink Christian Louboutin high heels. Her slick hair is parted in the middle, and pulled back in a tight bun, making her appear more sophisticated. Nobody needs to know that Diana, bless her heart because I know she's truly trying, is the worst worrywart in the whole of New York City. Marco walks toward them slowly in contemplation, perhaps trying to figure out what he's walked into, but Diana pulls him immediately closer to Eric. He stumbles forward. Fortunately, he is able to save himself from a major mishap.

"Mr. Park, this is Marco Evans. He will lead your publicity team." He bows. This has a potential to be a long conversation, and so I quietly take a step backward and slowly turn around to escape. "Bianca, come on over and let me introduce you to Mr. Park as well." I hear Diana's voice behind me. I close my eyes, and I stop mid-step. I turn around and walk toward them slowly. "This is Bianca Curtis, who's also part of your team. She will be your social media coordinator."

"Bianca Curtis?" I hear him ask. He reaches out for a handshake. I take it. When our palms touch, the feelings all rush back to me. He holds my hand longer than necessary, and we look into each other's eyes with the same familiar gaze. He's searching for something I don't have. I look away immediately.

"Hi, Mr. Park. It's good to meet you." I don't know what else to say. I pull my hand from his grasp.

"Here's your publicity team, Mr. Park." Diana excitedly says, gesturing her hand toward Marco and me.

"Call me Eric." His voice sends shivers down my spine.

"We'll walk with you to the executive floor," Diana says.

Van rushes toward me with two notebooks and pens. She pulls off my coat, grabs my purse from my shoulder, and hands the supplies to Marco and me. "Happy Birthday," Van whispers close in my ear. Eric looks at us curiously. Marco pulls me next to him while Diana punches the executive floor on the kiosks and leads Eric to the appropriate elevator. Marco and I stand side by side waiting for Diana to give us further instructions. I sense Eric stealing a look at me. I try ignoring it.

"Is he the *Oasis* dude?" Marco asks softly. I nod. When the elevator opens, Eric makes way for Diana. He then waits for Marco and me before stepping in himself. I think about the time we were at the elevator going up the Empire State Building and how close our bodies were. I feel heat rising up to my face. He steals another glance at me.

"I'm sorry if you were given the wrong floor. But our meeting is in the executive conference room. Robbie will meet us there," Diana explains.

I don't remember having this meeting in my calendar. I don't remember being invited to the executive conference room. Ever. I quickly turn to Diana and then to Eric. Eric and I both know Robbie. A few months after I started my job, I was surprised to find out that he's the network's big boss. We met briefly two years ago when I was with Eric at Piedmont Lounge, but on my few run-ins with him, I could tell that he didn't remember who I was, for which I'm most grateful.

"I knew where it was. I just wanted to explore the building, and I landed on your floor," he explains. He is businesslike but kind, cordial, respectful, which is quite the contrary to other famous celebrities I've met. "It's a great building. Are there studios here?"

"Small studios, yes. We do our news broadcast and live shows from this building. The others, we do on location."

"Are the studios nice?" Eric looks at Marco. Marco looks

startled and nods vigorously. "Have you been in a lot of shoots?" he asks.

"Not really," Marco replies, his voice cracking a bit. I chuckle quietly, but he hears it anyway and elbows me lightly.

"Why not? Doesn't the publicity team need to know what's going on with filming? I mean, I'm sure we'll have a photographer on the set, right?" He directs this question to Diana, and she looks like she's thinking about this deeply. "Photographers on set are a thing of the past though. We need social media coordinators to take pictures from their phones and directly post them on the social media platforms."

"Of course. Yes." Diana replies. "We send our team on location every once in a while to get a feel for how things are going on set, take some photos, and draft blurbs for social media use." In the two years I've been with the network, this has never happened—at least, not with me involved.

"I think it's really important to get our audience and followers to be part of what we're making, no?" Eric reiterates.

"I agree." Diana concedes. The elevator dings, alerting us that we've reached our destination. Again, Eric holds the door for us and steps out last.

This floor is where the powerful reside. It exhibits expensive taste, elegance, and authority. Black marble floors and black granite walls comprise the foyer. The interior design is a thousand times more upscale than the communications department, and a five-star hotel lobby has nothing on this one. There is a large vase filled with dozens and dozens of flowers on a center table as you step out. The flowers look real, and I wonder how often they replenish them—they also look expensive. I now feel self-conscious realizing that I'm wearing denim to this occasion. It also doesn't help that Diana looks at me and then at my skirt. I give her a weak smile as an apology. As we enter the reception area, Eric's team from the elevator earlier walks up to him questioningly.

"Where have you been? Tim has been looking for you and searching from floor to floor," says an American guy, who is likely his US agent.

"Tell him to come back up," he says slowly and clearly, and no one dares to ask any more questions.

Marco and I stay as far away from the group as possible while Diana introduces herself. Marco looks at me, and mouths, *What the fuck*? I give him a wide, pretend-smile as if to say, *I don't know what the hell is going on either.* To our surprise, Eric moves toward us and introduces us to his team.

"Bianca and Marco, this is my team. Lee is my manager, Francis here is my US agent, Eun Dong is my assistant, and Lucas is one of my bodyguards. And Tim who is on his way back is the other. Not that I don't love you guys," he says to Lucas, "but I don't think I need a bodyguard here. And these are Marco and Bianca who are going to handle my publicity." Eric beams as he says this. There are handshakes all around. Diana stares at us, and I can tell that she's trying to understand this very odd dynamic.

The receptionist, who looks like a celebrity herself, welcomes the group and graciously walks us to a large lounge area at the far end of the floor. The room is complete with a lavish breakfast buffet spread and a coffee bar that would embarrass the Starbucks headquarters. Marco and I eye the coffee machines longingly. Eric walks up to get a cup and Eun Dong, a beautiful, young Korean lady, rushes to assist him.

"I can get my own coffee, don't worry." Eric says this nicely. No ego in him at all. "Black, two sugars?" He turns to look at me. "And you, Marco?" No one noticed what he just said to me. It was in passing, a quick reference to the past. My heart skips a beat.

"I'll take mine black, thanks." Marco walks up to him and helps with his brew. He then turns around to hand me mine as if it's the most natural thing in the world.

"Eun Dong, I need you to do something for me, if that's okay?" Eric says as he pulls his phone from his shirt pocket.

"Of course, Park Hyun Min."

"I'll forward you a text message and I want this handled immediately." Eun Dong scrolls though her phone as soon as she hears it beep, looks at Eric, and walks out of the lounge.

"Eric, my man! Nice to see you back in town! This is it. We're really doing this!" Robbie, in his expensive pinstripe navy suit and bold red tie, walks in with his big thundering voice. He walks straight to Eric and gives him a big tight hug. I want to be invisible right this minute. "Let's not go to the conference room, let's all just stay here in the lounge. I've not had breakfast yet. Trina, can you lock the door and not let anyone in? We're meeting here instead."

Trina, the receptionist, sashays out of the room with her long legs and tight miniskirt. Twelve more people enter the room. One of them is Vanessa—Serendipity Vanessa. I brush my hair sideways with my fingers to cover a bit of my face and bend my head down some more. Everyone who's important takes the center seats. Marco and I remain standing at the far back. Eric takes the big couch. No one seems to dare sit next to him.

"Marco and Bianca, there's lots of space right here." He pats the space next to him. I quickly take the spot on the opposite end. Marco doesn't have a choice but to sit uncomfortably in the middle. Diana continues to stare at us curiously. It's actually funny to watch.

"Okay. This is it!" Robbie begins. "We're doing this. Contracts have been signed, Eric and his team have approved the scripts, the Korean team will be landing next week to set up their offices. We'll have our first reading in two weeks. Here's Mavie, one of our executive producers. She will give us a run through of what to expect in the next couple of weeks. We will have costume fittings, makeup tests, rehearsals, trainings, and stunt coordination."

Two years of working behind Diana and alongside Marco have taught me a great deal about television publicity. I love this job, and this right now should be the biggest moment of my career—to be among people who have created great television for decades. Instead, I sit here self-consciously wondering what Eric is thinking. It's my turn to steal a glance at him. Unexpectedly, he is looking right back at me from behind Marco. His lips curve into a small inconspicuous smile. I return the gesture. Our eyes lock for a good few seconds until I break our gaze.

Marco doesn't notice a thing. He's probably still wondering why we're in this room with the big leagues. I put my hand on his shoulder. He turns around to me. He's nervous, no question about it. His eyes widen to confirm this.

"Are you prepared for this?" he asks. I shake my head. "Well, we'll just run through our usual laundry list."

"Yeah. I'll be right here to assist you." I open the notebook Van gave me earlier and start jotting some social media ideas. If only they'll let us handle their personal Instagram and Twitter accounts, that will definitely resonate well with fans.

I feel Marco relax a bit and lean back on the sofa, giving me an open view of Eric on the other end with his legs crossed and his steaming cup of coffee on his lap. If you want to talk surreal, this is the most surreal thing I've ever experienced. Not long ago, in a faraway dream, I met this beautiful man sitting next to us. He was both happy and a little sad. He was talking about a television show he's thinking of making here in the United States. He was uncertain of love. I was uncertain of my entire life. Now, here we are sitting together under very different circumstances, strangers and yet connected by the honesty of our souls on that fateful beautiful night. From the way he looks at me, that night seemed to have had as much of an impact on him as it did on me. Perhaps he remembers because I was the girl who turned him down, unlike Vanessa here, who sits across from us, giving Eric some massively flirty glances.

Executive Producer Mavie clears her throat and starts talking about schedules, rehearsals, scripts, and shoot locations. Diana is earnestly jotting down notes. Marco draws stick figures. Eric sees it too and chuckles lightly. Marco covers his notepad quickly, embarrassed.

When Mavie is done speaking, Eric's team starts asking questions—mostly logistical stuff. He's not even paying attention. He looks at me and looks at my untouched cup of coffee on the table. I couldn't move even if I wanted to.

"Your coffee is getting cold," Eric says, interrupting the meeting. He gets up and heads to the coffee bar. Minutes later, he comes back with a new cup of coffee, which he hands me before returning to his seat. All eyes are on him and then on me. I take a sip of my coffee because I don't know what else to do. Conversations resume. Marco gives me a puzzled frown. I slowly shrug my shoulders in response.

Finally, it's Diana's turn to speak. She talks about the campaign strategy for the show, which she says is separate from her publicity plan for the actors. She talks about the show ideas first and how she wants big billboards in Times Square, spots on television shows, and celebrity magazine ads. She also talks about social media and how—she gestures with her hands to

Marco and me—she is working with her team to get it all set up.

"More importantly, our plan is to make sure there is a focused publicity campaign for every cast. Mr. Park coming to New York for this is something we should leverage. We can set up his social media accounts like HyunMinUSA, and he can start posting on Instagram and Twitter. Bianca, who is our social media coordinator, will handle those accounts." Robbie turns and eyes me curiously. Eric smiles at this.

"Good. I like this. Bianca will handle all my social media accounts and we will have to discuss content every day," Eric says.

"Yes. I'll send you content ideas and we can help you craft them." Diana adds. "You can email me or call me for any ideas you or your team may have."

"I think Bianca can handle that, right?" Eric looks at me fixedly. I want to disappear right now. "I'm sure you're working on multiple projects, Diana, and I'm confident Bianca here is capable and will report back to you." He turns to Diana. He's not asking. He's telling her what he wants to happen. Everyone is silent.

"I think that's a great idea!" Robbie agrees with Eric.

"Then it's done."

❧

I'm the first one up and out as soon as Robbie ends the meeting. He asks Eric to stay behind. His team walks out with us too.

"What was that about?" Marco whispers to me as we wait for the elevator to take us back to our floor. I look at him pretending not to understand his question. "That was weird and you know it," he insists. I don't say anything. As soon as we land on the sixteenth floor, Marco and I walk toward the small conference room, adjacent to the kitchen.

"Let me get coffee," I say casually.

"Bianca Maria Curtis, I swear to God if you don't tell me what's going on this instant, I will skin you alive!" I laugh at this because if Marco were not in PR, he'd be great in standup—or maybe, in one of our shows. "And don't laugh at me, sister."

"Can't a girl get coffee first? Geez!" I walk to the coffee machine and pour myself a cup. I add two sugars. Marco looks at this suspiciously.

"You know him." It's not a question.

Instead of answering him, I walk toward the conference room. Then Diana shows up.

"Okay, team. I guess, Marco, you and Bianca are going to handle this. Robbie and Eric insist on it. We need to talk about this some more, but I need to run to my next meeting uptown. In the meantime, Marco, choose your team, put it together and start planning. We have two months before the show starts production, but we have to start cracking on it immediately. We are talking big creative teasers, press releases, stories in the papers about Hyun Min, feature articles, profiles in men's magazines, even *Vogue* and *Bazaar*, press conferences, and late-night show appearances. The works. Okay. I have to run. Give me something by Friday." Diana dashes out of the room. Marco rolls his eyes.

"I can do all that in half a day, but for right now, I'm more interested in how you know the famous Park Hyun Min!"

I get up and I close the door.

"No one knows about this," I say. "Not a soul."

"Okay." He sits down, clasps his hands together, and leans forward on the table. I sit across from him.

"I met Eric almost two years ago. The night before Tommy died." There is silence. Marco puts his hand over his open mouth in shock.

"Holy shit. . . ." he whispers. "Pam doesn't know?"

"She'll kill me if she finds out that you know and she doesn't."

"So, so, what happened?"

"We spent twelve hours in Manhattan. From dusk until dawn."

"And?"

"It was one of the best nights of my life." We hear a light tap on the door.

"Who is it?" Marco asks angrily. Van opens the door.

"Your ten o'clock is here."

"What? How could it be ten o'clock already?" He looks at his iWatch, and true enough it's already five minutes to ten. "I hate this! I hate this suspense!" He pushes his chair backward noisily and gets up. "This is not over. We are going out to lunch to brainstorm our new project. Van, put that in the calendar."

"Yes, boss!" Van teases, and they both walk out of the room.

ॐ

I sit alone in the conference room with my coffee and stare into space. I don't know what to make of this coincidence. But God, he looks good. No, he looks better than good. He looks great. Perfect. He looks taller and healthier. Happy. Engaged.

Engaged. There is no destiny in this. This is a freak chance.

I didn't have the time to mourn losing him that night, because I had to mourn Tommy's death. That morning, I lost both the past and the present. But I see where I am now, and that fateful morning gave me this future. I shouldn't complain. There shouldn't be drama over this. There should be gratitude. Eric and I spoke about a lot of things that night. I knew in my heart that I needed to walk away from Tommy to set myself free.

It's been two years. I'm healing, getting there, braver,

prouder, and more confident. I'd been in the darkness for far too long with Tommy and I let it trap me when I knew I deserved sunshine and lightness and hope. I look around again, the crisp white walls of the office conference room, the humming of the fridge next to the door by the kitchen, and the buzzing of people out there making magic with their creativity—this is my reward. I feel tightness in my throat. I've not cried in more than a year, and I'm not going to start today.

Marco walks by the conference room with a group of people from the printing company. He gives me the look and leads the team to the meeting room next door. I get up, rinse my coffee cup in the sink, and head back to work.

When I reach my cubicle, I stop in my tracks. On top of my desk is the most beautiful flower arrangement of peonies and pink roses and a balloon attached to it that says *Happy Birthday*. Van is the best. She probably planned this for weeks, emailing the entire office for contributions. I run out to the reception area to give her a hug. As soon as I let her go, she hands me a dozen red roses and a box of my favorite cupcakes.

"There's more?" I ask her smiling while still holding her hand.

"What do you mean?" She looks confused.

"The flowers and the balloons on my desk, they are the most beautiful I've ever seen."

"Oh, those were not from the office. These are." Pointing at the cupcakes.

"Then who. . . ?"

"I didn't receive them." There is confusion written all over her face. "Carol covered for me when I ran to the bakery. Are they great? Let's go see them. I'm sure there's a card." Van pulls my arm and drags me back to my desk.

She gasps when she sees it.

"My goodness, Bianca. They are amazing!" There is real astonishment in her stare. The entire arrangement literally occupies my entire desk. "Let's see who's it from! C'mon!" she cajoles me, bumping her narrow hips to mine.

I see the card tucked on the side of the basket. It's shiny and pink, which matches the flowers and my desk's color pallet. I pull it out and I slowly open it.

"Happy Birthday, B. Fate is crafty, isn't it? It's so nice to see you again—E."

I'm speechless. I stand there staring at what Eric can bring me—not the material things, but the joy of his unpredictability.

This is what happiness feels like—the kind that hits you when you least expect it and hoists you to a new greatness from within. It's not fabricated or forced. It's honest. Raw. Real.

Chapter 20

"You're not making this up?" Marco asks as he scrutinizes me closely at lunch. I knew there was no way I could get out of it.

He pulled me from my desk twenty minutes ago as I was tracking Twitter chatter over our competition's new show to see how much traction it's getting from the audience demographics we're targeting. To be honest, I didn't mind the break, so I let him drag me out and into our favorite salad bar across the street. This place is packed today, and Marco and I had to squeeze in between two big dudes to get to the smallest table in the corner.

I shake my head in response and shove a fork-full of spinach and strawberry in my mouth.

"Do you think he likes you?" There is obvious disbelief in his expression. I don't feel offended. I'd react the same way.

"I don't think so." It's not important what I think. He is South Korea's most famous actor. He's so famous that the US market also wants a piece of him. Let's also not forget that he's engaged to a gorgeous celebrity.

"Are you sure?" I sense the wheels turning inside Marco's head. He's hot and cold on this one. "I mean, why would he spend twelve hours with someone he's not attracted to?"

"I was funny," I joke.

"Focus, Bianca." Marco eyes me sternly.

"We were strangers having a very open conversation. There were no judgments. It was freeing. I think we came out of it as friends." I don't tell Marco that the grand birthday gift on my desk was from Eric. I told him it was from my family in Jersey.

"Then why was he giving us—*you*—special treatment earlier?"

"Because what are the chances of us seeing each other again? We were friends, at least for that twelve hours."

"Are you attracted to him?"

"What kind of question is that? Look how hot he is. I'm just another fan, Marco. Dude, don't think too much of it. It's nothing."

"And now you're single. . . ." he whispers this as he stares into space above me.

"Ha! And he's engaged." I try to wake him up from this fantasy.

"Fine. Fine. Okay. This is not a romantic relationship?"

"Not at all. I'm sorry to burst your romantic bubble."

"But you earlier said it was the best night of your life?" He's still quizzing me.

"Yes. Because he was . . . is an awesome person. And he treated me like a human being. I was having a rough day, a rough year, and he lifted my spirit. He talked to me like we'd been friends for a long time. He was being honest, and I trusted him. He trusted me."

"Were there any juicy scoops?"

"I'm not going to tell you that. Geez, Marco."

I think this is the furthest and the safest place I can go with the truth. All I know is what I see and feel and think. I'm not privy to Eric's feelings. These are all from my side of the story.

"Are we going to tell Pam?"

I shrug at this. "It's not a big deal, but I'll find the time to tell her." I don't think I'm ready.

"It's kind of a big deal because he is a big deal, don't you think?" Marco points out sarcastically. "His latest drama ranks the top rating show in all of Asia, beating that zombie thriller of that other famous Korean actor." I've heard of it, but I decided not to see it. I made many excuses to Pam. She did see it because I heard her rave over it countless of times. But I was glad that, instead of watching it in the living room, she binged it from her iPad in her room.

"I guess." I don't want to say any more. The important bits I keep to myself.

"How do you want to celebrate today?"

"Oh, we did plenty of celebrating last night. I'm thirty-eight, not twenty-eight. I can't drink two nights in a row. I'll die. I'm actually surprised I don't have a pounding headache today after all that wine and vodka you guys made drink."

"Miguel was a party pooper the entire time, geez. He was blocking everyone from having a good time. Which reminds me, what are you going to do with that guy? God, he's so in love with you it's so painful to watch."

"Stop it. Miguel and I are not like that, and I've been telling you this the past two years."

"Whatever. Sure, pretend to be blind. Anyone within a five-mile radius can tell."

❧

The next day, Diana is extra pumped because of a complimentary email she received from Robbie. What's making Diana even more motivated is an apparent dinner invitation from Eric to meet with him once a week when he's in town. This means the location is probably not going to be in New York. I don't know anything about this project and, to be honest, I don't think I was meant to be part of this team. I just happened to be standing at the right place at the right time that morning.

"Washington, DC?" asks Marco. "I was thinking Pennsylvania, or Upstate." Well, that answers it.

"The story is in DC, but we're setting up a studio in Baltimore," Diana confirms. "That means you and Bianca will be heading to DC every few weeks. We have a hefty budget for this one, so money is not a concern."

"There goes our social life, Bianca."

"I went to William and Mary, so I'm familiar with DC. It'll be fun."

"Is it as fun as New York City?" He pouts at this.

"Not even close." I chuckle.

"People there are pretentious smarty pants. I might murder anyone who talks politics to me."

"No one will do that unless, of course, you start the conversation. DC people are very cliquey. They only talk to their own people. But we can still go to great bars and restaurants, and concerts and ballet and stuff like that," I explain.

"Ballet? Are you kidding me?" Marco exclaims. I laugh some more and strangely, Diana joins in albeit a little restrained. She's wearing big bold gold earrings today so she's a bit careful not to make big movements. They do look painful. Her earrings match her yellow pantsuit superbly, though. She is no more than maybe ten years older than me, and she looks really put together, in control, an adult.

"Okay. No ballet, I guess. We can go to museums."

"Do I look like someone who goes to museums?" I can see real despair—he's almost in tears.

"DC is not that bad. It's the power capital of the world." I reason.

"Whatever. Anyway, what else did this Eric say?" Marco rolls his eyes before finally changing the topic.

"He's inviting the team to dinner in his apartment in the city." Marco and I look at each other. "This is not uncommon," Diana affirms.

"I've never been invited to a main talent's house before, and I've been doing this job for more than eight years," Marco sarcastically interjects.

"Well, consider this the first of many. And stop complaining, will you? He says it's a casual dinner and just the four of us. I guess his fiancée doesn't come in until at a much later date."

That hits me hard in the middle of my chest. It hurts to hear it. I shake the feeling off.

"Is she moving here, too?" Marco is curious.

"I don't know that, and I honestly don't care. We just do our jobs and stay away from our client's private affairs as much as possible. In the meantime, Bianca, I want you to send me some ideas for social media strategies. Just a quick list. I don't care if it's outrageous, or bold, or out of this world. This endeavor is out of the box in itself, so explore and be creative but not controversial or tacky. Oh, and before I forget, here's the script of the first episode. Another thing, don't tell anyone about this until we get all our campaign ideas approved."

Marco and I nod and get up to leave. Marco's office is adjacent to my tiny cubicle, so we walk out together. Navigating this floor is second nature to me now. I like the open plan brightness and how everything flows toward the center of the floor, which we call the core creative space. Once a week we sit around there for our digital team meeting. It's one of my favorite spots, sitting on beanbags as I crank up on my social media planning.

"I didn't even know about this project until yesterday, and now it's all we need to focus on. Did you know about this?" I don't say anything. "Bianca Maria Curtis?"

"Kind of."

Marco stops walking, puts his hands on his hips, and looks at me like I've committed one of the seven deadly sins. I abruptly stop and turn around to face him.

"What?" I give him an angry glare in return.

"Spill, you bitch."

"He spoke to me about it two years ago. It was the reason he was in town to begin with, but I didn't know it's with CWS."

"This has been in the works for two years, and we're only finding out about it now?" Marco's theatrics are a constant fascination. I hope he doesn't stop. I laugh. I pull his arm to get him to start walking again.

To our surprise, Eric is waiting outside of Marco's office. Marco pulls his arm away from me. Eric sees us and waves. He smiles. You can feel the authenticity in it. It's how I remember them. His eyes sparkle in the most unguarded of moments.

"Hey, Mr. Park, what can I do for you?"

"Call me Eric." He shakes Marco's hand and bows at me. "I just want to drop by and see if Diana has informed you guys of my dinner invitation tomorrow night at my place."

"Yes, she did. We just came from her office."

"Are you guys coming?" He looks hopeful.

"Of course!" Marco responds with an exaggerated squeal.

"Bianca?"

"Yeah, I'll be there." I brush my hair off my face with my left finger.

He stops and stares at me in what appears to be shock. I return his gaze curiously.

"Did you forget your wedding ring again?" he asks softly. I stop cold. Coming from him, it stings. I put my hand behind my back instinctively.

"She's no longer married." Marco declares matter-of-factly.

"Oh." The look of surprise on his face is clear. I glance up at him from under my lashes, not knowing what to expect from this revelation, and when our eyes meet, there are questions.

"This lady right here is a single woman in New York City," Marco declares.

"Like Sarah Jessica Parker in *Sex and the City*?" Eric asks curiously.

"That's showing our age. We can say *Girls* instead," Marco offers.

"What's that?" Eric inquires. I don't think he's one to be following such programs.

"It's another television show about single girls in New York City," I say softly.

"Oh. Well. Do you guys want to grab a cup of coffee downstairs, maybe?" Eric looks at Marco and then right back at me.

"I'm busy," Marco says, "but Bianca here can spare half an hour."

"Are you sure? I have that thing that Diana was asking for."

"Well, who best to brainstorm than the person you are ghost-tweeting for?"

"That is a great idea, Marco," Eric chimes in.

❧

Eric effortlessly looks perfect. His hair, his skin, and everything else about him appear polished and refined. This is, of course, expected of a superstar. He's wearing khaki pants and a black, long-sleeved Balenciaga T-shirt with a plain black ball cap. I'm wearing black pants and a black top that has seen better days.

We are at opposite ends of the elevator. Neither of us says a word. It's been two years since we've been alone like this. The once casual banter, the comfortable teasing, and the laugh-out-loud moments—they're gone. Instead we are two awfully uncomfortable humans right now. There's a tight knot in my stomach.

"How long has it been? Almost two years, right?" He finally breaks the silence when we get in line for coffee at the lobby Starbucks.

"Yup. Shit, I forgot my wallet!" I exclaim and I hold his arm instinctively. I move it away immediately.

"You don't think I can buy you a cup of coffee?"

"Not that. I don't want to assume." I don't mean to upset him.

"Bianca, it's me, Eric." I smile at this. I remember this man. I was the most real with him. That is not lost to me. But two years ago, we were in a bubble. Things are different now.

We put in our orders. He pays. When we get our coffees, we make our way to the furthest booth in the corner by the window away from the crowd.

"How are you, Bianca?" He sits down and crosses his leg over the other with grace. He leans his back against the glass window and moves his head to stare at me.

"I'm fine. Everything's fine. How about you?" God, this is painful. We are more strangers now than when we first met.

"Good. You work in the city, which means you moved out of Jersey." I nod at this. "And you're not married anymore?" He doesn't let that one go. "Did you get a divorce recently?" There's a hint of bitterness in his voice. My marriage and how it ended is not something I'm particularly keen to talk about now or ever, but I suppose he needs answers.

"My husband died the morning I came back from the city that day . . . with you." Shock is written all over his face as I say this. There is silence between us. He stares at me with gentleness and sympathy, but I look away.

"God, Bianca, I'm so sorry." There is true grief in his voice. He reaches out from across the table to touch my arm, which presents unknown and frightening emotions I'm just not ready to explore. Having the same feelings for someone after almost two years of absence seems ridiculous to me, but I'm living it. My sentiments for this man are as fresh today as when I walked out on him that morning.

"Don't be." I see confusion on his face as I say this. "He died of drug overdose. He was sick, an addict." His face shows surprise but slowly transforms into understanding.

"I want to hug you right now," he whispers, and I smile at this. His nearness makes me want to indulge. Now I can. *But can he?*

"Don't pity me," I say as he looks at me with compassion. "It's been two years. I've moved on."

"I'm happy to hear that," he whispers.

This is the man I fell in love with two years ago during the lowest point of my life. I fell in love with him not because of his fame, but because in the quietest time of our friendship, he saw me and heard me and sincerely cared.

I tell him the details of that morning. It's starting to get fuzzy now, but I tell him the story as best I can, stripped of emotions. I no longer want to relive my moments of distress, my rage, and my guilt. When I finish, he's speechless. He sighs. His expression reflects the weight of that morning's tragedy.

"Bianca, I can't imagine what it must have been like to go through that pain. Death is devastating for those who are left behind."

"It's fine. I'm fine. I'm here. I'm doing well."

"I'm so sorry," he says again.

The sun is shining spectacularly outside. The entire lobby is flooded with rays of silver and gold. I lift my head up and welcome the heat it provides. I soak in it. I feel his fingers touch my cheek. I angle my face slightly toward his hand and I welcome the comfort. I'm in another one of those dreams.

"I hope this is the last time I talk about this." That part of my life exhausted me. I never want to relive it again. Eric is the last person who deserves to know this story. It should no longer be told. It ends here.

"Thank you for telling me. I wanted to know from the moment I saw you again what changed and today answers that."

"Did I change?"

"Yes. You look happy and healthy. Your eyes are smiling now too."

"Thanks. I aimed for that. I'm glad someone noticed."

"I noticed. It was the first thing I saw at the elevator." There is no denying the chemistry between us. My desire to touch him is potent, but this time I don't indulge. What I was the last time is what he is today—committed to someone else.

"Forget about me. How about you? Congratulations!" It has to be said and I'm curious how he would react to it.

"You told me to find love." There is disdain in his voice as he says this.

"And you did." I take a sip of my coffee and I turn around to look at the people milling about close to our table. The ladies may not know this famous actor across from me just yet, but I see their admiring glares. He lifts his eyes to look at them too and as if on cue he smiles, sending the giggling women their merry way. I shake my head at this, but I get it. Pam and I are one of them. The fans. "Do you ever get tired of it?"

"What do you mean?"

"You know, being famous," I tease. But then again, this probably comes second nature to him. He's lived this life for a long time now.

"It comes with the job. Are you jealous, Bianca?"

"Offended." I smirk at this and I lean back against the chair. "Does she feel this way, too?"

"No. She loves it. It's the air she breathes." He lowers his head in melancholy. "And we both know it isn't love. It was the easy thing to do. I proposed to her the night I came back to Seoul from being with you. I was angry and bold. It wasn't revenge, but it felt like it, and it gave me vindication."

I don't quite understand the anger that came from being with me. Was the revenge toward me? I search his eyes for answers. He doesn't cave in and looks at me head on.

"So many things have happened since that night." I exhale. I reach for his hand on top of the table and I stay there holding it. This confidence is empowering. He then moves the same hand over mine, and I let it stay there because it feels good, safe. I remind myself that he belongs to someone else now. I pull my hand away, but he doesn't let it go. Instead, we move in synchrony, our palms touch and our fingers intertwine. We stay like this for a while. Enjoying the motions and emotions our hands and fingers arouse as we stare at them. I can sense the nervousness and the thrill that pass between us.

"I tried to break off the engagement before I came here. I was hoping to see you again. It was wishful thinking. How could I wish this when I knew you were married?" I look up to him. Could it be that he too was thinking of me? "I thought about you every single day the past two years." There, he says it and my heart soars. "When I saw you at the elevator, I knew I should try harder.

We should. Now, it feels like its fate. Do you feel the same way?"

"There was not a single day that I didn't think about you, no matter how guilty I felt." It has to be said. I have to tell him my truth.

We both know there are implications to our confessions. The meaning, although still undecided, lingers—that we didn't truly disconnect, that there were still parts of us that stayed with each other that night, and that we still want that story to hold today. To talk of love seems irresponsible and illusory, but both our eyes speak it loud and clear. We stare at each other, looking for answers, expressing the truth of the past two years, and opening our hearts though words defy us. Then calm washes all my worries away.

He's not just a dream.

"Bianca?" I pull away from Eric's space, and I turn around to the sound of the anxious voice that spoke my name.

Miguel—carrying my gym bag and looking undeniably annoyed.

Chapter 21

"I forgot you were dropping by today," I stand up immediately to face Miguel. His annoyance turns to apprehension.

I'd left my gym bag in his apartment when he and I went for a run last week. I need it tonight.

"You weren't answering your phone, so I went up to your office and saw Marco. He said you're probably here. Is everything okay?" His eyes move from me to Eric then back to me. There is suspicion in his posture, and his desire to protect me is obvious. He's been in this role since before Tommy's death.

"Yes."

Eric is suddenly standing next to me. "Hi," he greets Miguel enthusiastically, "my name is Eric." He takes a step forward to offer his hand. Miguel still looks uneasy.

"I work with Eric," I explain. "He's also one of my good friends from the past." Eric tenses at the mention of the past. It makes it sound like the said friendship is over. But I also don't know why I need to explain this to Miguel. "Eric, this is Miguel, my friend from Jersey." Finally, Miguel takes Eric's hand. I sigh with relief.

"Dropping off your gym bag, which you left in my apartment last weekend, just as I promised." I don't know why he has to say that. "Anyway, I better get going. I'll call you later. Nice to meet you, Eric." He turns around and walks away.

"A jealous boyfriend?"

"An overly protective friend."

"Then why did you leave your gym bag in his apartment last

weekend? You know what, don't answer that. I'm sorry. I can't believe I just asked you that. I'm sorry." Uncertainty is apparent in his stance. It is so unlike him. He looks away from me like a nervous young man. I smile at this. *Is he jealous?*

"It's fine. How about we just finish this coffee?" I sit back down and slowly sip from my cup, and he does the same. We look at each other with an expression that is fraught with meaning. For some reason, fate thinks it's funny to put us right here, right now, without a plan. Again.

"God, it's great to see you," he says after minutes of silence. His eyes are steady, only on me, and I know beyond a shadow of doubt that I love him. Still.

❧

In a screwed-up way, pieces of this thing I have with Eric are now revealed to my friends. Marco is aware of the twelve hours Eric and I spent in Manhattan two years ago, and Miguel has seen us holding hands. What part do I introduce to Pam? That's another snag here. I bow my head and I hit it hard twice on my desk with loud thuds.

"Miguel saw you, didn't he?" I hear Marco from inside his office. Everyone is at lunch so our little space is empty. "Were you doing something inappropriate?"

"Stop!"

"Were you?"

"No. Yes. I don't know." Marco gets up from his desk, walks toward me, and leans over my tiny cubicle. I can sense his intense glare at the back of my head—I can also sense suspicion.

"You lied to me. There was more to it than you think, wasn't there?"

I lift my head back up to face him. He narrows his eyes in his attempt to start the interrogation.

"I don't know, but for some reason we ended up holding hands, and then Miguel walked in."

"So fucking what? It's not like Miguel is your boyfriend. But wait? Why were you holding hands?" His eyes widen with this realization.

"I told him about Tommy. I was feeling sad, and he wanted to be there for me. He told me about his thing, and I wanted to be there for him. So we touched." I lean my forehead on my desk again. Marco pulls my hair to get me to face him.

"What is that *thing* he told you?" He's still holding onto my hair to keep me upright.

"Stop!" I protest. He finally lets go of my hair, and I slump back against my chair.

"Look, I think there is some attraction there. Either you're lying to me, or you don't want to make assumptions. But I saw it on the first day. The look he gives you is beyond friendly, and I'm pretty sure you see it too."

"I don't know. God, this is complicated."

"Why?"

"Because he's engaged. Or I think he still is. I don't know." I look at him in confusion.

"Shit, right. I forgot about that."

Marco's eyes shoot upward, and I can tell he's analyzing this information in his head.

"This has to stop right here, right now. I might not even go to dinner tomorrow," I say.

"Well, that's silly. Tomorrow is work. You have to go." He's glaring at me now.

"Fine. But you have to protect me. Or stop me or something."

I wish I could articulate how distressing this is without sounding like a delusional fan.

"Diana is there. She'll do that for all of you—dampen the mood." And right on cue, Diana walks in with a big box full of binders. She walks straight to my desk and dumps the box on top of it.

"Are you done with that thing I asked you to do?" I hand her a clear file folder with three pages of ideas for a social media campaign. It was the first thing I did as soon as I came back from my disconcerting coffee with Eric, and it helped clear my head. She opens the folder and flips through the pages. She doesn't say anything, so Marco and I stare at her and wait.

"Fine. Sort out that box of old campaigns we worked on so you can familiarize yourself with them. You need to learn fast. I don't think you're ready to take on our biggest budget project, but they asked for you, so there. If you screw up . . . well this is a high-prolife campaign, so please don't screw up." She turns around and walks away. She is the most peculiar human being on the planet. Her navy blue Valentino shoes are amazing though.

"Don't turn out to be like her, okay? No matter how messed up your love life gets." Marco points at Diana's retreating figure and rolls his eyes in annoyance.

꙳

I asked—no begged—Marco not to mention anything to Pam about Eric. Not even about the work dinner that we were invited to. I need to find a way to tell her myself. I need to tell her everything. Everything. Yeah, I'm not looking forward to this at all.

I jump into the bath as soon as I get home. It's Friday, and I need a few hours to calm down before I head back out to go to

Eric's dinner. I've been jittery and out of sorts the entire day. My phone is in my bedroom. I'm alone in the dark with two aromatherapy candles flickering softly, creating calming shadows in this tiny space as a luxurious bath bomb sizzles in the tub. I close my eyes and let the silence wash the toxins of the day away.

I've not seen Eric since we held hands yesterday, and I've been sick to my stomach with nerves. I don't know what to expect tonight. *We're friends.* We're not anything more than that. To think any differently would be reckless. I can see no future, from whichever angle I look. I live in New York City, and he lives in Seoul. Sure, he's here now, but I know that's temporary. Let's also not forget the significant fact that he is South Korea's national treasure. A celebrity. There's also the other not so minor detail that he's probably still engaged to his longtime girlfriend, and all of Asia, if not the world, knows about it.

"Honey, I'm home!" Pam calls from the living room. *Here we go.*

"I'm in the bath," I shout back. She shoves the bathroom door wide open and sits on the toilet.

"I've been calling you," she exclaims with an obvious pout.

"My phone's in my room, sorry," I whisper, trying not to disturb the calm atmosphere. The sequenced drip of the water from the bath faucet is the only sound we hear.

"Oh, that smells divine," she says, inhaling the luxurious flower scent. "What's the plan for tonight?" she asks while mindlessly scrolling through her phone. Pam is big on Twitter and Instagram, with followers reaching around one hundred thousand on each platform.

"We have a work dinner tonight. Didn't Marco tell you?" I lather the silky suds on my arm, trying to act calm and natural, like I don't have a big secret to reveal in a few seconds. My apprehension is slowly overriding my peace.

"No, that stupid bitch!" She lifts up her eyes from her phone to look at me.

"I need to tell you something but promise me not to flip your shit." I look at her intently, waiting for her to agree. She nods her head twice looking skeptical.

"Fine," she finally answers.

"We're going to dinner at Park Hyun Min's apartment." I brace myself for her reaction, sitting at attention in the bubble-filled tub and still making sure I'm modestly covered.

There is a long pause. I'm holding my breath.

"What do you mean, Park Hyun Min?" I let her figure it out. I wait some more. "Like Hyun Min the actor?" She gawks at me as if what I just said was the most absurd thing she's ever heard.

"Yes. But we're not allowed to say anything to anyone at this time because of contract clauses." I speak slowly and clearly as if addressing kindergarten students on life-saving measures. I wait again.

"Are you shitting me?"

I finally exhale. I don't really understand what that means, but I don't say anything. She jolts up, stamping her feet in place as if preparing to march into battle. Her eyes are on fire, and they are directed at me.

Pam is not just a K-drama fan; Pam is a Park Hyun Min fan. She stalks him on social media, reads every news story about him, and has his photo as a screen saver on her office computer. All this started more than two years ago when she—or we—got into the whole *Oasis* craze. Her infatuation with him is so intense that she even started planning a trip to Seoul at one point. It's the reason why I couldn't just tell her the truth. She starts pacing back and forth in our tiny bathroom. She stops, turns around, looks at me, and starts all over again.

Again, I wait until she has fully processed the extent of what I just told her. And I wish I can stop here. Obviously, there is more to say, which I'm not totally keen on doing.

"When were you planning to tell me?" She looks irritated.

"Now?" I don't know what else to say. "You do understand the work we're in, right? We can get sued if someone finds out I actually told you about him. You know that, right?" Although she's nodding her head in understanding, it's quite obvious that I'll never hear the end of this. "And there's more." I close my eyes and I take a deep breath.

"More? What else can be more shocking that this!" She throws both her hands up to emphasize the ridiculousness of this news.

"I met Hyun Min two years ago. Here in Manhattan. We be-came friends." Even I can't grasp the sense of what I just said. If I were receiving this news rather than delivering it, I'd say I was full of crap.

"What *the fuck* are you talking about?" This time, Pam takes a step backward and shows genuine hurt in her eyes. "And you're telling me just now?"

This is totally on me. I should have said something sooner—but I wanted to forget about Eric and telling people about our encounter, how I felt, would not help me move on. I mean, seri-ously, what are the chances that we would ever see each other again after all this time?

"I met him the night before Tommy died, and you know things got crazy after that." Thankfully, after a full minute of si-lence, the shock on her face turns into understanding. I'm re-lieved. She had been witness to all of the events of that day and the weeks that followed. "We became friends but we didn't keep in touch until I saw him at work again a few days ago. Funny, right?" I try to joke about it. I'm not ready to tell her more.

❧

Pam follows me around the apartment as I get ready for dinner. She's either biting her nails or twirling her hair with her finger. She's clearly in an anxious mood. I reach for my black dress from the closet and pull it over my head carelessly. It's my go-to dress, which is not too fancy and not too casual either. It's just right. It's a little snug on my chest, but it A-lines from my waist to my knees so it's comfy enough. It's safe. I'll probably end up walking tonight, so I settle on my black flats with rhinestones. I let my hair down.

"Let me straighten your hair and style it a little," Pam offers. My hair has a life of its own, that's for sure, so I sit down at my dresser and let Pam do her magic. She sections my hair into four pieces and works on each one. The end product is lovely and I don't normally use that adjective to describe myself. I look like I'm attending the Oscars. Okay, fine, maybe just the SAG awards. She parts my hair to one side and places a crystal encrusted hair clip on it.

"Should we also do your makeup?"

"Nah, my hair is already the highlight of my look. Thanks so much, Pammy!" I touch my hair and it bounces right back like in one of those shampoo commercials.

"You're having dinner with Hyun Min. The least you can do is dab on a little lip gloss."

"Fine, that I can do." Again, I let Pam play with my face.

❧

I'm a nervous wreck as I sit fretfully inside my Uber on my way to Eric's apartment. I don't feel prepared. I hold on to my black bag tightly. My palms are starting to sweat, and I feel a light tingle in my fingers and toes. I close my eyes and I take a calming breath, but it doesn't work.

I get out of the car a few minutes later and stand in front of the building feeling slightly nauseated. This is a work dinner, I remind myself, and I walk right in. I declare myself to the door-man who, after talking to Eric, escorts me toward the elevator with enthusiasm.

"Have a good evening, now, miss," the doorman says as he punches the *P* button inside the car. This is not a date. Marco and Diana are going to be in the same room. This is part of my job, and it has nothing to do with our encounter of two years ago. I clasp my hands together in front of me. When the elevator door opens, Eric is waiting. His eyes sparkle like stars in my dark blue sky. I shake my head and try to erase the poetic image in it.

"Welcome to Chez Park." He smiles widely. Standing on one side of the door, his arm is outstretched across the other side with his hand resting on the doorframe as if blocking my entrance. There is no denying his current mood—chill and relaxed, and a little cocky. He's wearing a pair of tight blue jeans, a cashmere sweater, and shoes. I wondered about that earlier, whether he would impose a Korean no-shoes policy in his apartment. I had put a fresh coat of nail polish on my toes, just in case. He doesn't move when I walk toward him. He lets me stand there, mere inches away, looking at my mouth. Instinctively, I bite my lower lip. He leans forward and releases an admiring sigh.

"Eric," I say sternly but quietly, just in case Marco and Diana are already in the apartment and can hear us. He sighs again, this time in frustration, and makes way for me to enter the apartment. He smells good. Exactly how I remember, Chanel Homme.

A big foyer welcomes me as I step in. Farther down the room is the perfect view of the Empire State Building, seen through the floor-to-ceiling windows that line the living room. It's mesmerizing, and it instantly draws me in. The living room is a massive space pulled together by a majestic, vintage chandelier dangling from a high-vaulted ceiling.

Diana and Marco are standing at the corner by the piano. I can tell from Marco's hand gestures that they are talking about the intricately-designed chandelier. It's like one of those you find in old English castles. Iron. Old. Rustic.

"Most of my things will arrive next week," Eric says. It's then I notice that, apart from basic furnishings, the apartment is bare. There is nothing in the room that speaks of him. "Let me get your coat," he says, moving behind me to help me out of it.

"Thank you," I mutter. Marco sees me, gives me a wide-eyed thank-god-you're-here look, and walks toward me. Diana remains standing by the piano, looking fabulous in an elegant red, white, and black block sheath dress. Her face is expertly painted in nudes, and her hair is brushed with wet gel. There is no casual day where Diana is concerned. Every day is runway day. I smile at this.

"Hi, Diana." I put up my hand for a small wave and I see a little curve on her lips. It looks like a smile. I'll take it. She takes small steps, taking her time, and finally joins in. The three of us regard her in anticipation.

"Bianca." The coldness as she says my name gives me chills. Marco rolls his eyes at this. I pretend to shiver a little.

"How's Pamela doing? Did you tell her about what we discussed earlier?" Curious George Marco here just couldn't wait, so I nod at him without volunteering any information and then lightly shake my head.

"Red wine," Eric offers as he walks toward me with one hand in his pocket. The vision of him walking down the hall is like watching fashion week live. Marco and I look at each other, breathless.

"Sure," I say. "Sorry, I'm late."

"You're not late," Eric replies. "It's two minutes before eight, which in truth is a little early."

"Did you Uber over?" Marco asks and sips on what looks like a vodka tonic.

"Yeah. I wanted to walk, but it's a bit blustery outside."

"I should have offered to pick you up. My apologies."

"No. It's fine. You didn't need to do that." I instinctively put my hand on his arm, then pull it away immediately. He smiles at this.

Eric hands me an empty glass, which I take.

"It's the same one," he murmurs. He shows me a bottle of the wine we had the night we met. Eric pours the red liquid into my glass with grace and turns the bottle lightly as soon as it reaches the perfect fill.

Marco and Diana take a seat on one of the large sofas in the middle of the room. I sit across from Marco.

"My apartment is not a home yet. My apologies. We didn't plan this well. We weren't sure it was going to happen until the last minute."

"Oh? How so?" Diana asks.

"This project has been on the table for some time now—about two years. And logistically, it's a big thing to plan. Then I had two movies the past two years and a television series in

South Korea, so Robbie agreed to put it on hold for a while. Two months ago, I sent them a green light, so here we are."

"What was the reason for the green light?" Marco asks, crossing his leg over his thigh and leaning his body forward toward Eric. I'm glad he's asking all these questions for me, and we didn't even plan it.

"It's time. Two years is long enough." He gives me a sideward glance. There is meaning in it, but what, I'm not entirely sure.

"Are you excited to do this project?" Marco eyes Eric with genuine interest.

"Absolutely." The gleam in his expression shows when he's truly enthusiastic about something. It's one of the many beautiful things I remember about him—his ability to share his brightness. Marco shifts his position and looks at me as if there's a secret message he's sending out.

Grabbing his beer from the side table, Eric sits next to me on the couch and stretches his arm on the backrest behind me. I don't lean back for fear that it will look, at least to these two across from us, like we're too friendly. I sit still and stiff. He then crosses one leg over the other toward me.

"So, Eric, tell us what you want from the team here?" Diana turns businesslike, clasping her hands together as she asks this; her gold earrings dangle heavily with her movement.

"I just want to get to know the people who will protect my image. My life is very private. I keep it separate from work. My job is acting, but I'm not in it for the fame." Marco nods his head thoughtfully.

"That may be a bit hard considering you have a huge American fan base. We've done some analysis on this recently."

I look at Marco inquisitively and he shakes his head. This is the first I've heard of this. Eric takes a sip of his drink, and so do I.

"Bianca, what do you think?" he asks. I turn my head slightly to look at Marco and Diana. Marco nods, encouraging me to speak up.

"Go ahead." Diana says.

"I think. . . ." I start uneasily, "this can be achieved if we pretend that you're actually handling your own accounts. We must show your personality and the things that you're interested in. You should post on your accounts from time to time. Show them you're holding your phone and not have someone take the video for you. You should take a few selfies. People love that. It makes it personal. Like they are part of your life. And so, if you have a plan for what your life should look like, we can work on keeping your private life private."

"Brilliant." Eric places his bottle on the coffee table and claps his hands once. I think he's overdoing it. "I like this idea. Now I understand why my team kept asking me to take selfies." He booms with laugher. The expression on Diana's face is priceless, and I can guarantee that this brilliance will cost me something—my dignity, perhaps, as she screams at me on Monday for contradicting her.

"Also, we shouldn't keep your followers waiting. We should post something a few times a week. Obviously, it would be out of character for you to post every few hours. That could hurt your brand."

"Ah, the brand. What is my brand? Do you guys know? Because I sure don't."

"You're more an action superstar than a romantic comedy actor. But we know you're also versatile because your last movie that smashed the Asian box office is a romantic comedy. We have to decide which side of you we leverage here. Your brand is the action star. That's why the girls go wild when they see you fall in love every now and then in your movies." As Marco continues his analysis, I ignore Diana's reaction.

"Diana, these two can run the world! You have an amazing team here."

"We've chosen the best to take care of you," she replies. I see Marco roll his eyes again. Eric sees it too.

"Are there red flags in your life that you want to keep out of the spotlight? Your engagement? Or is this something we should highlight." I don't know if Marco is fishing with this line of questioning.

"Yeah. That's a red flag." He pulls his arm from behind me and slides forward and rests his elbows on his knees. I lean forward with him and so does Marco. "I broke off the engagement two weeks ago, but she's not buying it. I don't want that anywhere near the public eye. My ex-fiancée is going to try. She thinks her life is for public consumption and I don't want us to fall into her trap."

"Is there a reason behind the breakup that we should be aware of? In case we get some weird trolls on this?" Marco is on a roll, and I love it.

"Love. Someone once told me that I should find love. And it's definitely not with her."

Chapter 22

Dinner is art in its truest form. Robbie sent Eric one of the network's celebrity chiefs to prepare tonight's meal. The scallops are the stars of the night; each one delicately melts in your mouth and slowly explodes in a variety of delightful flavors. I'm not a foodie, but Pam is, and I tag along with her sometimes to try the latest restaurants in town for some gastronomical adventure. It's usually pretty impressive. New York City always tries to outdo itself. The nature of its ever-evolving identity, the beauty of its constant need for change, and the brash tendency to make everything bigger and better and bolder—this is what New York City is all about, and its food scene proves it. New York City on food is in full exhibition here tonight.

"This is the most exquisite meal, Eric. Thank you," Diana says formally. Eric bows his head in acknowledgment. Marco, sitting right across from me, just plows into the lobster pasta with fervor. I can't help but laugh at this.

"Stop," he warns me.

"You're just the cutest when you enjoy your food, which is very rare. This is a great compliment to the chef." I tease Marco some more.

"I'm glad, and I'll let Idris know. More wine, Bianca? I have a case of it." I almost choke as I hear this.

"Sure," I say.

"It's her favorite," he tells the group, and I can feel my face heat up. Diana raises an eyebrow at this. Marco widens his eyes and turns to look at her. "I remember you mentioned it in passing as we were drafting the list of my dos and don'ts a few days ago." That's a good save. "It's one of my favorites too. I think it's brilliant that my social media person shares my good taste in wine." An even better save.

"True," Marco adds.

If you think about it, there's really nothing to hide here. We met in the past, and I don't think it's that big of a deal. I get it, he's like a god, and obviously I am no one, so to even acknowledge that we knew each other previously would probably require an elaborate explanation, which I'd rather forgo.

"I suppose we also need to monitor Suzi's social media platforms, Bianca," Diana recommends, and I nod at her although I'd really rather not. It feels like stalking the competition. What am I even thinking?

"It's not necessary." I can feel him trying to gauge my reaction to this. But I have to be professional. It's a necessary task no matter how painful.

"I agree. We need to monitor Suzi's platforms. That way we can either go a different direction or jump on it," Marco adds.

"Is she planning to come to New York at some point? I think it's smart to know in advance so Marco and Bianca can manage it."

"Not that I'm aware of. We left everything pretty much broken. I don't think it's anything we need to talk about." That sounds certain. Final. Are we really both single tonight? Right this minute? At this very phase of our lives? I give him a sideward glance.

A phone beeps loudly. We all look at the living room where the noise is coming from. Diana gets up and rushes to grab her purse, pulls out her phone, and scrolls through it. Her expression changes.

"Fuck!" she says out loud and stumps her foot.

"Everything okay?" The three of us ask at the same time.

"A sex video of Arthur just surfaced on the web ten minutes ago. What an idiot! Who still does sex videos these days? I have to go to the office. His publicity team is heading there in twenty minutes. I need to be there too. So sorry about this, Eric."

"No. No. It's quite all right. Good to know that when my sex video surfaces online, I'm in perfectly good hands."

I slowly turn my head to look at him with an expression of disbelief on my face.

"Funny." Marco replies.

"Just for the record, as far as I'm aware, I don't have one." He's trying to make a comeback from this joke.

"Ha. As far as you're aware?" I sarcastically point out. I don't know why I reacted as such. I shouldn't give a damn if he has sex videos floating around the Internet every few weeks.

Diana gathers her things from the leather sofa and heads to the closet where Eric pulls out her coat from the hanger and helps her into it. She's huffing and puffing as she walks out the door.

"Coffee anyone?" Our host offers. Marco raises his hand. "And who is Arthur?"

"He's a comedian in one of our sitcoms. And he's trouble. He's always in the news, always in a pickle. He's Diana's biggest headache—actually, the network's—but he's raking in so much money they can't cut him out," Marco explains.

"Oh, Arthur of the show *Arthur*? I love him!" Eric says.

"Exactly. You are his demographic."

"But he's like what, almost in his sixties, right?"

"Yup! Sex, drugs, and rock 'n' roll. Never got out of that era. What a douche!" Marco adds.

"Bianca, coffee?"

"Nah. I'd stay up all night if I do."

"That's not too bad. It's a Friday night."

"I don't party anymore."

"Except the other night when we welcomed your birthday, and you didn't even get a hangover." Marco offers.

"That was actually a freak moment because I always get a hangover. Always. I was so excited to get older that I even went to work early the next day, and I was fine." I laugh at myself.

"Marco, you want to come with me to the kitchen so you can play with the coffee machine? Unless, of course, you only want plain black brew."

"Nah, I'll get it."

I get up from the dining table and walk around the room. I stop and stand by the window to look at the sparkles coming from the Empire State Building. And as I look at it again, I think of all the love stories written around it. Mine is one of them now too. No one can take that away from me—and I don't give a damn if it was a one-way love affair. A girl can have her fantasy. I stand there and stare.

"Freedom was what you asked for when we were there to-gether the last time. I didn't know what it meant until you left that morning." I turn around to see Eric staring at me. Marco is still in the kitchen. We are alone again. "Are you finally free, B?" I don't answer. Instead, I turn right back to face the beautiful city I now call home. The flicker of the lights down below ignites nostalgic sparks within me, reminding me that I was once young and feisty and brave. I'm slowly rebuilding her. There is nothing and no one holding me back anymore. I am mine. If that is freedom, then I suppose I'm free, so I nod my head without looking at him. I'm reaffirming this to the universe out there as well, inviting them to see me as the person I've become.

"I'm glad," he says. I sense him walking toward me, and he stops close enough for me to inhale his scent. The shadow he creates around me is comfort that I can't explain, a shield that protects me. He had been that for me two years ago for twelve beautiful hours.

We stand together in silence in the darkness. The subdued glow in his apartment makes the lights outside the city seem more enchanting.

"I've missed you."

"How is that possible? You don't even know me," I say, but my heart is pounding because I've asked myself the same question. How can I miss someone I barely know?

"But I do. You never really left me." I sense him taking another step closer. I feel his chest behind me, and I lean back against it. His chin is on top of my head just like the last time. He puts his arms around me and rests them just below my chin. I let myself go and exhale. In his arms, I relax. We stay like this for a while.

"I have to go. Sorry, guys. I have an emergency!" Marco says this from behind us, and I know he's lying. Eric and I break apart immediately, both of us turning red. When we look at Marco, he's already closing the door behind him.

⁊⌒

"Another drink?"

"I have to leave." I don't look at him as I say this.

"Is that Miguel your boyfriend?"

"No," I whisper, shaking my head as I walk to the living room to gather my things.

"Finding each other after all those years must mean something, right? We didn't force anything." I know this to be true. I even stopped watching his dramas so I could avoid aching for him. I slowly make my way to the coat closet, and he doesn't try to stop me. He's not asking me to stay, but why am I having a difficult time walking away? I turn around to look at him. There is pain in his eyes. He may be a great actor, but I know his truth. I know him.

"Are you running out of reasons?" he asks in a whisper, pleading for a chance. "All you have to do is stay. I don't expect anything more than that."

But I might, and it might break my thriving heart. I close my eyes and run the rationale through my head. My heart is winning. When I open my eyes, he's still standing there with his side-swept hair, big brown eyes, and soft lips hypnotizing me. Silently pleading.

"Fine. Fuck it." I run toward him and leap, putting my arms around his neck and my legs around his hips. I see his face break into a beautiful smile as he catches me with his big sturdy arms.

"That's the girl I know and love." I bury my face on his neck, his scent overpowering my senses. He holds me tight, kissing me on the side of my head. He finally lets me slide down, both my feet reaching the floor, and he looks into my eyes, searching for more, asking for me. Instead of enduring this push and pull between us, I stand on tiptoes and I touch his lips with mine. *God, it feels good.* He is taken aback by this and pulls away. "Are you sure?"

"Aren't you?" I giggle like a teenager.

"I've been sure for two years." And with this, he grabs me and plants his lips on mine with unrestrained passion. I join him. I've never felt this much force in my very core before, my lust is something utterly new to me, and touching him is almost like breathing. I open my mouth to welcome his tongue, to let him know that I say yes to him with my body. The desire between us is overwhelming. I want to soar, and be free, and jump into this with all of myself, because I goddamn well deserve it. I feel his hands pushing me deeper into him from behind and I oblige, and as I do, I kiss him with such intensity that my senses are heightened to full tilt. It's insane how much detail I see and feel as our bodies collide like this. Finally, we break apart, both out of breath. He holds my hand tight and I can tell that he's afraid to let go. I'm all in now. There is no turning back.

"Where's the bedroom?" I boldly ask. His mouth breaks into a charming smile—it is slow and light and beautiful—and he is mine . . . at least, for tonight. He pulls me gently and leads me to the second floor of his penthouse apartment.

❧

I am brave. Bold. It's been more than a decade since I've been this confident. I like this person. As soon as I hear Eric close the door shut, I pull my black dress over my head. He laughs as he watches me. I stumble a little, trying to get out of it.

"Stop laughing! I'm trying to be sexy here." I squint my eyes and give him a stern warning.

"You don't need to try." He laughs some more and crosses his arms over his chest.

"Well, we waited two years for this, so we might as well get on with it! Come here!" I joke and jump backward in my bra and undies onto his enticing California king bed with gray satin sheets. They are the softest sheets I've ever touched in my entire life.

"Yes, we've waited two long years for this, so we don't need to rush it. We have to experience it and explore it slowly and carefully and wonderfully." He sits next to me on the bed and leans back on one elbow with his body toward mine. I curl onto my side. My boldness disappears as I look into his brown eyes, almost the same color as mine.

"I've missed you." I trace my index finger along his face, from his eyebrow down the curve of his soft lips. He closes his eyes. I edge upward to kiss him lightly. How many times have I imagined doing this in the past two years? He opens his eyes as he receives me. We stare at each other as we kiss. We don't want to miss out on this moment. He lightly bites my lower lip, and my body shivers. He pulls me toward him, and I put my arms around his neck and link my bare leg onto his. He grabs my behind and pushes me toward him. We still don't close our eyes. We watch each other as this fiery moment unfolds. We're taking this and doing it wide awake and head on. I unbutton his shirt as we continue to kiss, and as I pull it off him, we quickly move under the covers. He removes the rest of his clothes and is immediately on top of me. I can sense his elation, his joy. He touches my hair and brushes it off my face with his fingers—lovingly, adoringly, and perfectly.

"I've missed you more than you'll ever know. And I've fantasized seeing you somewhere, anywhere. I've practiced what I'd say to you in my head over and over. It was shameful for a man like me, as old as me, to have such playful fantasies about a woman I spent twelve short hours with in Manhattan. But I did that. And now you're here, and I've found it. In you."

"What? Did you find?" I ask coyly.

"Love." As soon as he says this, I pull him closer to me. Our kiss is deeper, more forceful, yearning. He reaches for something on the side table and manages to put on protection while I bury my lips in his neck. Before I know it, we are one.

"Eric. . . ." I whisper in both shock and rapture. The feeling is much more powerful than I could ever imagine. We move in one direction with both our eyes wide open, looking into each other, taking it all in and engraving it on our memories.

"Bianca. . . ." he whispers. I arch backward and I feel him in full force, and I scream because I have him and I make it there with him. Seconds later, he joins me in ecstasy. I pull his face close to mine—we are both out of breath—and I stare into this man's eyes, and I know that what I feel is love in its truest form.

"I love you," I say.

"And I, you."

Chapter 23

*L*ove is patient. Love waits. The cynic in me wants to brush those fantastical notions aside. But it's here, staring me in the face. We are in bed, side by side, gazing into each other's eyes. He looks younger with his disheveled hair. His smile is unguarded. I touch his lips with my finger lightly, and I smile right back because he is with me again after two long painful years, and although it may only be for another twelve hours again, at least those hours are mine.

He links his fingers with mine. He raises our hands up in the air where we can both see how perfectly they fit together. His fingers are long and delicate; mine are short and stocky. I start laughing at this.

"What?" he complains.

"I'm not making fun of your popularity or fame or whatever, but compare your fingers to mine. Yours are impeccable. Mine are like, I don't know . . . not impeccable." We both laugh at this. "Is there like someone who goes to your house and does all these luxurious things to you?"

"Yeah. Well, in the beginning it irritated me, you know because it's not manly, but my manager insists that I do it. Then I got used to it, and it relaxes me. It's a pause where I can actually read books."

"Do you like reading?" The thought pleases me.

"Yes. I'm a nerd. I read everything."

"Wow. I'm impressed."

"Did you think I'm shallow just because I'm an actor?" Although he's teasing, I can tell that this hurts him.

"Not at all."

"Well, you always tease me about being a celebrity." He plays with our fingers as he says this.

"Stop. I didn't mean it like that." I pull myself up to plant a kiss on his forehead.

"How about you? What do you like to do?

"I love movies."

"What's the latest Korean drama you've seen?" he asks.

"I stopped watching." I bend my head to avoid his eyes.

"What? Why? Is it because of me? Man, I was hoping you were watching me in *Happy Ever After*. It's a romantic comedy, which isn't really my style, but I did it for you."

"What do you mean?"

"I improvised some lines to remind you of our night together."

"You did?" This fills my heart with love. "And the director let you?"

"Well, I had to justify all the changes, but yes." This is the weirdest, most surreal, yet the sweetest thing I've ever heard. He pulls me closer. Our faces are now just inches apart.

"OK. I'll watch it. I'll watch it with Pam." I put my arms around his neck and pull his face down for a quick kiss.

"Should I meet your friend Pam?"

"Oh, my god, yes!" I start kissing him all over his face, little, tiny pecks. He begins to laugh, and it brings light into my world. The past two years, I have learned to kindle the ember, but his nearness—he himself—ignites the fire within my soul. The chemistry between us is not something I've felt before. It's potent. It's wild. I don't think I've connected with anyone this quickly or this strongly.

"Okay, let's do that before we move to DC."

⁊◌

District of Columbia. I almost forgot about that until Eric reminded me last night. That means he's not settling in New York after all, and our time together will be constrained by his schedule there. Sure, I can go visit every now and again—especially since I have a great excuse, work—but still.

I turn the knob of our apartment door and walk in as quietly as I can. To my surprise, however, Pam is waiting for me at the kitchen counter with her hand on her hip. I don't even know how to explain this. I don't know where to begin.

"You spent the night with him, didn't you?" This question stops me in my tracks "You are fucking beaming like a glow stick, so please don't deny it," she hisses. Yes, like a snake—an angry one.

"Do you honestly think that a woman like me can get a man like him?"

"Well, you did, so stop denying it. Didn't you?" Her eyes are burning with rage. In her pink robe and a pink scrunchy holding her blond hair in a bun on top of her head, Pam looks like a furious teenager.

"I don't know how to explain it." I sigh in frustration. I want Pam to be part of this, but I didn't have the chance then, and I can't find the time now.

"Did you have an affair with him two years ago?" Her eyes widen and she drops her coffee mug on the kitchen counter with a loud bang. "Did you!"

"No!"

"Then what?"

"I walked away from him then. I told him I was married." I go to the living room and plop down to the sofa with Pam's glaring eyes still on me. "It was one of the biggest regrets of my life until last night."

"Did you sleep with him?" She strides toward me and shakes me.

"Yes!" She stops and puts her hand over her mouth in utter shock.

"Eek!" she screams like a madwoman, and then starts laughing. I back up and stare at her in confusion.

"What the hell is going on here?" I ask.

"Do you remember the nights we both wondered who the lucky girl Park Hyun Min was screwing? And that she probably was the luckiest woman alive on the face of the earth? Remember?" Now there's excitement in her tone.

"Yes."

"You were that girl last night, bitch!" She slaps my forearm hard, playfully.

"I guess. . . ."

"Don't be fucking coy with me!"

"Yes!" And I giggle. Pam grabs the decorative pillow next to her and starts whacking me on the shoulder.

"I can't believe this is happening to you! I can't believe this!" She continues hitting me hard. "You know what, you deserve it. Own it!"

"I will."

"And don't let drama get in the way, okay. I saw you with Glen and then with Tommy. Let this be calm and drama free."

"Drama follows me everywhere."

"Not the last two years."

"True."

To my surprise, my bedroom door suddenly opens, and it's Marco. So this is where he went last night. He's wearing a pair of my favorite baggy sweatpants and "I Heart New York City" T-shirt under my fluffy blue cardigan. He's rubbing his eyes with his hand as he sits down next to me.

"Is it all and everything you've ever dreamed about?" he asks hoarsely and rests his head on my shoulder with his eyes closed. "Pam and I stayed up late waiting for you last night. That sight, phew, I tell you, Pam. It's like a scene from a movie. You should be an actress too." I push his head off my shoulder lightly. "But it's true." Well, it is kind of true. "You should have seen it, Pam. It was like the K-dramas we watch. Were you guys crying? I was so uncomfortable, I had to flee."

"No, we were not crying . . . geez."

"Bianca, let's be clear. This should be a fun fuck, okay." Pam stares straight into my eyes for an answer, but I can't do that anymore.

"I think I'm in love with him. . . ."

"You are nuts!" Pam shouts. Marco also pulls away immediately and stares down at me. "Binky, listen to me. You don't fall in love with someone in one night. That's make-believe."

"Are you sure?"

"I'm goddamn sure. There is no possible way this is love. No way."

"Fine. Do you want to watch *Happy Ever After* with me this weekend?" I see her eyes light up.

"I thought you'd never ask."

❧

I'm in a bubble—similar to the one I was in two years ago. I'm ecstatic beyond measure, but at the same time, I'm anxious that all this will be taken away from me in a blink of an eye. I'm in my room, staring at the ceiling, trying to gauge the consequences of last night. Pam went straight back to bed, and Marco took the couch and fell asleep again. It's almost ten in the morning. I should be rejoicing, instead I am here, simmering on the negative.

Eric was asleep when I tried to get out of bed this morning. He immediately woke up when he felt the bed move, he reached for my hand, pulled me back in his arms, and we made love again. It was slower this time. We let the motions take us but didn't let our excitement rush us either. I can still see his face as he was gazing at me from the depths of his soul and can still feel my tears rolling down the side of my face. It's been a long time since someone made me feel beautiful.

I feel my phone vibrate on the bed. I pull it up close to my face and I see a text message from him.

"Why are you not in my bed with me right now?" the message reads. He then sends a photo of an empty bed with his arm on it, pretending to be searching for someone with his hand. I take a photo of my empty side of the bed and push it to him in return.

"What's your address? I'm heading your direction," he replies. I get up as I see this.

"You're nuts."

"Do you have plans today?" he asks.

"No. But I know you do."

"The thing about fame, which I intend to take advantage of, is that you can do whatever the hell you want. I can do my costume fitting some other time."

"I don't want people to blame me for your missed schedules. You have to go."

"Can I see you after?"

"What time does it end?"

"Around three."

"Okay."

"Okay, I'll see you then?" There is an endearing hopefulness in the tone of his text.

"Yes," I confirm.

"And then I'm clearing my schedule until tomorrow."

This conversation is a little dizzying. I do a double air punch with one fist, a silent scream, and haphazardly shake both my legs upward in sly display of pleasure. I am no different from an adolescent girl getting her very first text message from an ultimate crush.

I suddenly hear a light knock on the door.

"Come in." It's Pam, still in her robe.

"Hey." She jumps next to me in bed.

"Hey," I say, as I make room for her in my bed. She smells of watermelon, the scent of her night cream.

"What's your plan today?" she asks sleepily. She stretches her hand and yawns loudly. The bedroom door opens again. This time, Marco walks in and drops at the foot of the bed.

"I might go out around three-thirty."

"This is not work because I know your schedule. You're going to see Hyun Min, aren't you?" Marco accuses. Pam jerks her body to face me.

"You have a boyfriend." It's not a question. Pam is making a declaration.

"Guys, chill. I don't even know what this is. I don't think Eric does either."

"Why do you keep calling him Eric?" Pam asks.

"I'm used to calling him by his English name. It was before I found out that he's Park Hyun Min."

"What do you mean?" Pam asks this in confusion.

"When I first met him, I didn't know he was Park Hyun Min, and when he introduced himself as Eric, it stuck."

"How could you not have known that he was Hyun Min?" She looks at me like this is the biggest betrayal of all.

"I was in distress. I was trying to get drunk and then a stranger just started talking to me. I didn't right away assume he was someone famous."

"That's how you met him?"

"Yes, at my absolute worse."

"Now, you have to tell us the story." And for the first time, I relive the twelve beautiful hours I spent with Eric. I skip the part where I cried my heart out at church and the powerful connection we had at Piedmont Lounge and how we said goodbye. I tell them about how he was such a generous man—gentle, considerate, a great listener.

"Did you want to sleep with him then?" Pam curiously questions.

"Yes. But I didn't, because I couldn't."

"Well, I wouldn't blame you if you had," Pam replies after a long pause.

"I'm glad I didn't, or I would have carried that guilt in my heart forever." I believe this.

"Whatever. I'd jump right to it if I were you," Pam says with a wink.

"That's what made our friendship special. It didn't start like that. It wasn't like that at all. We were two perfect strangers who needed to vent, knowing we'd never see each other again."

"True." Marco finally speaks from his stillness at the bottom of my bed. "This way makes it less tainted. You guys did nothing wrong. And so you deserve all the wrongness that you do this time around."

"Let's stop talking about this," I say and get up. "Let's have breakfast at Bruno's. I'm starving."

"Yay, Bruno's!" Marco jumps out of bed too. Bruno's is our local breakfast diner that serves killer French toast and cappuccino.

"Let's do it!"

Chapter 24

Marco, Pam, and I are sitting in Bryant Park eating ice cream and cream pie when Eric shows up. As soon as I see him walking toward us, I involuntarily hold my breath. He's in khaki pants, a blue shirt with sleeves rolled up to his elbow, and a blue puffer vest that fits him like a glove. I don't remember him mentioning a stylist, but whoever puts his clothes together is a fashion genius. I should ask him this. He sees me, and his eyes light up. To witness his reaction like this, a reflection of how I make him feel, lifts me up from insecurity to elation.

My phone vibrates from inside my jeans pocket. I pull it out and see Miguel calling. I smack my forehead with my palm.

"Shit!"

Eric is a few feet away and sees me.

"It's not the reaction I was hoping for, but okay," he teases.

"I forgot I was supposed to go see a movie with Miguel today. Shit!" He bends down and kisses me on the cheek anyway.

"Are we still on for this afternoon? I'm running late. Should I get tickets?" Miguel asks as soon as I answer.

"Something came up," I start to explain. "I can't do movies, but we can still meet you for drinks, if you'd like. I'm with Marco, Pam, and Eric."

"Eric?" I sense indifference as he speaks his name.

"Yeah, my friend you met the other day at my office." I let this simmer.

"Oh. . . ."

"Yes," I say and I turn around to observe Eric in conversation with Pam and Marco. Pam looks starstruck but, thankfully, Marco is his usual jovial and teasing self. I don't know what he's telling Eric, but I see him blushing, rubbing the back of his neck, and then turning to look at me a bit anxiously. I give him a wide smile. He sighs.

"Okay. I can meet you at Sergio's in an hour," Miguel says with obvious testiness.

I look at my watch. It's almost four o'clock.

"Sure. Five?"

"See you at five." We hang up, and I head back to the group. Eric and Marco are now talking like old friends, but Pam is still standing quietly, looking comically stunned. When I finally join them, Eric immediately puts his arm around me, which sends Pam's eyes in a wide tailspin. Marco is cool with this now, especially after last night's display.

"I forgot that I was supposed to meet Miguel today." I eye Eric apologetically, and I feel him tensing up. "We planned to watch a movie tonight, but we decided to just go for drinks at Sergio's instead. Do you all want to join?" I'm not letting Eric out of my sight tonight, so I look at him first.

"Yeah, I supposed I should meet all your friends and introduce myself as your boyfriend." Pam chokes on this. Man, I can't even describe in words how this wild and sudden declaration makes me feel. Pam and I stare at each other in a wide-eyed buzz.

The fuck? Pam mouths.

"Should we just meet you there?" Marco asks after we all pull ourselves together. "I need to run to the apartment and change. I've been wearing this since last night." True.

"Sure."

"I should change too," Pam says. She doesn't need to change, really. She looks perfect in her faux leather leggings and white off-the-shoulder sweater with a gray newsboy hat.

"We can meet you there," Eric says, reaching for my hand. Nothing feels more natural than to be connected to this man.

I exhale.

Marco and Pam turn to leave. Eric then takes a step closer to me, and finally envelops me in his arms—right in the middle of the crowded park. As he is more than a full foot taller than I am, he bends down to take me in closer. This is the fairytale I've been looking for my entire life, and in one magical moment every-thing in the universe is aligned, complete, mine. The wind swirls around as sunshine dangles golden rays of cozy light toward us, locking this instant in history.

"In a couple of months you'll lose your invisibility cloak," I whisper closer to his ear. He hugs me tighter, and I can sense that, just like me, Eric doesn't want this fantasy to end.

"I'll still hug you like this anywhere." He kisses the top of my head. "I've waited this long. I won't let you go."

When he finally lets me go, I'm both frightened and over-whelmed. I don't want this dream to end like it did the last time. I don't want my life's history to repeat itself. I have taken big strides to rebuild this life. He notices my anxiety. "What's up?" he asks.

"Every time life seems perfect, I get scared." He holds my hand tighter.

"This is not perfect. Bianca, you have to push your expecta-tions further. Walking in the park hand in hand like this may seem magical, but we don't want this to be the ending to our story. I want more. You should want it too." Elation bubbles through me. "You should want more. You should ask for more. You deserve it." And this time, I throw myself at him, ignoring the stares of older gentlemen playing chess in the park on this chilly spring afternoon. All my life I've always tried to devalue my contribution to the world, to my life. When I gave up on my first relationship to think about myself, about wanting more, it broke me. When I fell in love with Tommy, knowing he was sick, I told myself it was the best I could do. But in this man's arms, I want more. I *am* more. "You told me to find love, and I did." In his eyes, I see myself as a different person—deserving, worthy, a queen.

❧

We're back in Times Square where it all began, but this time our hands are clasped tightly together, not letting each other go. There is a different sense of ease and comfort between us now. I know it's been less than a week since we found each other again, but our connection defies time and space. We've proven that before. He moves behind and puts his arm around me while I lean against his chest.

"It's difficult to walk like this," I complain.

"It's difficult to walk here. Period." Times Square and Saturdays. Looking up, obviously, there is no denying the magic from the lights—but soon as you bend your head a little and stare at the crowds, it's pandemonium. Eric and I chuckle at this. Again, he kisses me on the top of my head.

I pull away and reach for his hand. I lead him toward the street that will take us to Sergio's. It's almost five o'clock. Finally, after walking a few blocks away from the Square, the noise dies some.

"Do you know that my parents are dating again?"

"Woah," he replies and tugs my hand in surprise. So I tell him about my dad, about how my mother kept everything from me, and how I now have three siblings I didn't know existed until a couple of years ago.

"It's just weird that they're together," I say, but in truth I'm ecstatic that my parents found each other again. I'm happy that I have three siblings that I'm starting to have relationships with and an entire new set of people I call family.

"Why is that? We found each other again—it's a wonderful thing, love . . . I finally realized." There is sincerity and affection in his eyes as he says this.

"I don't know," I say in pretend protest.

When I found out that my parents were seeing each other again behind my back, I was livid. I felt like I should have had a say in it. But Dad is like pixie dust to Mom; he makes her more magical, alive, and love high. She deserves this after not dating anyone else after he left, devoting her entire life raising me, and even so, I managed to screw things up.

"It only goes to prove that love always wins."

"I thought most Korean men were not very articulate about love?"

"I'm not most Korean men, I'm not even most men." He has a point. He's a bleep in an otherwise boring flat line of expectations.

We make it to Sergio's at exactly five o'clock but Miguel is nowhere to be found. He's usually punctual. The waiter who welcomes us at the door leads us to the furthest U-shaped booth at the back, decorated with heavy red velvet drapes and purple ropes. Sergio's used to be a small theater in Broadway that was later transformed into a jazz bar. I suspect no one is scheduled to play live jazz until later tonight, but there's faint oldies music playing in the background. Eric lets me slide into the booth first and then sits next to me.

"Are you finally living the life you wanted when we first met?" I feel a pang of guilt as I hear this because it means I've somehow wished for Tommy to die so I can live. But it is the truth, and I just need to get better at managing my guilt, especially now that I have someone new in my life. Eric sees it and stops. "I'm sorry," he says, but he shouldn't be. He didn't know what my life was like. I may have mentioned something about my husband's addiction, but I don't think he understood the enormity of it—how it also almost ruined me. It did, actually. I was just able to rise back up again with the help of amazing people in my life. I think of Mom, Pam, Marco, Miguel . . . and Dad—my precious tiny circle.

"Don't be. And yes, this is the life I envisioned two years ago. You don't have any idea how much I wanted this . . . to be free with you like this."

I turn my head to face him. To make sure I capture all of him at this moment in time. The cynic in me wants to take everything all in, just in case I end up losing it again tomorrow.

"How are you middle-aged lovers?" Pam finally appears and jumps right in front of us. She winks and throws herself at us for a tight embrace. Eric and I catch her, and she stumbles against the table, moving it slightly out of place. Finally, she gets up and pulls herself away from us. The real Pam has returned, no longer shocked or starstruck, as she was earlier. I'm relieved.

"Okay, somebody needs to explain to me now how all this happened," Pam demands as she slides in the other side of the booth and moves closer. She winks at me as if we're setting Eric up for some intense interrogation.

"Apparently I was a little too forward when we first met," I say.

"Well, you asked me if I was rich." He laughs out loud at the memory.

"Like loaded with money rich? You asked him that? Dude, you sound like a gold digger." Pam throws the table napkin right at my face. I chuckle.

"I was probably already drunk." I put my hand up in defense.

"No, you weren't." We laugh some more.

"Man, I made the worst first impression," I say.

"And yet here you both are," Pam teases.

The waiter finally comes and takes our order— beers for the three of us. A few minutes later, Marco and Miguel walk in together. Eric gets up again to welcome them, especially Miguel.

"Hi, I'm Eric. I think we've met the other day." Eric reaches out to Miguel for a handshake. He takes it although I can sense reluctance, but that's good enough for now.

"Yeah. Miguel," Miguel takes the end seat, which is smack across from Eric. He doesn't look very happy to be here. I don't need to feel uncomfortable around him. I give him a stern look to tell him I don't need this right now. He should be happy that I'm happy.

After a few more rounds of beers, Pam pulls out her phone and turns her back to Eric and me for a selfie.

"Smile!" she shouts at the two of us.

"Pam, don't check in or post where we are, okay," I say.

"It's all right." Eric lightly stops my hand from grabbing Pam's phone.

"I'm not stupid. I won't post it until tomorrow," she says, giving me the evil eye. "Don't be such an overprotective girlfriend. Geez." Marco and Pam high-five to this, and I see Miguel shift on his chair uncomfortably.

Apart from Miguel sulking away and nursing his drink, it's a good evening among friends. Eric looks relaxed and never once mentions show business. Pam and Marco are both their usual loud, jovial selves, and our table is a riot. I laugh my heart out unabashedly, loud, and unguarded, and free. I turn around to Eric, and he's watching me fondly. He holds my hand under the table, which Pam notices and shoves me just to tease.

Finally, I can now rightfully say, I am happy.

℘

"Good morning," says the voice I want to wake up to every day of my life, if it's ever possible. I open my eyes gleefully, stretching my arms over my head, and I smile as I see his beautiful face next to mine. This is not a dream, I remind myself.

"Hi." I say, planting a kiss on the side of his lips.

This thing, what Eric and I share, is the calm and yet effervescent kind. It's easy and effortless, and yet it is everything and more. He brushes the hair off my face and kisses my eye gently.

"I can't get enough. . . " he whispers, as if only to himself, "of this. . . of you."

With a beaming smile, I put my arms around his neck and let the silence envelop us.

"But though we have love big enough to feed us, I need to get to work." I tickle him on his sides and I jump out of bed, naked. He grabs me from behind and we both tumble back in bed, laughing.

"I'll ask the driver to take you." He gently presses my breasts with his hands as he pulls me from behind playfully. I can feel his excitement next to my hips. "See, what you're doing to me." I laugh some more.

"You are not getting a driver for me. I'll take Uber or the subway. I just need to get ready now." He pokes me on the side of my waist. "Stop it!" The freedom of my laugher in his arms is novel to me, and it's one of the most beautiful gifts he has ever bestowed. *Freedom.*

I turn around to face him and plant a strong kiss on his lips. He puts his arms around my waist, not letting me go.

"Where do we go from here, B?" His intense glare sends my insides into a backflip. I don't know if the question is literal or metaphorical, so I don't reply.

I sigh.

Where do you want to go from here? I silently ask, uncertain where this conversation is heading.

"I'll be here for as long as you want me. I don't think I ever knew what all this means until you. And I don't want to lose this, Bianca. I don't want to lose you again." To hear this, my soul floats into the highest form of bliss.

"Eric . . ."

"I can't guarantee it will be perfect, but I promise I'll be right here. I'll be here with you and for you every step of the way. How I feel about you beats everything I thought was possible."

"Is a love like this real, Eric?"

"I didn't think so until that night with you." His soft lips find mine.

I open my heart further to him and to this heady passionate emotion that is so new to both of us. As we make love, I let him own me from the tips of my toes to the ends of my hair, and he lets me do the same as I take him—screaming, moaning, and crying his name as I peak into oblivion—while he gazes deeply in my eyes. And toward the end of my stupor, he holds my hips and moves me to his own rhythm until he makes it there with me. "I love you, Bianca." He pulls me down into his arms again, and there's no place I'd rather be.

Chapter 25

I 'm at my desk at exactly eight o'clock this morning. It's a Monday. No one comes to work on time. People from our department are mostly night owls. I am too, but Eric and I woke up early this morning. We took our lazy, lustful time though, and then he thoughtfully prepared me breakfast. We've been in this slice of heaven for a few months now. I'm getting used to being up at dawn when I'm at his apartment, with the curtains drawn wide open, watching the city wake up—lights turning on in buildings one at a time, the fading glitter of the previous night, and the sun peeking through the skyscrapers—and pondering the excitement of conquering the world. I never used to think this way. I was a sad, lonely, miserable woman who didn't seem to have a shot at anything.

I turn on my computer, and a loud reverberating ding breaks the silence. I wait until it loads up my email.

"Hey, Bianca," Tony from creative arts walks by my cubicle with a venti coffee from Starbucks.

"Hi, T!" I give him a wide happy smile, which in my opinion everyone deserves this morning. Finally, my email loads and right at the top is from Diana.

SUBJECT: Hyun Min SEOUL TRIP THIS WEEK

I open the email. It was a forwarded message from Robbie, cc'd Marco. I skim through it.

Bianca,

See Robbie's email below. Let's talk this morning. Come to my office at 9:30.

—

Diana,

We do not want to lose any more time in making sure that Eric and his publicity team are in sync. I heard from his management company back in Seoul, and they want him back there this week now that the premiere night for his latest movie has been confirmed. He didn't think this was going to happen with the "Suzi" issue, but I guess it's back on track. I would suggest you send one of your guys with him, preferably Bianca, to make sure we are part of this event—take photos and start posting from our network social media platforms announcing that after this movie premiere, PARK Hyun Min is doing a season of American drama with CWS. Better we start drafting language now. Eric is on board. We need this handled ASAP.

R

I read the email again. I shake my head and I read it again. After the fourth time, I get up and I walk to the kitchen to start the coffee machine. I stay composed. I prepare the pot and wait. I lean back against the sink deep in thought. Marco is not in yet. I desperately want to talk to him, but I try to maintain my calm though I'm a topsy-turvy of emotions inside.

This is confusing. Eric has not once mentioned anything about a premiere night for his latest movie, and we've been together almost every night for the past month or so. I don't even know what movie they're talking about. I pull my phone from my jacket pocket and search for "Park Hyun Min movie." The top searches that pop up are photos of him and Suzi in a seductive embrace—it's a movie poster for sure, and it's in Korean. I hit translate. It says, *Critical Affair.* I look at Internet Movie Database for the synopsis. It's a kidnap-for-ransom film, and Eric plays the bad guy. I search for the trailer on YouTube. I watch them kiss. I hate watching it. There is undeniable chemistry between them. Suddenly, I feel a little prick of resentment. I flick the site away with my finger and shake the vision out of my head.

"I'll eventually get used to this," I say under my breath. I'll have to.

"There you are. I've been waiting in my office for you to come back. Did you see that email from Diana?" Marco appears at the kitchen and slowly leans on the refrigerator next to me as if waiting for me to start explaining. Like I know something.

"Yes. What's that about?" I ask. I tuck my phone back into my jacket pocket.

"I don't know. But it came from Robbie. Did Eric say anything about it?" Marco asks, squinting his eyes as if in deep thought.

"Not at all. That's why this is a surprise to me. And I was with him this morning." I can hear my voice rising, almost a whine.

"Nice." Marco smiles and nods his head mischievously.

"Stop it," I hit him lightly on his arm.

"Well, you get to go to Seoul. Isn't that something you've always wanted to do?" He reminds me of this once faraway dream.

"Yeah. But this is a little uncomfortable, don't you think? It's a premiere of his movie with his ex-fiancée. I bet you their publicity team is strategizing how it will look like everything is all fine and dandy between them."

"Dandy, really, B?"

"Focus, Marco," I whine again.

"Are they really broken up?"

"Well, I certainly hope so." I stand at attention as the possibility of what he just said hits me. I feel myself starting to panic. Marco holds both my arms and steadies me.

"We talked about this, remember. Fun fuck. No drama. No panic. None of this." He's looking me straight in the eyes, and there's no humor in his expression.

Finally, we hear the last push of the coffee machine and then it pops. Marco walks to the cupboard and grabs two big mugs. He pours each cup full to the brim and hands one to me. He pulls two packets of Stevia from one of the drawers. I hold on to the cup. It's scorching hot, but I take on the pain and sip a little.

"Bianca, look at me. You've only been together a few months. Let's not make this a *thing*." I should listen to him, not just as my friend but also as my kind of boss. "You have to let go of the notion that this can be forever."

I slowly lift my head up to face him, tears forming in my eyes, because that's exactly what I was doing from the first night we slept together. I let down my guard—all of it. I went all in, head on. Marco's expression turns to worry. He's seen it all. He's seen me build everything up from ground zero—from the moment he helped me get this job.

"You've been through a lot—from shit that most people can't come back from." I nod my head and sip more of my coffee. But I can't speak. I start walking back to my cubicle with my mug. Marco follows close behind me. "Are you okay? Talk to me." I abruptly stop and turn around to face him. He almost stumbles in surprise.

"You're telling me to go on this trip and make sure I don't overreact when I see them together, right?"

Marco looks upward in deep thought and puts his index finger on his chin.

"Yes," he finally answers after a long, lingering, and painful pause.

"I go to Seoul, meet him there, take photos, do some social media for the network, and come back—and all will be well?"

"In theory, yes, as expected of you by the company," he says matter-of-factly. I turn around and walk toward my cubicle again. Then I turn right back around. "Stop it," he warns, "you're going to spill your coffee."

"Fine. I'll go. I'll go as a social media manager for CWS. Period."

"We expect nothing less."

We find Diana restlessly pacing around my cubicle.

"I said nine thirty," she says as she walks toward me. I show her my watch that says 9:28. "That's late. Follow me to my office."

"Should I come, too?" Marco asks as he loiters near us.

"Yes." The three of us stroll down the hall in a silent, straight line. I give Marco the I-am-so-scared look, and he returns the gesture with an even scarier face. I almost laugh at this. Once inside the room, Diana closes the door shut. "So, I guess you're going to Seoul. Did you know about this?"

"Nu-uh." I only hope that Diana doesn't know about me and Eric. We've been careful. I specifically told him not to show me any special attention at work or anywhere near work. We were in DC a couple of weeks ago, and we didn't even talk to each other in public. Plus, Marco was great at covering for us at night, when we would go out for dinner and drinks, or just stay in the hotel room and make love until dawn. Marco always makes sure that his room is next to Eric's, so there's no confusion in case someone from the crew sees us in the hallway together.

"Are you sure?" Diana looks skeptical. She glares at me, then at Marco, then back at me. "Eric is nice for sure, and his entire team too, but I don't understand this need for you to go to Seoul. Do you have any idea why?" Marco and I shake our heads in perfect synchrony. "Eric leaves tonight. Your ticket is for tomorrow *morning*. Thank me, because I fought to get you in business class."

Marco and I doubt that very much. If anything, it's probably because it's company policy to bump up all flights to business class when they're more than seven hours. We're looking at around fifteen hours to Seoul. *Hold on. Did she just say Eric is flying out tonight? I don't remember him saying anything about this.*

"Was this a sudden thing?" I finally speak.

"Apparently, this premiere night was canceled because of that breakup drama. Now, their producers want them there or they'll sue. I guess it was turned on last night or this morning.

"Get your tickets from Van and ask for the company credit card. Van normally books us at the Palace, which is in the city centre close to the markets and Namsan Tower. One of our people on the ground will be in touch with you to discuss details about transportation. I don't know where the theater is, but it's likely to be at the Lotte Cinema World Tower. Bring something nice to wear. Not too nice. Something efficient."

"What do you want me to do?"

"Take our go-pro and the best phones we have to take photos. You're going to manage the network Twitter and Instagram while you're there. Take photos of Eric and of the premiere night. I guess Robbie already wants us to announce the show. In which case, Marco, tee-up all the materials we need for this. Language for press releases, photos from fittings and trainings."

"When is the premiere?"

"It's on Friday. You leave tomorrow and lose a day, so you'll get there Thursday morning or late Wednesday."

I'm starting to get a little excited. I've never been anywhere.

Since we emigrated from the Philippines decades ago, I've never been outside the United States. It's one of those luxuries that I'm not even permitted to contemplate. Thank goodness I have a passport. Mom checks every few years to make sure it's still valid and reminds me to renew it six months before it expires. I asked her once why renewing my passport was so important to her. She said it's the only tangible and handy document I can show to prove that I'm a US citizen. With all the stories of people getting deported by mistake, she worries a lot about that.

"Now, get out." Diana snaps. And we do. Marco gives me a wide-eyed stare.

"He didn't tell me this. And we were together the entire weekend," I say in a whisper, in distress, thinking I'm in a parallel universe where things are about to end, where I always feared it would go.

"Look, it's a great opportunity to explore a country you've always wanted to see. So go explore and enjoy."

It's almost three in the afternoon and still no word from Eric. I don't usually call him during the day to avoid suspicion among the staff and crew. I also don't like getting in the way of his work —stunt trainings, photos shoots, and fittings. If he's flying out tonight, I at least expect him to let me know.

It's almost six o'clock, and I've not heard from Eric. I got my ticket from Van earlier today, the credit card from the finance department, and all the materials I need from Marco. My flight is at six tomorrow morning, which means I need to be at the airport by three-thirty. This will be painful.

❧

At eight o'clock, I finally call him. It goes straight to voice mail. This is a first. I time my calls perfectly, as I do now, so he always answers them. Whatever confidence I have is slowly dying. There is a push and pull to the dynamics of my trip—on the one hand, I will be visiting a land I've always dreamed of seeing, and on the other, Eric's silence is sending me into a tailspin of distressing emotions. I trust Eric. I know him. I know there is a reason for all this.

I start packing.

"Are you sure you're going to be fine?" Pam asks, worried. I nod my head. I can't help but crease my forehead in apprehension.

"I've not heard from Eric since this morning, and he's normally very conscientious about making an effort to reach out to me. So, this is a little bit disconcerting." I tell her my truth. It's not something I can hide because it's written all over my face.

"I'm sure there's a reason to it. Eric's been very consistent. He'll call. I mean these first-class flights have phones anyway, right? I'm sure as soon as he gets settled on the plane, he'll call you."

❧

It's midnight, and still nothing from Eric. I need to wake up in three hours. I reach for my phone next to my bed and punch in his number. Again, it goes straight to voice mail.

Chapter 26

My layover in San Francisco takes more than five hours because of an Internet malfunction on the plane that delays our departure. Instead of getting to Seoul at six o'clock, we are expected to land around midnight. It's the silliest reason I've ever heard, but I'll take it if it means I get there in one piece. Thankfully, I have access to the VIP lounge and am able to sleep some and take a shower.

I give up worrying about Eric. He'll call when he can. I know this. Also, I trust that as soon as he finds out that I'm on my way, he'll fuss over arrangements to guarantee that I get the best Seoul experience of my life. I'm certain of that. What's the point of having the most famous Korean boyfriend? I relax some at this thought and even manage to titter quietly.

We finally land. I check my watch as soon as I hear the wheels screech on the runway. It's midnight. I look out the window, and it's raining. Not quite a torrential downpour, but impressive. I sit in place awaiting further instruction. I pull out my phone from my backpack perched in the big cubby under the seat in front of me and turn it on.

"Had to fly to Seoul. I can't reach you. Where are you? Sorry was out of range yesterday." I exhale upon seeing this message from Eric.

Another one comes in.

"Where are you?"

Then three more beeps make their way into my text inbox.

"B, call me please."

"Tell me where you are?"

"I'll explain later, but I'm in Seoul."

I feel the urgency and distress in these messages. Not that I'm saying I'm happy that he's in distress, but I'm happy that he feels it's important to inform me. I get it. There are contracts to complete and commitments to fulfill.

"Surprise! In Seoul too! See you at the premiere of your movie." Send failed, it says. I try again. It's not working. I check my iPhone's roaming switch, and it's on. My system is probably not syncing just yet. I'll call him when I get to the hotel. Maybe he can come see me tonight. This is getting cooler and cooler by the minute. I smile inwardly.

Now that I've finally heard from him, I can relax. The extreme uncertainty of the last twenty-four hours was excruciating. I can't wait for him to find out that I'm here too, if he hasn't already.

I'm in Seoul!

When the plane finally comes to a full stop, I look at my surroundings. Flying business class is definitely the way to go. I might get used to this. Not that I travel all the time or anywhere this cool before. In fact, the furthest I've been was to California. *I'm not in Kansas anymore, that's for sure!* I laugh at this, looking at the man next to me who, without a doubt, notices my craziness. I get up, gather my belongings from the overhead bin, and make my way to the exit. I pull my puffer jacket tighter around me as I step off the plane. The night chill from the wind outside slides through the cracks in the jetway.

It's a short walk from the plane to the immigration hall. It's quiet this time of night, and I'm in and out in five minutes.

There is no denying my giddy enthusiasm as I arrive in this

place I've only seen on television. I walk farther down where the carousels are and see a larger-than-life mural of the famous Korean girl band, Black Pink, on one of the walls welcoming arriving guests. The wall is painted in pink and yellow, so many bright, colorful hues that's delightful to look at. This is definitely Instagram worthy, so I pull my phone out and I take a couple of selfies. I have to make sure the world knows that I actually made it here. I chuckle softly.

"Miss Curtis?" I turn around and see a Korean man in a black suit and black hat holding up a sign with my name on it. He smiles at me immediately. "Welcome to Korea," he says, repeating the sign on the wall. He bows his head and I return the gesture. There is no limit to the number of bows you can do here, I was told. You just have to go for it. Pam mentioned this numerous times while I was packing last night, or was it the night before last? I don't know anymore. This time difference will definitely screw me up. "My name is Lee Seo Jeong. Should we wait for your bag?" He gestures to the carousel.

"I don't have any. I'll only be here until Saturday." I give him a wide happy smile.

"But why only a couple of days? There's so much to see in Seoul." He looks disappointed.

South Koreans are very proud of their culture, as they should be. What they create, whether technology or film or fashion, they make sure it exceeds expectations. I see that in Eric. He doesn't do things by halves, or as he calls it, *half-assed*. He goes all the way. He makes sure he pours his heart and soul into everything he creates. If I'd known I'd be in this part of the world with the man I love, I would have planned this better. There is so much to see in this little paradise. And the food! Not just their famous BBQs and side dishes, but the thought of chicken and beer makes my stomach rumble. I doubt there's anything open at this hour in the city, so I should probably wait until I get to the hotel and figure out something to eat.

Lee Seo Jeong instructs me to wait outside while he gets the car. The wind is picking up, and the weather is no different from New York City. After a few minutes, he appears in a black Hyundai sedan. He gets out, helps me with my spinner bag, and holds the door for me. I bow before I enter to show gratitude. One other thing I learned from Pam is never to tip in Korea. I keep this in mind as Lee Seo Jeong drives through the streets of Seoul. From the airport, we pass by the Han River, and although it's dark, and it can pass for any river on the face of the earth, I'm still overjoyed. How many Korean movies have I seen that has this river as its backdrop? A lot!

"You've done well, Binky," I whisper to the wind, as I look out into the night.

Success is subjective. A success for one may be a failure for another. But here, right now, is a milestone. Something I can look back on. This is where I can finally say that my life is moving toward the right direction. At my age, I should be married with kids. But life didn't hand me that template. I tried it. I suppose I'm meant to be here, at this very moment in this very place, because this is how and where my life will finally start moving to where I'm destined to be—in Seoul with Eric. I beam at this thought. I can't wait to see his face when he sees me. I expect him to be shocked at first, of course, and then he'll smile and walk toward me and hug me in the middle of the crowd as we do all the time in New York City, like a movie.

We drive up a narrow hill to get to the hotel. It's one of those massive five-star buildings attached to a casino. Funny, the casino features the face of another famous Korean actor, Lee Jung Ho.

His face is plastered over every wall on the left side of the hotel building at the entrance of the casino. Note to self: selfie required tomorrow. As we circle toward the driveway, there is a life-size Lee Jung-Ho cutout greeting arriving guests with flowers. I laugh at this. Lee Seo Jeong turns around to me.

"You know this actor?" he asks. I nod my head with a wide grin on my face. This is like my Disneyland. Pam would love it here.

It was a forty-minute ride from the airport to the hotel, so I stretch out my legs and arms as soon as I step out of the car. I turn around and there I see the Namsan Tower, the Seoul Tower—the tower I only see on television. It's standing tall and bright and colorful. This is Eric's very own Empire State Building, and maybe we can steal some precious time to get up there and see the view of the city from the top. We can recreate our time at the Empire State Building and throw another wish into the sky.

"You should go there," Lee Seo Jeong says, pointing to the tower. "Great parks around the tower," he adds as he reaches for my bag in the compartment.

"Thank you. Thank you." I bow twice. And Lee Seo Jeong does the same.

So far, so good.

⁊⊃

I pull out my iPhone from my pocket and take a photo of the Namsan Tower staring at me from a great height. I turn around and stretch my arm in an attempt to get the perfect selfie with it as a background. It isn't easy. The light on my flash only focuses on my nose and blurs the tower behind me. It doesn't matter. I'm here, and I have the blurry background selfie to prove it.

I walk into the hotel as I drag my spinner bag behind me. It's almost two in the morning, and I'm starving. I was asleep when they served dinner or breakfast or lunch, I don't even know, on the plane.

"Hi, my name is Bianca Curtis, I have a reservation until Saturday."

"Hello, Ms. Curtis. Welcome to the Palace. Yes, we have you here until Saturday. Do you have a credit card to put on this reservation?" I reach for my wallet inside my purse, pull out the company credit card, and hand it to the pleasant, tall Korean lady behind the counter. She wears her hair up in a neatly coiffed bun, bright red lipstick, and a blue, white, and red uniform that replicates that of a flight attendant. She gives me a sunny smile and thanks me.

"Is room service still available?" I hear my tummy grumble again under duress.

"Unfortunately, our room service is not open twenty-four hours." This I find silly. I look around the massive, grand hotel and see two restaurants and a wine bar off the lobby, both closed. "But there is a twenty-four-hour convenience store across the street." My eyes widen at this. I've always wanted to visit a Korean convenience store with its wide selection of Korean food and beer—and yes, soju! I'll have a soju tonight!

"Great! I'll do that. Is it safe though?"

"Yes. It's very safe in Seoul, madam." There, she says it. I'm already a madam in her eyes. I can't blame her. She looks like she's in her twenties, and when I was in my twenties, everyone over thirty-five was already a madam. She clicks on the computer some more and finally hands me a small envelope with my room keycard and my credit card. "You're in room seventeen twenty-two. We have free breakfast at our lobby restaurant with a view of the city from six thirty to ten thirty daily. We have a gym on the fifth floor, and next to it is the indoor pool. We also have a spa in the building. Please let us know if you want us to book you a service." She bows as she finishes her spiel. I bow right back.

"Thank you." I turn around and head for the elevator where a man in a black suit and earpiece escorts me. I bow to him too. I step into the elevator, and I feel bold—alone in an elevator in a faraway land with so many unknowns among strangers. I giggle again. Mom and Pam will be very proud of me. I feel my phone vibrate and pull it out of my pocket.

"You made it?" A text from Marco.

"Yup. Elevator. Alone. Two in the morning," I reply. It's two in the afternoon back in New York, and I'm sure he just got back in the office from a lunch somewhere.

"Tell me when it's a good time to call." I look at this text with furrowed brows. Why would he call when he's well aware of the twelve-hour time difference? I get into my room and although the bed is magnificently enticing, I drop off my stuff and turn right around out the door on a mission to get food. I now have a sudden fixation to invade a South Korean convenience store. I can't wait to discover selections of cold coffee, hot coffee, rice, noodles, tea, energy drinks, sodas, and microwavable food—oh it's never-ending. I've never been in one before, but I've seen many of them on TV.

It's freezing cold and dark outside. I have my jacket zipped up to my chin as I run across the street from the hotel to the well-lit convenience store at the corner. It's not a narrow road so I make sure there are no cars driving by fast to hit me, or I'd die, and no one would ever find out. Oh, the silly things that come into my head sometimes.

Next to the store is a chicken and beer restaurant, which I

should definitely try out tomorrow. I hope it's open at lunchtime. When the sliding door opens after I lightly push a tiny button, a young man behind the cash register greets me in Korean. I bow to him and he bows right back. Walking in is like navigating a new world, where cute packaging of anything and everything is enticing me to buy them all. Pink Band-Aid canisters, green kitty mascot on a coffee can shaped like a bottle, and a probiotic concoction that doubles as a refreshing yellow drink. This display of drinks is photo-worthy in itself, so I take one. The young man probably thinks I'm a lunatic and will likely call the cops if I stay here much longer. Next to the refrigerated drinks are the prepacked foods. My eyes beam upon seeing the array of microwavable meat—pork belly, bulgogi, and pork knuckles—deliciously displayed in one of the refrigerated sections. I grab one of each, and on my way to the counter, I also snatch a couple of packs of microwavable rice, which make my Asian genes jump up and down with glee.

"Soju!" I remember. The nice young man shyly snickers and points at the refrigerator next to him that holds different flavors of soju and a variety of domestic and imported beer. I pull out two bottles of Cass beer and one green bottle of original soju. I'd love to browse around some more but it's ridiculously late and I need to get back to the hotel room and try to call Marco.

I pay for my haul, microwave them all, and run back to the hotel.

I put my food on the table. Everything is in cute multicolored plastic containers. I tear open my chopsticks wrapper and dive right in. The pork belly is to die for, and this is just prepackaged convenience store food. I can't wait to eat at a proper Korean BBQ restaurant tomorrow.

I feel my phone vibrate inside my pocket. I pull it out and see Marco calling.

"Do you know it's three o'clock in the morning here in Seoul, South Korea?" I have to say it out loud for laughs because it's simply unreal.

"Hey, sorry. Yeah." Marco sounds off.

"Is everything okay?" I ask. He suddenly makes me nervous.

"Have you read your email yet? It's doesn't matter. I'll tell you anyway. Eric was hard to reach on Monday because he was on the phone with his lawyers the entire day. Suzi made a big fuss about this premiere night and said she was going to sue if he didn't appear with her at the event." I feel my heart start to palpitate. "He was forced by his management team to fly back to Seoul." I stop at this. No one can force Eric to do anything. If there's one thing I know about him, it's that nobody can make him do anything against his will. He is too proud to succumb to that. He has money. He has power. He can walk away from this life.

"Marco, why am I here?" I whisper. I inadvertently drop one of my chopsticks on the table, and it tumbles onto on the floor. I stare at it, but I don't pick it up. I have a bad feeling about all this.

"I don't know much. All Van told me was that Robbie came down to see Diana last night after you left, and because she wasn't in, he left a message with her. These were his exact words, according to Van. 'Tell Diana to confirm with me that Eric's girlfriend, Bianca, gets to Seoul and makes sure that he comes back here to New York.' And he was livid." I lean back on my chair as the horror of this hits me. Robbie knew who I was. "Bianca, are you still there?"

"Yeah," I say hoarsely. "What do I do?" I sigh.

"I'm telling you so you're not caught off guard. I don't even think Eric knows you're there." I figure as much. "But do what you were asked to do and come home. Don't get into whatever drama Eric has with his ex-fiancée. Okay?" I nod my head slowly, though he can't see.

"Marco, this feels like a trap." I feel chills up my arms and around my back.

"I don't know what it is, but it's certainly about Eric and his ex, and Robbie thinks adding you to the mix will help his case." There is undeniable worry in Marco's voice as he speculates. I need to talk to Eric. "Look, I like Eric a lot. He's good to you. I can honestly say he cares about you deeply, but at the end of the day he's also a celebrity, and we don't want to get involved in their screwed-up life." I've never heard Marco this concerned before. There is no humor in what he says.

Marco hangs up with a promise to call if he finds out more.

I don't see a point calling Eric at this hour, but he has to know first thing in the morning.

"Hey. I'm in Seoul. Please call me immediately. We need to talk." I type this message and send it. I don't expect a response.

I open a can of beer and gulp half of it in one go. I also unscrew a bottle of soju and mix it in. This is the big leagues now. This feels like a trick. Suddenly, I feel tiny and alone in a huge, strange city.

❧

The phone wakes me up with a loud thundering buzz. I didn't ask for a wake-up call so I don't know who's calling me from the landline. Still in my traveling clothes, I grab the phone next to me.

"Hello?"

"Bianca, it's Robbie." I get up immediately. "You know me. We met at a bar the first time when you were with Eric. I was impressed by you and followed all your advice."

"I didn't know you were the big boss in the network when I started working there." I don't know what else to say. He's cornering me right now.

"I figured as much. I'm calling because I need your help. I can't get in touch with Eric." I look at the bedside clock that says eight o'clock. I've only been asleep for four hours. "Look, I didn't plan this and neither did Eric. But I feel like his management team is onto him about this whole Suzi breakup and their movie." I don't know what to say but I can't be someone's pawn in this battle.

"Robbie, I don't know what you want me to do," I say. He's asking me to do something beyond my job.

"A massive amount of money is on the line here. And I don't know what else to do. I'm sorry." At least there's an apology. I don't think he's a bad man, but he's still a businessman, and we're talking about millions of dollars here. "Just show up at the premiere. I made arrangements for you to attend it. The VIP packet is down at the concierge waiting for you."

"And then what?" I almost scream this, but I restrain myself.

"Look, I know he values you. I even think he's in love with you, and I'm sorry I'm using this as leverage, but he needs to come back and fulfill his contract, or the entire production is on the line." This is not power. This is blackmail. I hate that he thinks I have any control over this because of a personal relationship I have with one of his talents. "I'm not using you. I'm asking for your help."

"I don't know what I can do, Robbie."

"All I ask is that you show up. I've had my team prep everything for you to attend the event. You have scheduled appointments at the spa and the salon. Just think of this as attending a red carpet event. They are big at these kinds of things. I also had them send clothes in your size. I asked your friend Marco to give me specifics. God, I'm so sorry to be doing this."

"Robbie, just don't promise me a promotion I don't deserve."

"Fair enough."

I see my phone vibrating next to the landline. Marco.

"I shouldn't have sent you there by yourself. Again, Bianca, I'm sorry. And know that I value you as an employee and took your advice two years ago to heart."

"He doesn't know I'm here…" It's not a question. He doesn't answer.

"I made sure you're well taken care of. I had to try." I know this. I just don't want to be part of this high-stakes battle just because I love Eric. "Thank you." I don't say you're welcome, I just hang up. There's nothing left to say.

My phone continues vibrating on the bedside table. I don't want to talk to anyone right now. But I do want to know what Marco is calling to say; I'm sure it's not about work. It stops. After a few minutes have passed, my iPhone vibrates again, and I see Pam's face. I need time to gather my thoughts. I need to understand what I just got myself into. The difference about this and my life in Jersey: then I knew I needed to get out and it had to end. With Eric, I thought it was forever. I'm an idiot, plain and simple. Who did I think I was? I stare at the phone with rage, but I don't know who I'm angry with. I finally grab it.

"Binky!" Pam screams at the other end of the line. I clutch the phone tightly trying to stop myself from bawling. This is so embarrassing. "Talk to me!" she screams again. I can't get myself to speak, and yet there is comfort knowing that the people I love actually care. There is light coming out from the blackout curtains I haphazardly drew last night. I cover my eyes against the brightness.

"Pam," I finally manage. I don't want another conversation about how pathetic this all is. How pathetic I am to submit to this.

"Binks, you okay? Come home. Nobody should treat you like this." I can hear Marco shouting in anger in the background.

Then I cry.

I feel my tears rolling down my cheeks—in anger, in pain, and in shame. Once fucking trash, always trash, and no amount of perfume or luxury can mask that.

"You don't need to do anything you don't want to. Come home and we'll figure it out. We'll find you another job." But I love my job. It's who I am. That hurts even more. "We can do this. Marco is right here, and we'll figure it all out." I wrap my arms around myself tight and bend my head down as my tears continue to flow. I'm goddamn humiliated. "You are loved, sweetie. Don't think otherwise."

There are many moments in life that define us. This is one of those in mine—questioning my strength as well as my worth, of who I am, and who I truly want to be. Do I even know it? Do I simply react to circumstances in my life? Do I not encourage change? Do I not push for it? Do I just float through life because I exist?

Am I forgiven? Did I forgive?

"Why do I always find myself in this position after a fucking relationship?" I scream and let myself go. My body starts to shake like I want to get out of myself, out of all this.

"You have a heart that loves. It's your flaw. But it's a good flaw. It makes you a great human being. It makes you pure. You don't judge or think ill of people. You just love without conditions. You have to be grateful. You don't need to go tonight." Pam says this in a whisper. I need to hear it. I need to know I am loved, that I love.

There is silence on both ends.

"I have to go," I break the quiet that distance us.

"Why?"

"Because if I don't, I will forever ask myself why I didn't try hard enough. Why I didn't see it through."

"But you always do—by begging Glen to understand, by taking it all for Tommy. You always end up broken. I know you're not fragile because I fucking saw you fight 'til the very end. But you don't have to put yourself in a situation where you are likely going to get hurt further, Binks." I quietly howl in pain and in anger to myself, clutching the bed as if my life depends on it. "I'm envious of how brave you are sometimes. I wish I could be like you. You don't give up. You push hard. You try until the very end. But sometimes, weakness can save us. Don't face this alone. Come home."

"I have to do this," I say calmly.

"Okay. But the first sign of doubt, run as far away as you possibly can and come home to people who love you. Fine. Go tonight. Enjoy it. Then come home."

Chapter 27

I look at myself in the mirror. My black dress has been discarded. Tonight, I wear a red lace dress with nude underlining. My face is fully made up with red lipstick and smoky black eyes. My hair looks like it's been tumbled at the beach. I look golden . . . an impostor. The two hours in the spa helped. I was able to sleep for a couple of hours as they prepped me for this evening. When I woke up, I was calmer. I stare at the person I was created to be tonight—someone who looks elegant enough to make it through the door. I don't know how I got from that-girl-whose-husband-killed-himself to this-girl-who's-all-glammed-up-but-doesn't-feel-any-better.

The car is waiting for me downstairs. Robbie's people told me so. They rang not too long ago, and they've been checking in on me every few hours making sure I get to the premiere as planned. I don't know what they think I can do. I'm no magician. I'm no princess either. I grab the Chanel bag on the nightstand. Not mine. A borrowed dream like this one I'm living right now. A dream, and yet my heart is heavy. I walk out of my room feeling the weight on my shoulders. I'm not a quitter. People know that about me. So I walk one step at a time until I get to the car, sit in it as I watch the tantalizing world pass me by. I check my fully charged phone in my purse. I'm here to take pictures, I remind myself of this bullshit.

As planned, my car is marked to stop at the red carpet. I give out a heavy sigh when the car comes into a full stop. The driver doesn't say anything. He was given instructions to pick me up right here as soon as I send a text message to a number provided. He'll be parked a few blocks away.

I step out into the flashes of cameras. People are curious so they start taking photos—sure, I can be an unknown heiress from wherever. I don't stop to pose. I continue walking because I'm here to see a movie, and it's the only job I need to do tonight. They were very clear about that.

I don't expect Eric to be here yet. The featured stars are usually the last to arrive. I saw his wrap-up party event for *The Oasis* on YouTube a few years ago, and he arrived last. I remember how he was with his fans that night. He walked and talked to them and offered to shake their hands. He looked sincere. He was sincere, at least that much I know. He kept telling me he owes all that he is to his fans, and so he makes time for them. I pull my VIP pass from my purse and show it to the muscular security guy in a black suit at the end of the red carpet walk. He lets me through without a second glance. As soon as I enter the building, I notice the cocktail bars at every corner. I need a strong drink to get me though this night.

The party is already in full swing at the reception area as I walk in. Crowds are milling about, posing for cameras, making sure they are seen. I bend my head to make sure I do not get any form of attention from the press. I'm afraid someone will notice I don't belong here and escort me out. I get myself a drink and settle at the farthest cocktail table at the other end of the theater. Everyone wants to be at the entrance to the cinema. I'd rather be away from it all.

The lights dim, and a loud welcome music suddenly fills the air. I feel a bang at the center of my chest.

There he is, in his tuxedo, looking so perfect, Park Hyun Min

—South Korea's most celebrated actor. He wears his radiant smile with confidence. This is where he belongs. Though I know him in this persona, this man I see here tonight is a stranger to me. He captivates the crowd. He is larger than life. He is pure bright star. Magic.

I'm way at the back and can't see all the actions and interactions around him, but I see him reach his hand toward someone. I stand on tiptoe, and on his arm is a goddess in a gold dress. I don't need to guess who she is. Suzi.

God, they look good together. No, they look perfect. Their smiles sparkle together. They belong on stage where people can see their luster because it shines mighty bright. I choke and start to hyperventilate. I'm more than twenty feet away from him and yet I feel him, I remember the touch of his hands all over me, his lips on mine. But tonight, he is far from my grasp. I don't know this man.

He works the crowd, shaking people's hands, stopping for cameras—all this, with Suzi on his arm. The woman he said he doesn't love but was willing to marry. Is that, right there, truly just for the business they're in? The smiles, the light touches, the way he guides her on the floor—they all look real to me. She looks radiant, luminous, like a perfect star that she is. I swig my martini. I'm angry. I'm sad. I'm defeated. I'm no one.

When it's time to enter the theater, I take my time. I don't want to be rubbing elbows with these people. I look at my seat number and Robbie is not kidding when he said I'd be in the VIP spot. I'm seated two rows behind Eric and his leading lady.

The movie begins with action-packed scenes. I hear *oohs* and *aahs* from the audience, and all I do is look at the man who is two seats in front of me. I see Suzi leaning in and whispering something to him. He whispers right back. I see this and I think of all the probable lies he has told me. A tear unexpectedly rolls down my cheek. I let it because no one can see my pain in the dark. A few minutes into the movie is a scene of heavy dialogue between the two main characters, and then they kiss. It is bold. It is hot. Then comes the sex scene. I want to cover my eyes with my hands. How can I un-see that? It ran for about two minutes, or maybe more. For me, it ran forever.

❧

Two hours later, the lights come back on. People are clapping with great admiration. Eric gets up and gestures for Suzi to join him, turns around and waves at us. Our eyes meet. I don't smile. I simply stare. Expressionless. There is a question in his eyes but he immediately pulls himself out of it and smiles wider for the crowd. God, he's a professional. Suzi, standing next to him, doesn't notice anything; she shows her pearly white teeth and waves to the expectant crowd. I avoid his stares now. Then they walk on stage, where the crew has quickly set up three comfortable armchairs.

I don't understand a word. They are all speaking in Korean. Well, at least the movie had English subtitles. There is a lot of teasing, laughing, and clapping. I can't just take off because people will notice, and I don't want to be *that girl*. I don't want any attention on me. I don't know their culture enough to try to do anything out of the ordinary. I don't want to offend or insult anyone, so I stay.

He laughs, he smiles, and he jokes with the moderator. The crowd roars with excitement when he blows a kiss to Suzi. Suzi in turn leans in and gives him a real kiss on the cheek instead. Then he looks right at me. There is no signs or secret messages. He is simply giving me a piercing stare.

When the conversation between the host and the two stars is over, I'm the first one to get up and run out of the theater. I pull my phone from my borrowed Chanel bag and am about to text the driver when someone grabs my hand from behind. Eun Dong. Eric's assistant.

"Hi," she greets me. "Did you like the movie?"

"I did," I say as I pretend. Tonight, I'm one of them living in a world of aesthetics and make-believe. I give her a wider, faker grin. She can tell I'm lying and gives me a weak smile in return.

"Eric wants to know what you're doing here." I certainly hope it doesn't mean what it sounds like. So much for dreaming that he'd be pleased to see me, that together we would explore his home.

"Is he angry?" I ask.

"No. Not at all." She waves both her hands in front of me.

"I wanted to surprise him. The movie is great. Tell him I like it, but I've got to get going."

"Where are you staying?"

"At Myeong-Dong."

"He'll call you later. Until when are you planning to be in town?"

"Not very long."

I see him walk out of the theater with Suzi in front of him. He's standing tall, searching the crowd, patting people on the arm, and shaking their hands. There are photographers and videographers right in front of him. Our eyes meet again. I can tell that he's about to walk my way when Suzi pulls him for another photo opportunity. He's trying to escape her, but she's deliberately tugging at his arm.

"I've got to get going," I say again. Then I hear the crowd scream. I look where the cheering is coming from, and Eric and

Suzi have locked lips. It looks so real I want to throw up. No, I need to get out of here because I *am* about to throw up. I run out the building. Swarms of fans are on the other side of the rope, waiting for the big stars to walk right out. No one notices me. I'm nobody. When the lights fade away in the background, I start to cry. This is not for me. This is not and is never going to be my world. This is Eric's, and from the looks of it, this is not a life he can leave behind, no matter how much he insists he wants to. He is great in front of a crowd. He is perfect in front of the cameras. He is real with Suzi in his arms. I hear more screaming fans from a distance.

I can't take this away from him. But I also can't be in this with him. And so I run as far away from it all as I possibly can.

❧

On the plane, I let go. Thankfully, no one is sitting next to me because I can't stop crying. It's not hatred or pain. I cry from self-pity.

I'm back to where I once was—uncertain of myself, unsure about my worth, unloved.

The champagne keeps flowing, and I'm in and out of sleep. I'm in my pajamas. I'm disgusting. I just can't be bothered.

As soon as I got back in the hotel from the event, I asked the concierge to change my flight to early Saturday morning instead of the planned Saturday night. I called Marco and Pam to let them know I'm coming home. They didn't ask any questions.

❧

Miguel is in his car waiting for me when I walk out of the airport. He gets out as soon as he sees me. He doesn't say anything but grabs my bag and puts it in the trunk. He then opens the passenger door, and I get in. He walks around slowly, looking at me from the windshield, and gets into the driver's seat.

"Where to?" he asks.

"Home." And we don't cross the bridge, and we drive toward Jersey City.

❧

Yesterday, I emailed Diana and informed her that I need to take two weeks off. I didn't offer any other explanation. This morning, I received a snarky email from her with an obvious implication that I could lose my job if I don't come back in three days.

I call Robbie. He answers on the first ring.

"I heard."

"You heard what?" I ask sarcastically. I don't think I can come back from this, talking to the network president in such an informal manner.

"That you left earlier than planned. He called me. Screamed at me for a good twenty minutes. He got the message. Thank you for helping me out."

"Robbie, I'm no one's pawn, I told you that."

"I know. I never saw you like that. I was desperate, and I'm sorry." I can tell that he means it.

"Now, it's your turn to return a favor."

"Anything."

"I'm not asking for a promotion. I just need a month off and I want to be taken off Eric's project."

"Done."

"I'll see you in a month when the whole production finally moves to DC—if I even see you in the building."

"You will. I'll call Diana as soon as we hang up."

⁊◌

I'm back in my room at my mom's house. I remember coming back here after I broke up with Glen too. I'm glad that this little shelter still exists, and that my mom is healthy and happy and can still take care of her hopeless, almost forty-year-old daughter. It would be easier to justify this if I were thirty, but almost forty is really pushing it. It's hilarious how my life turned out. Laugh-out-loud hilarious. Pam and I once declared that we would never ever get married—well, I obviously broke that promise and was later left badly broken. My marriage didn't really end, did it? The other half of the whole died—does that mean I will forever be a half? That's fucked up. I was a whole for two years—or at least, I tried to be. Then Eric came, and I'm weak again. Some people simply don't learn, you see.

"Binky?" It's my dad at the door. I was surprised to see him having breakfast in the kitchen when I walked in this morning. My parents were both in shock. I was in shock. He opens the door and sits on the chair next to the window. It's an old, tattered armchair I bought at a thrift store in Hoboken. He looks like a giant sitting on a dwarf's chair.

"I don't need a pep talk," I say nicely. I really don't. I'm a middle-aged woman, and I don't need my father to give me a lecture right now.

"I want to be here for you."

"I know. I'm okay. I'm glad that you're here, though." As soon as I say this, he heaves a heavy sigh. "I don't hate you anymore, Dad. I'm sorry I did. But I don't now."

"Is it okay if I stay here over the weekend to be with you and your mom?" he asks.

"Of course. Yeah, I want to be surrounded by family. That'll be nice."

Chapter 28

"**I**'m on fire, people! On fire!" Pam screams after hitting a strike. My dad punches the air in defeat. Mom laughs right next to me. These are the two most competitive human beings I know. Mom and I are like, *whatever*, which drives Pam and Dad insane. I didn't use to have this. I'm now a daughter again to a father and a mother. Life right here is perfect.

"So, Diana bitch is letting you take a month off? That's very generous."

I shrug my shoulders at Pam. I rather not talk about this in front of Mom and Dad.

"What's happening?" Mom asks, worried.

"Nothing, *Tita*," Pam says and kisses my mom on the top of her head.

"I'm taking a month off work so I can finally go to this art writing seminar I've been wanting to attend. It's at the MoMa. I can walk around the city and be lazy. I just need a break. I'll keep my job, Mom. Don't worry."

"I'm not worried about the job. I'm worried what's happening to you."

"Nothing. I just need a change of pace, you know."

"Perhaps it's now time to mourn." She whispers this avoiding my gaze and then gets up and takes her turn at the bowling lane.

I'm holding a steaming cup of tea with both my hands as I sit by myself in the kitchen in deep thought. I think of what Mom said about mourning earlier tonight. I've been fine the past two years after Tommy's death. I don't need to internalize it. He died. He killed himself. He did it. I moved on. I sold the house, started over in New York City, and lived the life I deserve. I think that shows how steady I had been the past couple of years. If she tells me I need to get married and start a family, I'll lose it. I tried that, though it was hell, I didn't give up, even when I wanted so bad to walk away. I stayed. I thought that was enough.

Mom joins me in the kitchen, her head wrapped in a white towel.

"You want tea?" I ask, as I nurse mine.

"I'll get it." I remember her this way. In this kitchen with me as I did my homework every night. It's always been just the two of us. She grabs the kettle and fills it with water; then she turns on the stove and puts the kettle on. It's like a dance I've seen a million times before. She just looks a little older now, but everything else—her movements, this kitchen, she and I—they're all the same. A few minutes later, with her own cup of tea in her hands, she sits across from me at the kitchen table. "I'm sorry about earlier." She knows I'm still thinking about it too.

"That's okay," I lie. "You're my mom, you should say things like that." I smile weakly.

No one speaks for a long, lingering minute.

"But what did you mean though?" I finally ask. I can't let it go because it's been nagging at me since the bowling alley.

"Binky, no one questions how strong you are, or how brave. . . ." she begins. I can see she's uncertain as she says this.

"I'm not that brave, Mom."

"You are," she counters. "But if you don't give yourself time to mourn, grief will fester inside you. It might not be obvious, but it will remain in there." She points to my heart.

"Mom, I was okay after Tommy's death. God, I don't want to say this—but I was actually . . . relieved."

"I understand. But I'm not asking you to mourn over him." She pauses. "You should mourn over yourself—not over losing him, but over losing yourself because of him. I saw how you quickly rebuilt your life and moved on as fast as you possibly could. After a major life blow like that, you need to take a pause. Somebody close to you died. It's okay to mourn, even if it's not about him. There is a process to goodbyes." Two years and she's telling me this now. I'm a little irritated.

"When I kicked your dad out, I convinced myself that it was for me. So I should be fine, right? I wasn't. I was too proud to think I needed to heal." She sighs. "I pushed everything down inside me, and so when another pain came along, I crumbled and I couldn't escape it."

Mom reaches out to hold my hand. I can't cry in front of her. This is something I've avoided all my life. I don't ever want her to see me weak because she's already got enough on her plate.

"I knew about Glen too. I knew about your visit to the clinic. God, I sat by you every night as you slept, and I just wanted to take you in my arms and let you know it was okay, but I couldn't. I didn't want you to know that I knew. But the next day, you jumped right back into life as if nothing happened." I bend my head at this, controlling tears that threaten to spill. "I didn't know the extent of Tommy's illness, but I knew something was wrong. You pretended in front of me. You pretended to everyone. And so when Tommy died, nobody knew how to carry you."

"Mom. . . ." Still with my head bent down, I wipe my eyes with the back of my hand—like the girl I once was when I found out

Dad had left, at this very table, more than twenty-five years ago.

"I'm so sorry I didn't tell you the truth about your dad. It's my fault that you think you need to be brave around people. It's okay to fall apart, baby. It's okay to simmer and understand your pain. More importantly, it's okay to mourn over yourself because once you're done crying and screaming and being selfish, that's when you'll truly be free." At these words I lift my head up. Freedom. All these years, and I'm still struggling to find it. And so tonight, in my room, I let myself cry again—not for Eric, or for Tommy, or for Glen—but for the girl that I lost that day at the clinic, the woman who is less of herself after marrying Tommy and living a horrible hell because of drugs, and for the woman who is too insecure to love Eric because of who he is. I'm still stuck in this world where I play all these personas without really growing up or owning who I truly am.

☙

It's been more than three weeks since I came back from Seoul, since I ran back to my parents' house, and since I decided to mourn. Most days I'm inside my room, wallowing in misery, running through the memories of my past life. I already know where it began and when I changed, but I want to figure out how I can untangle the mess that is my heart and my head. My mom said I'd be silly to do that because no matter what, those moments are integral to understanding my present and who I am today. There is no going back. "You need to accept the person you've become. Love her. Be proud of her. Don't live with regret. Don't let insecurity eat you alive. You are worth it. Forgive her," she said. I want to stand by it.

I scroll through my phone as I sulk in bed on a Monday

morning looking at the many stories written about Eric's movie. There are a lot of photos too. Some are stills of the movie, some from the premiere night, and some from all the other press events he has done with Suzi the past few weeks. He looks good. He looks fine.

Since I got back, I've received a few calls and text messages from him, but I decided that this is not the right time to engage. He's still in Seoul doing press and promotion. Pam sends me Instagram clips almost on a daily basis now. I've seen in some clips how he was the perfect gentleman to Suzi, guiding her on the stage, making sure her path was clear, a bottle of water next to her, and in one clip he was seen removing dirt from her hair. They were intimate gestures. They looked real and sincere. They looked in love. But I don't avoid looking at them anymore. I'm not going to run away from reality.

My phone vibrates in my hand. "He's back here," Marco's text message says.

He and Pam have been over a few times the past two weekends. Pam was surprised to see my state after our bowling night. My mom told her to let me fall apart among loved ones because it's a healthier process in the long run. I've withered away, and my mom is letting me.

"How is he?" I ask. The old me would not have.

"He looks different."

"Like how?"

"Not movie-star-like."

"What does that even mean?"

"He looks sad. He looks exactly like you. He doesn't even smile as much anymore." I don't feel good about this. This is not a validation of my pain or my love. To wish him to be this way is not just selfish, it's also not good for my soul.

"Is he going to head to DC soon?"

"Yes."

"Did he ask about me?"

"Yes. We're heading up to the executive floor again for a meeting. Diana is all over the place. I'll keep you posted." I have to steady my beating heart knowing that he is near.

I'm alone in the house today. My mom, who retired recently, is now volunteering at the Memory Care Center—dancing and singing and playing games with older citizens who are suffering from mild dementia and early onset Alzheimer's. They offered her a part-time job a couple of weeks ago, and she's still thinking about it. My dad is at work in the city and drives here every night to be with us. Was this the kind of normal I craved when I was younger but never truly admitted to myself? Yes. I know this now. I'm glad for my parents' second chance.

I finally get up from my misery and jump into the shower. My hair is way too long now and needs to be handled this week. A visit to a hair salon is a must. Maybe Mom can take me. Today, I wash it, scrubbing away several days' grime. Over the weekend, Pam brought over my favorite Lush shower gel. I lather it all over my body and inhale its calming scent. I close my eyes as I let the warm shower take over me. Mom said I should take all the time I need to be still. Sometimes, she said, stillness is the moment in which your heart and your soul weave your body back together again. I don't know where she got all this wisdom from, when most of my life I saw her moving in every direction just to support us, to stay alive.

I feel refreshed as I walk out of the bathroom—like a brand new human. I smile at my childishness. Perhaps, this is where I need to go back to in order to move forward.

I grab my phone off my bed and find a missed call from Marco.

I punch in his number and call him back, but he doesn't answer. I call again. Nothing. I throw my phone back on the bed and put on jeans and a sweatshirt before pulling my wet hair up in a tight bun. I slip my feet into my pink UGG slippers. It's still a little chilly outside, and the heat is cranked up in the house big time, which drives Dad crazy. I grab my phone and run down to the kitchen. Thank God, Mom put on a pot of coffee before she left. I reach for a mug on the cupboard and pour myself some. I stand there as I stir sugar in my cup, and I stare at nothing deep in thought.

I feel good. I breathe in and out—and I notice the difference today.

I didn't understand the beauty of being still until recently. Life is not a race. I sit at the kitchen table looking through the window into the backyard. Dad has been working on some planter boxes to house Mom's vegetables, and they've been at it for over a month now. It's what they do together on weekends. It's actually very endearing to watch—a couple in their sixties getting a second chance at love. Real life is stranger than fiction. I can guarantee that.

I stay like this for more than an hour.

The doorbell breaks my silent reverie. *Who could be visiting me, or Mom, at ten in the morning?* I get up and walk toward the door, open it, and freeze.

Eric.

My heart melts at the sight of him. He looks nothing like the polished man I know and love. There are dark circles under his eyes, and they are sunken in what looks like sadness. I see Marco behind him. He gives me a weak smile in apology. I make way for them to come in. As they walk past me, Eric looks straight into my eyes—and for a second, I feel the world take a pause, and there we are, holding each other's stares looking for answers.

"I'll head to the kitchen for coffee. Do you want some, Eric?" Marco asks.

"No, I'm fine. Thanks," Eric replies, and time moves again after our eyes break apart. I blink incessantly as I close the door behind us.

"Hi," he whispers as soon as Marco makes an exit for the kitchen. We stand face to face in the foyer. He looks at me from head to toe and smiles. This is not the first vision I want him to see of me, but we're here, and there's nothing much I can do about that now. I turn and lead him to the living room— the room we only use for visitors that are not family or friends. This thought hurts me somehow. *He is neither family nor a friend.*

"I hear the movie is a box office success," I begin. I don't know what else to say.

"Yeah. I think it's also showing in some art cinemas here in the US. Robbie thinks it's a good preview for the show."

"Good idea." I nod mechanically.

"I head to DC tomorrow," he says, but I already know this. I planned around it. It's when I intend to go back to work. "And I want to talk to you before then." I don't say anything. I don't really have much to say. I can't just start screaming and tell him how much he hurt me. I don't even understand why I'm hurt. Seeing him on screen and on stage like that, I knew it was what he was good at. It's a job, he told me, so I don't have any reasons to be mad at him. "Robbie told me the ridiculous thing he tricked you into." I nod my head again and look away. "He doesn't have the right to do that to you—or to anyone." What Robbie did was just a trigger to my downfall, not really the cause. It was the fact that I can be deceived to do such stupid things because I don't stop and simmer. I just go.

"He apologized profusely," I say.

"It's still in bad form," Eric counters.

"And he knows that." I don't know why I'm defending Robbie.

"Then why are we here, standing apart?" There is silence between us. This is the moment where I can actually tell someone my truth, advocate for myself, and not keep it all bottled up inside like I've done all my life. I don't know how to do it. I bend my head and exhale.

"You ignored me, and it hurt," I finally say. He takes a step forward, and instinctively I take a step back, moving my arm away as he tries to reach for it. "When you looked at me while I was in your world, we both knew at that moment that I don't belong there. And it made me think. I welcomed you into the only world I know, but you never really introduced me to yours. It all seems so silly to feel this way, when we only found each other again a couple of months ago." He stares straight into my eyes. I can sense his brain working overtime. I stare right back, coaxing him to respond.

"I found you four months after the morning you walked away from me." My brow furrows as I hear this, and I don't quite understand what it means. From the expression on his face, I can tell that he's trying to decide whether or not to say more. I dare him with my glare. He turns around, brushing his fingers through his hair in distress. His hair is longer now too.

"Huh?"

"Robbie helped me track you down. And I think it was simply an act of fate when you landed a job at the network like that." My eyes widen at this revelation. "I didn't want to get in the way of your freedom, so I stayed away. I asked Robbie to check on you every now and then, to see how you're doing."

"Eric . . ."

"I've loved you from the moment at church when you poured

your heart out to the universe. I wanted so bad to be that pillar for you. But I, too, am a proud man. You left me heartbroken." There are no words I can find to respond to this. My mind is blanking, but my heart has a life of its own—exploding in a million pieces of both hurt and joy.

Love. There is nothing more confusing or more complicated.

I feel weak in the knees all of a sudden, so I move toward the sofa away from him and slowly sit down. I raise my chin to look at him.

"You asked for freedom, and I wanted you to have it, and I wanted you to take it, own it and see your dreams come true. To know that you were thriving and making it in the world on your own brought me so much pride," he says.

"Did you know that my husband died?" I ask this shamelessly. He nods his head slowly, pulling his gaze away from me.

"I didn't want to show up until I knew you were healed. I didn't want to take you away from your mourning."

"My mom said I never really mourned. I just existed without really moving on." My voice cracks as I speak. "And so, I decided to start mourning after my heart was broken three weeks ago."

"By me?" He slowly sits on the ottoman in front of me. We're way too close, and I fear that my weakness will betray me.

"By circumstances. By me." I lean backward to keep my distance.

"On that Monday after you left the apartment, Suzi called with her lawyers. She threatened to sue my management company together with all my employees if I don't go back to Seoul to walk with her at the premiere night of *The Critical Affair*. My lawyers started reading through contracts, and we didn't have much time, so I had to jump on the plane that night. Soon as I got to Seoul, I called you a few times, but there was no answer. Suzi also threatened to sue if I broke the engagement, because she said that, too, was a business arrangement. I didn't know what to do or how to explain it to you. I didn't even have time to explain to Robbie, so he probably thought I was bailing on him." He bends his head and clasps his hands together on his lap.

What he's saying all makes sense.

"I was in Seoul to see you, Eric." He lifts his head to face me. I want him to see me and so I stare into his eyes unblinkingly.

"I know. Seeing you in my world frightened me." He looks away as he makes this confession.

"Were you embarrassed by me?" I whisper under my breath.

"God, Bianca, not at all. If any, I was embarrassed by my superficial existence." He looks upset as he slowly rakes his fingers through his hair. "I was embarrassed by the lights and the fame when all I talk about is anonymity. That day, I stood in front of the crowd, with you in it, a fraud. I complain about that life, and yet I still do it." There is shame in his stance.

"It's a job, you said." I repeat to him what he tells me all the time.

"I was an idiot to believe I could walk away from it. What I didn't understand was that it would affect a lot of people around me if I did—people's livelihoods. I didn't think of it that way until that legal battle Suzi pulled me into. I was selfish to think everything was just about me." Park Hyun Min is not one person. He's a company with people who depend on him. My heart is not the only thing that matters. Neither is his. He has responsibilities. "That night, I realized that I was trapped. I can't just walk out on all this, even if I want to."

"Eric . . . this . . . what we have . . . is not television . . . " I look away from Eric's expectant gaze. There is no easy way to say this. "This is not something we can wait out and hope for a happy ever after." I feel a tiny pain at the center of my heart. "Ours is a fantasy . . ."

"Bianca . . . "

I put my hand up to stop him.

"This is not a love story. . . . "

"It is to me . . . " He whispers.

"To love someone, I need to do a better job at loving myself first. I don't want to be trapped again in a world where I won't be myself. Your world is unknown to me. The flashes of light that you welcome will blind me. The people screaming after you will drown me. I'm a simple girl, with simple dreams, but to love you means to stand up and to be brave. I don't think I'm there yet. I forgot that there are repercussions to loving you."

"I can't lose us again. . . . "

"Please let me go. My problem is not about you. It's me. I need to understand myself first and my life choices. And when I'm ready, when I'm finally truly free, I'll try to find my way back to you. If you're still there."

"There is nothing more important to me than your happiness. Heal. Don't think about me. And when you're ready, I'll be right where you left me. If you decide that you don't want to see me again, please always remember that I love you, Bianca. I love you like I've never loved anyone else in this world. You keep me going just by knowing that you're walking in the same world with me. If I can't make you happy, knowing that you are . . . is good enough."

He doesn't say goodbye. He gets up, turns around with his head bowed, and walks out of my life.

Chapter 29

"Run, run like the wind, Bianca Maria Curtis!" I scream, though I'm out of breath, puffing, looking around for someone to take my place. I can see Marco running as far away from me as he possibly can, waving me off.

Today is the first day of our two-day annual company retreat in Long Island. Tonight, Marco and I will smuggle Pam in and enjoy the rest of the evening at the beach. We own our evenings except for the last night, which is the company's awards ceremony.

Thankfully, Van shows up to take the baton from me and continues running for our team. I drop down on the floor and start panting like a dog. I'm so out of shape, it's ridiculous. Diana walks behind me in her neon-yellow leggings and black athletic top with her neon-yellow sports bra peeking out at the sides. As usual, she looks spectacular. When I went back to work five months ago after a four-week sabbatical, she didn't ask me any questions. She gave me a new assignment and moved on. What's more puzzling is that she's more understanding of me. She checks in with Marco about how I'm doing and regularly sits next to me at meetings. She never used to do that.

"Hey, you okay?" she asks, her bright colored leggings complementing the sun as it beams right at me. I cover the top of my eyes to see her clearly. Her face is bare of makeup, and she's beautiful.

"Yeah, I'm good. Thanks," I say and she reaches out her hand to pull me up.

"You should get a bottle of Gatorade at the booth. You don't want to get dehydrated." Then she walks away. She's been acting really bizarre. She's mostly alone in these company outings because no one is comfortable enough to socialize with her. She isn't that bad.

"Is she still acting off?" Marco appears next to me, and I nod my head with creased forehead. "Maybe Robbie told her to lay off giving you crap."

"I don't know. It's as if she's mourning something too. Like she's sad."

"I noticed that too. What do you think it means?" Marco puts his hand on his paisley print boardwalk-short-clad hip.

"I don't know. I actually feel bad for her sometimes. I don't think she has any friends either."

"Not our problem," he adds.

"But it is. She's our boss. When she's not in a good mood, we're screwed." We've seen that happen countless of times. I get most of the wrath. "Van is coming back, Marco. I'm not taking that fucking baton again. It's your turn!" Van throws the baton at Marco, and he starts running.

Van and I look at him as he flounces on the track, and we start to giggle.

❧

Pam is already at the beach waiting for us when Marco and I arrive. The ocean looks magnificent with the moonlight providing an amazing backdrop like a painting. I take in the fresh air, and in my white sundress, I drop down next to Pam on the sand. I give her a big lip smack on the cheek. She turns around, pulls me in, and kisses me on top of my head. Marco, ever efficient with everything alcoholic, is making sure our beer bucket has enough ice and our tequila bottle is intact.

"It's great to get out of the city sometimes," Pam says. "I feel like my soul needed the water for so long, and yet I refuse to get out of Manhattan." I sigh at this. I lived in Jersey most of my life, and yet I never go to the ocean. It's pathetic. Here we are, three city souls, mesmerized by the enchantment of the ocean in front of us. We are all silent as we stare.

"It's like the three of us are waiting for a mermaid to appear or something," Marco jokes and hands beers to us. No one speaks for a few more minutes.

"I asked Miguel on a date." Pam says to no one in particular. Marco and I turn our heads to look at her with so many questions.

"Finally!" Marco declares. "You've been simmering on this for more than two years now. What made you decide?"

"We bumped into each other at the book signing of one of my authors and started talking. Obviously, he's still very worried about you, Bianca. Then I asked him point-blank about his feelings for you."

"What the hell!" Now, I'm embarrassed. This is one part of my life I didn't really have the time to confront. "And?"

"You're right. He said he's constantly worried about you because he'd seen you fight for your life and for Tommy's for five years, but that it's not what I think." To hear this is a relief. Miguel is a great man—perfect—just not perfect for me.

"I'm so happy for you, Pam!" I really am. We all lift our beer cans, toast, and drink big gulps.

"It's tequila time, babies!" Marco declares. He pulls out plastic cups from our tote and passes them around. He is about to pour each of us a shot when Diana walks past us.

"There's your mermaid right there," Pam whispers.

"Hey, Diana." I have to acknowledge this. I'm not evil and obviously, she too seems to be having a rough time the past few months.

"Hey," she responds with hesitation. She looks like a goddess in a bright orange off-the-shoulder linen dress. A light white shawl is draped around her.

"Do you want to join us for a beer?" The two dingdongs look at me like it's the worst idea in the world, and probably it is, but I can't leave her standing there without reaching out.

"Are you sure?" She looks at the two looking at me. I shove Pam to speak up.

"Yeah, c'mon. We have enough beer here to serve an entire battalion," Pam affirms. She pulls a can out of the bucket, gets up, and hands it to Diana.

Diana sits gracefully next to me on the sand and slowly opens her beer.

"Everything okay?" I ask.

"Yeah." She nods, but I can see flickers of sadness in her eyes under the bright moonlight. "The shoot for *Deception* is doing great, by the way." That's the tentative title of Eric's new show.

"I'm glad. And I think Van is doing a great job with social media. I'm very happy for her on this promotion," I add.

"Yeah, she'd been at that receptionist job way before you joined us, and we all thought she'd get the new junior associate job. Then a name started floating around."

"Huh?"

"Your job was created for you, Bianca." She turns to look at me. Our eyes meet. The hot wind sweeps my hair sideway covering half my face.

"What are you talking about?"

"Robbie told me to take your interview. He swore by your brilliance, and he wasn't wrong."

"How did he even know about me?" I'm taken aback by this revelation. For the past two years, I've made sure I stayed out of Robbie's sight.

"Robbie has his ways. He didn't make it to the top by not knowing the things he should know. You apparently made an impression." That night with Eric, he knew where to find me. How though?

"How did he find out my connection with Marco?"

"He didn't. I did." At the mention of his name, Marco moves closer to us.

"But how?"

"Robbie showed us a photo of you. I don't know how he got it but, it was a blurry one taken at a bar somewhere."

"Okay?"

"I told him I've seen that woman before. Then I remembered where. It was at a birthday party at Jamba's. Marco was there . . ."

"With me and Pam. . . ." I finish for her softly.

"And I was there for dinner with a friend."

I remember that vividly. "Didn't you think it was a bit odd that he has a photo of a woman he wants to hire on the spot?" My heart sinks.

"His job is to seek out talents. That's not uncommon. He also knew your name. Bianca Pierce." Marco is listening to this now too, curious.

"But you never mentioned Bianca to me at all," Marco counters.

"But I made the announcement in your office. It was a long shot, but it worked. I didn't think it would be so quick."

"That's pure genius, Diana."

"I think it was pure chance." Diana gets up, removes her expensive Marc Jacobs sandals and walks to the shore, letting the tide wash over her feet. I follow close behind her.

"Did you know why? Did he tell you why?" I ask.

"I'm not stupid, Bianca." Diana turns around to look at me. Her blue eyes are luminous and clear. The darkness is turning her into an incandescent vision. "I eventually figured it out after Eric entered the scene." She stares right back out in the ocean. I move next to her. "I have loved once too. Just like you, I thought it was a lie. He was famous, so why would he want to be with me, right? He can get any girl he wants, but apparently he wanted me." She pulls her thin shawl tighter around her, not from the cold but for emotional support. I can feel her burden. "Don't let anything get in the way of a chance to love and be loved, Bianca."

"Diana . . ."

"Arthur is sick. He's dying." She breaks down and cries as she says this. She is talking about troublesome Arthur of the show *Arthur*. I had no idea. Just like Diana, Arthur never married. "He told me I robbed him of the chance of happiness because I was selfish and ambitious. I was afraid. I was just starting my career as an executive in CWS."

"Diana." I put my hand on her shoulder for comfort. I don't know how to navigate this openness. This is the real Diana underneath the tough exterior. She continues to sob as she bites on her fist in an attempt to control it. When her tears won't stop, I put my arms around her waist, my head on her shoulder, and I hug her closer to me. All of a sudden, the beach becomes quiet. Even Marco and Pam stop talking. The bellowing evening breeze is the only sound that provides a mask to Diana's painful moaning. The ocean is quiet too, as if it's mourning along with us. Suddenly, Diana turns around and looks at me.

"Eric did everything to protect you, to make sure you make it out in the world strong, as he waits in the shadows for you. I know you love him too. I'm almost fifty, Bianca, and I'd like to believe that I still have a chance with Arthur as we fight this thing together."

"Diana . . ."

"Don't let pride or cowardice get in the way of your happiness. Take it. Own it. It's yours." Then she puts her arms around me too.

We stay like this for a little while.

❧

The next morning, at breakfast, I see Robbie at a big table with a bunch of CWS executives that are rarely in the New York building. He sees me walking toward him, and in his golf attire, he gets up and walks to me with a glass of orange juice in one hand. We move to the corner of the restaurant to avoid people's curious glances. No one at my level would dare talk to Robbie the way I'm about to do now. But our relationship is a little unusual.

"Bianca," Robbie nods in greeting.

"Did you seek me out to get a job at the network a few weeks after we met at the bar?"

"Yes."

"Does Eric know about this?"

"No. But he eventually found out that you worked for me after a few months."

"Did I get the job because I was someone's love interest?"

"Are you being serious right now? Do you think my job is to be a matchmaker?" His tone is snarky, and I don't blame him.

"Then why?"

"Because I think you're smart, you get me, and you get the business. You impressed me during our conversation in my suite with Eric that night. I'm a businessman, Bianca. I hire people who I think could take care of my business. Your love affair had nothing to do with you joining the CWS team. I was surprised when Eric reached out to me for help finding you. I told him that by chance you already actually worked for me. I'm not going to lie. Having you on my team got Eric to sign the project quicker though he had other commitments then."

I stand there small in front of a big powerful man. I look up at him and listen.

"Bianca, here's a word of advice. That man is a good man—a great one. He loves you, and he's not afraid to let the world know it. If he hasn't introduced you to his world yet, it's because he's trying to protect you. People can be vile in the world of show business, Bianca." I nod at this. I have seen how relationships are shattered because of fame.

"Where is he now?"

"He's still in DC wrapping up. He'll be back in New York soon to do press rounds. You know this." I do know. "After the press rounds, the show premieres, and he'll fly back to Seoul. We've sold out advertising spots and we're expecting to get major audience shares on that time slot. That show will be a success, but Eric doesn't want to commit to another season."

I can sense all the other CWS employees staring at us. This is not a casual conversation, and people can tell from the emotion on my face.

"I feel it's too late," I tell Robbie.

His face softens as he shows compassion. "Show business is a fucked up business, so what purity we can find in it we should cherish. You are two beautiful souls. Nothing is too late when it comes to love. And here I say that I'm not a matchmaker." We both smile at this.

Chapter 30

I'm back at work bright and early this Monday morning after the retreat. I didn't win any awards, but Marco did—a trip for two to the Bahamas. He was miffed because he doesn't have anyone to go with, but he has an entire year to work on that before the ticket expires. It was a fun weekend albeit full of revelations. It also finally makes sense now. How I got this job. How Eric found me again. How I am back here pondering everything that happened to me the past three years.

For the most part, I think I operated under the theory that being miserable is easier than being happy. I reason, intuitively perhaps, that getting used to pain is a safer bet than getting used to happiness and taking a big fall. There might be some truth to that, but I don't think it's a good way to live.

I still love my job. These days, it's the reason why I get up in the morning. I don't save enough, but money isn't a big issue for me now since I've not touched the equity I received from the house when I sold it more than two years ago. Dad didn't want to take it back either. This week, I'll get to learn more about data analytics with our digital team, which I'm excited about.

I see Diana walk by coming into work. She's still as breathtaking as always, but now that I know her on a more personal level, I understand the sadness in her eyes better. The bright colors of her lips and the perfect contour of her cheeks can't mask it. I give her a weak smile when she turns to look my way, and she returns the gesture. Perhaps in another life, Diana and I can actually be good friends. Perhaps in another life, she will choose differently. She will choose love.

Yesterday was the last day of Eric's DC shoot. I know this because Marco still handles his publicity with Van. He continues to pass me tidbits through forwarded emails from the team on the ground. He asked me once if I wanted to continue getting information, and this time I said yes. I want to know what's going on in Park Hyun Min's life.

My phone vibrates from inside my purse on the floor. I grab it and see Pam calling.

"Are you in front of your computer right now?" she squeals on the other end of the phone. I don't know how her office lets her do all this screaming. She is one loud woman. It's actually part of her charm. It makes me smile.

"Calm down. Yes. Why? I just got in, so I still need to turn it on."

"Turn it on now! Hurry!"

"Hold on, geez. What's it about?" I tuck my phone between my ear and my shoulder as I turn my computer on and a loud ding echoes inside my tiny space.

"It's big news."

"Then why don't you just text it to me."

"Because I want to be on the phone with you when you read it."

"It's loading. Send it to me via email." Pam stops talking and I can hear the clicking of her keyboard.

"Hang on. There. Sent."

I open my email, and there at the top of my inbox is a note from Pam with a subject, BIG FUCKING NEWS. I click on it.

PARK Hyun Min RETIRES FROM SOUTH KOREAN ENTER-
TAINMENT INDUSTRY: Famed actor, Park Hyun Min, who
is currently in the United States filming his latest television drama under CWS, an American television network, today announced that he is taking an indefinite
break from show business. This news sent fans weeping
all over the world as they clamor for more movies and
television drama from the popular actor. Neither Hyun
Min nor his management people were available for further comments after this announcement was released. It
was known earlier this year that Park Hyun Min broke
off his engagement with pop icon Suzi after years of dating and more than two years of engagement. Suzi has
now moved on with actor Yoon Byung Joon.

I read it again. I sigh.

"Did you know about this?" Pam probes.

"No." And on cue, Marco walks into the office and rushes
toward me while reading something on his phone.

"Are you reading this?" he asks in shock. I nod my head. A
few minutes later, Diana joins us. She just looks at me. She
knows better than to ask.

"Marco, let's strategize. We don't have anything to do with
this. His management should take care of the media inquiries,
but I bet we'll get a call or two from the Asian media assigned
here in New York and Los Angeles." Diana is in her element
again. "Let's go to my office now." They leave me alone with Pam
still on the line.

"Is he back in New York?"

"I don't know." I can't believe he's finally walking away from
all this.

I miss him. I miss him every single day. It's been more than five months since the last time we spoke. Each night, I look at my phone trying to gather the courage to call or text him. I was, still am, a coward. This, I know is not pride. I'm worried that when I call to say *I'm ready*, he'll tell me it's too late.

"Why don't you give him a call? Ask him how he's doing. Be a friend. There's nothing wrong with that." I guess I can do that. There's no harm calling a friend. "Do it!" Pam cajoles.

"Maybe I will," I say to myself rather than to Pam.

"This man invested time and money and energy to make sure that you're okay. You're simply returning the favor with no strings attached. You're heartless if you don't reach out, Binks."

"I will," I whisper, unsure.

"Will you, really?"

The office is filling up. Everyone is now at their desks, starting their Monday routine. I can hear chatters about the weekend and how they are all hangover and sunburnt. I'm happy to be here among these people.

"I'll call right now. I promise." Finally, Pam hangs up.

I read the news article again. I plug Hyun Min on Google and the top search results are all about his retirement. One news report is linking his retirement to Suzi's new relationship, speculating that he's heartbroken over it. I click on his name on my phone contacts. It goes straight to voice mail.

My office phone rings. I immediately answer it.

"Bianca," says Robbie, "do you know anything about this?"

"I've not spoken to Eric for about five months now. So no. Have you heard from him at all? Is he still in DC?

"His team called me last night and said Eric plans to travel to New York today. They wrapped up yesterday in DC. He should be on the way here now."

"Do you think he's okay?" I have to ask this. I want to know that this is something he's doing for himself and no one else.

"I'm sure he is. I'm just checking to see if you've heard from him at all."

"Sorry, I can't help."

"Give that guy a break. You've forgiven me, why don't you forgive him? No one tried to deceive you. If anything, everyone has your back." Robbie and I are now in this surreal non-friendship friendship. I don't use it as leverage to get ahead. And in an odd kind of way, I actually like him.

⁂

CWS is hosting a big event for the premiere of *Deception* next week. I know this because Marco comes back from Diana's office all hyped about the publicity surrounding Eric's announcement and that the network plans to leverage on its popularity to promote the show. *Deception* will be his last work before he goes into retirement. They don't include me in any of this. But being a great friend that he is, Marco gives me a readout at lunch.

It's five fifteen, and I decide to leave work early. Pam is busy with a new client. Marco, Van, Diana, and two other people from the creative department are staying late tonight to make sure everything is all set and ready for premiere week. I can't just call Miguel any more, not until I know everything is okay with Pam.

I think of Eric as I walk out of work. I tried calling him a few more times during the course of the day, but there was no answer. My calls went straight to voice mail. He's probably screening them. I don't know if he's flying or driving from DC, but it's not a long trip, so he should be here by now. This announcement is not an easy decision for him, I know. A lot of people depend on him for their livelihood, and I also know that he loves his job. He loves the part where he influences his audience toward goodness. It's one of the reasons I adore him—his selflessness and his kindness.

The sun is still up. The humidity is a pain, but I decide to walk home anyway. I think of Eric and about how this will change his life completely. Also, as soon as *Deception* hits television, his anonymity here in the United States will be finished. I've heard so many good things about the show from people at work. They are all impressed by his professionalism, and about how he is inspiring and a great person to work with. Makes me even more proud of him.

It's a busy Monday. Hordes of people are going places in a hurry. I sometimes wonder why. Needing to get to a dinner party with friends, picking up their kids from daycare, lists of errands to run tonight? I don't have any of that. I have me. I should be content and be at peace with that. I no longer crave freedom because I have it. I've created this whole spectacle of blame over what transpired in my life, and now that I've done it all, I'm okay. In the end, it's all about coming back to me. It's all about me. There is some selfishness to that, but I think that's okay. I know I won't be able to cultivate healthy relationships with people if I don't have a strong one with myself.

I take a detour and turn to the flashing lights on Seventh Avenue. As soon as I enter the bubble that is the Square, it takes me right back to the time with Eric. This place will forever be about him, about us, about our night together years ago. Maybe I'll never see him again, especially now that he's closing his life to the public eye. There will be no new movies of him to watch or television shows to gape over. I walk over to where the bleachers are, at the far end where Eric and I once sat. I remember how we pretended to be together to trick some fans away. I remember how he walked this street with childlike fascination. I remember how I fell in love with him.

I climb the steps and take a seat at the top. I put my bag on my lap and I take it all in—the beauty of its loudness, the magic of the lights, the place where people fall in love. I smile as I stare at all this. I own this. In my heart this is ours—Eric's and mine. At least, we had Times Square. We'll always have Times Square. I giggle at this a little. The fondness in my heart has blossomed.

If I end up being alone in this lifetime, I will forever be grateful for the chance this place has brought me—for the love I found in Eric and the grace I found in myself. I'm not getting any younger, and I should anticipate that there is a good chance I will end up alone, like Diana. Motherhood is also not off the table. Maybe, when I'm more stable—emotionally and financially—in a year or two, I can have a baby on my own. I can buy a small apartment somewhere close to a good school district not far from here, and I can be an older modern momma. This thought excites me. I can't wait for the next chapter of my life. Maybe, it's the reason Eric came. Not so we can spend our entire lives together, but to shake things up. To show me that I am worthy of someone's love, that I am capable of loving myself, and to realize that I can still stand up after all the painful things I went through. Maybe it's time to go back to St. Patrick's Cathedral. It's been a long time since I've had a conversation with the higher power I call God. Maybe I should get myself a big hearty ice cream at Serendipity, and maybe I'll end my night at the Empire State Building to thank the universe for the best of opportunities.

When I bend my head down, I squint in an attempt to confirm what I've seen. I've noticed changes in my eyesight the past few months. My eyes stray away because what I thought I saw is close to impossible. My poor eyesight is playing tricks on me. I laugh at myself.

The figure stays right there at the bottom of the steps, staring at me with confidence in his stance. I take a second look. He climbs the steps toward me with wide strides. I stand up. I see him. He looks different. He is different. More relaxed than the last time I saw him. The sparkles in his eyes are back. He is beautiful. He is perfect. He has my heart.

Finally, he stops right in front of me, one step below mine.

"Hey," he says with a hint of playfulness.

"Hey," I reply with a twinge of naughtiness. He lifts his head backward and laughs at this. There is pure joy in his laugher.

"Did you call me?"

"I did."

"Why?" He looks expectant.

"Because . . . I'm ready." And with this, he pulls my face to his and takes my lips with all of his strength. We kiss and I melt and I love . . . and then, finally, I live.

"I love you, Bianca Maria Curtis."

The thing is, I never really thought this was a love story. As it turns out, it actually is.

BREAKING NEWS: Park Hyun Min attends premiere of his new American TV show with a mystery lady.

ASIAN NEWS ALERT: Park Hyun Min engaged to his Filipino American girlfriend, Bianca Maria Curtis.

SCOOP USA NEWS: Park Hyun Min is set to direct his first American movie in December under his American company, Park Curtis Productions, in cooperation with CWS Network.

ENTERTAINMENT ONLINE: Park Hyun Min welcomes twin daughters with his wife of two years, CEO of Park Curtis Productions, Bianca Maria Park.

ACKNOWLEDGMENTS

Oh, this journey!

When I published *After Perfect*, my first book, I didn't know where that road would take me. But here I am. It took me here—writing this acknowledgment to the many people who welcomed me with open arms, who accepted my voice, and rallied on my story for my second book. Second! It is because of you. Yes, you! And I will forever be in your debt.

It goes without saying, but nevertheless I want to thank my She Writes Press team for making *Twelve Hours in Manhattan* possible. Brooke Warner, my publisher, for trusting in this project—and in me, again. Shannon Green, oh you my editorial manager, who keeps me in check every step of the way—I heart you. Jennifer Caven, my editor, who knows my innermost thoughts and feelings enough to make this book come to life. My publicity team at BookSparks—Crystal, Tabitha, and Rylee—I mean c'mon, you guys know you are rockstars! And of course, Julie Metz, for the perfect cover design that captured my heart. Thank you!

This book is a fanfiction of sorts. I wrote it at the beginning of the pandemic. I needed to find ways to fortify myself from the uncertainty of the world. Though not lighthearted by any means, working on this project provided comfort and a fantasy. It is a fantasy of creating a world where my favorite celebrity is at the center of my story, where I get to see an adventure—from the front row—and see how two worlds can meld into one heart. More importantly, it also allowed me to try to capture the very essence of hope and love and, ultimately, self, in times of despair.

Again, I thank from the bottom of my heart the cheerleaders in my life. My college BFFs— Jazel, Rascel, Lace, Jojie, Alex, and Sarah—who have constantly provided inspiration and joy, hope, loads of love, and, most importantly, the belief that I could do this again. All my St. Scholastica's College, Manila classmates, AB402A, Class of 1994—you showed me what true support is all about. Thank you. To Tif Marcelo and Maida Malby—your invaluable advice, guidance, and friendship mean the world to me as I trek this road of fiction writing. To the Book Lover Titas—Diane, Joyce, and Kristine—thank you for being amazing book buddies and supporters of my book writing journey. Tita She, thank you for making me laugh out loud during our discussions. You all have my heart.

To Jamie Young, thank you for listening to me dream.

To the bookstagrammers, to the book bloggers, to bookstore owners, and to everyone in the publishing industry who took, and still takes, the time for me, I am grateful for you.

I thank my mom—forever, and always—for providing me a childhood and space that allowed me to dream and wander, for sewing my costumes for my moments of creative expression, and for praying that I would stay on the path that would get me where I needed to be. I was not an easy teenager, but we both made it through. Thank you to my brother, Nico, who is the true connoisseur of Korean drama, for keeping me up to speed on the latest entertainment bulletin. Thanks to Arnie.

Loving me is not always easy, but Chris, my husband, stands by me no matter how tough life gets. You are my rock. Thank you for constantly reassuring me, for telling me that I am remarkable, and for loving me beyond my wildest dreams—I don't know where I would be without you. To Jack—my life's greatest work, my heart, my life, my love—thank you for telling me how proud you are of Mommy, especially in those times I don't feel I've done enough. You make me the proudest.

And thanks again, you, for reading. It is because of you that I keep on dreaming.

ABOUT THE AUTHOR

Photo credit: Kir Tuben Photography

MAAN GABRIEL is a mom, wife, dreamer, writer, and advocate for women's stories in literature. She earned her BA in communications from St. Scholastica's College in Manila and MPS in public relations and corporate communications from Georgetown University. She has lived in Manila, Brussels, Dakar, and Mexico City. During the day, she works in strategic communications. She is the author of *After Perfect*; *Twelve Hours in Manhattan* is her second book. Gabriel, along with her husband and son, currently calls suburban Washington, DC, home.